Driving on the Left

The Fork in the Road

Margaret J Norrie

iUniverse, Inc.
New York Bloomington

Driving on the Left
The Fork in the Road

iUniverse books may be ordered through booksellers or by contacting:

iUniverse
1663 Liberty Drive
Bloomington, IN 47403
www.iuniverse.com
1-800-Authors (1-800-288-4677)

ISBN: 978-1-4502-3843-4 (sc)
ISBN: 978-1-4502-3845-8 (dj)
ISBN: 978-1-4502-3844-1 (ebk)

Printed in the United States of America

iUniverse rev. date: 7/23/2010

EPIGRAPH

"You have something to say, something to share with the world or with the people close to you. Your life is important, and your memories document how you have changed your corner of the universe."

ROBERT GOODMAN AND PEGGY LANG

"Life resembles a novel more often than novels resemble life."

GEORGE SAND, French Novelist (1804-1876)

In memory of my beloved husband

ACKNOWLEDGMENTS

A love of writing since childhood inspired not only the attempt to write this first novel, but initially the necessity to learn how to do it.

I am grateful for the training and inspiration afforded by the Course of Study—"Breaking Into Print"—provided by Long Ridge Writers Group, 93 Long Ridge Road, West Redding, CT 06896, and for recognition of my successful completion of this Course by awarding me their Diploma.

I am indebted to the knowledge and encouragement, in particular, of Connie Shelton, herself a successful author, at that time assigned to me as my Instructor/Tutor, and well-known for her "Charlie Parker" Mystery Series.

Any success I may enjoy is also due to the dedicated efforts of William Zinsser—"On Writing Well," Jon Franklin—"Writing for Story," Les Edgerton—"Hooked," Renni Browne and Dave King—"Self-Editing for Fiction Writers," Stephen Wilbers—"Keys to Great Writing," Nancy Kress—"Characters, Emotion and Viewpoint," Cindy Rogers—"Word Magic for Writers," and, Donald Maass—"The Fire in Fiction."

My hope is that these excellent tutorials have rubbed off to some extent in the direction of "Driving on the Left."

Thank you.

Margaret J Norrie

PREFACE

Since the principal action in the book takes place in the United Kingdom, four maps are included at the back of the book to make locations and distances more comprehensible. Size of the pages makes it difficult to decipher words in small print but reference to current maps could facilitate this. Please note that no freeways are shown because at the period covered by the book there were none. These are old maps.

1. Southern England, including Wales.

This map extends as far north as Manchester, which lies northeast of Liverpool on the west coast. Below Liverpool is Chester, in England, and the north coast of Wales, extending west to the Isle of Anglesey, which is accessed by a bridge from Wales. The coast follows the peninsular of Carnarvonshire, known as the Lleyn Promontory. This map includes the southwestern counties of Devon and Cornwall. Devon is abutted on its eastern boundary by the counties of Somerset and Dorset. Jeannie, the principal character, lives in Devonshire, about eight miles from Exeter, the County town, whereas Neil, the young soldier she meets, lives in Derbyshire, south of Manchester.

To the southeast lies the mouth of the River Thames, Southend-on-Sea, and the City of London. Dover is shown on the southern coast, just twenty miles across the English Channel from Calais, in France, with Dunkirk being situated a few miles east of Calais.

2. Northern England, including part of the Lowlands of Scotland.
The area includes Yorkshire and extends across the country eastwards to Newcastle and to the Cheviot Hills, forming the boundary between England and Scotland, with the City of Carlisle on the west coast. The Isle of Man is situated in the Irish Sea, accessed by ship from Liverpool on the west coast of England.

3. Scotland, extending to the Northern Highlands and Ross and Cromarty.
Edinburgh, East Lothian, Berwick and Carter Bar in the Cheviot Hills are all towards the east coast. Kilmarnock and Glasgow lie to the west, leading northward to Oban on the coast and Fort William on Loch Linnhe, with the famous road leading from Fort William to Mallaig on the west coast. The Queen's castle at Balmoral is situated just above the "lands" part of the Grampian Highlands printed on the map.

4. Northern Ireland and Eire, the Irish Republic.
Dublin is situated about halfway down the east coast. Our intrepid travelers cross the country to County Mayo and drive south from there to Killarney in County Kerry, lying south-west, and from there across country to Cork, up the east coast to Waterford, then Dublin for the watery journey back to Liverpool in England.

Contents

CHAPTER 1
"A Body of England's, Breathing English Air"—The Soldier—Rupert Brooke 1

CHAPTER 2
Convergence in Conflict 5

CHAPTER 3
The Steering Wheel—The fork in the road determines the life to be led 19

CHAPTER 4
Survival 29

CHAPTER 5
The Partings 37

CHAPTER 6
In the Service of His Majesty, King George VI—Camberley 49

CHAPTER 7
In the service of His Majesty, King George VI—Wales 55

CHAPTER 8
In the Service of His Majesty, King George VI—Awakenings 63

CHAPTER 9
In the Service of His Majesty, King George VI—Friends and Frustrations 70

CHAPTER 10
Under the Hood 79

CHAPTER 11
Southend-on-Sea—Memories 85

CHAPTER 12
Southend-on-Sea—"Doodlebugs" and Other Things. 93

CHAPTER 13
The Thames Estuary 100

CHAPTER 14
Means to an End. 103

CHAPTER 15
A New Company, a Parrot, a Goose, a Telegram and a Stranger. . .108

CHAPTER 16
Close Encounter on the Subway 114

CHAPTER 17
"Civvy Street" 120

CHAPTER 18
An extra passenger—and a honeymoon. 131

CHAPTER 19
When a sense of humor helps the days go by. 140

CHAPTER 20
Discoveries 149

CHAPTER 21
Tales of Triumph. 153

CHAPTER 22A
Decisions. 161

CHAPTER 22B
Decisions. 166

CHAPTER 23
Changes 173

CHAPTER 24
Turning Limitations into Opportunities 187

CHAPTER 25
Interlude 196

CHAPTER 26
Life-changing Times 204

CHAPTER 27
Reminiscences of a Maui vacation 216

CHAPTER 28
Normandy, the Car—and the end of the road? 221

CHAPTER 29
House swap 227

CHAPTER 30
Replanting Roots 232

CHAPTER 1

"A BODY OF ENGLAND'S, BREATHING ENGLISH AIR"—THE SOLDIER—RUPERT BROOKE

The train groaned gradually to a halt, steam escaping from its boiler, the sound reminiscent of the anguish of ancient oxen relieved from hauling a heavy load.

Neil stirred his aching limbs sleepily and raised the window shade: Wonder where we are? It's barely light and in wartime there are no signs.

Chesterfield!

The realization shocked him awake—only eight miles from home. *I'm getting off. Don't have any cash but I'll hitch a ride. Someone will take pity on me. Make sure I'll take my rifle, since I've carried it this far.*

He reached for his knapsack off the rack, stepped over prostrate soldiers' legs, struggled along the crammed corridor of the troop train, dropped down the window of the exit door, reached for the outside handle to open it, and stepped out at last into English air.

Jeremy, an early delivery van driver from Chesterfield, kissed his wife and picked up the flask of hot chocolate she always made for him.

"Which route are you on today?" she asked.

"Baslow and Bakewell, but I've got a special delivery at Matlock so I may be a bit later than usual getting home."

Determined to walk home, stoically overcoming the agony of his muscles, Neil covered several miles, when a van overtook him and he heard the brakes squeal as it slowed to a stop.

"Where are you going, son?" The driver rolled down the window and called to him as he caught up with the van.

"I'm trying to get to Baslow."

"No problem. Jump in. I'm driving through there to Bakewell.

And, as Neil climbed in painfully through the opposite door, he continued:

"Where've you been? You look pretty washed up. You live around these parts?"

Neil's mouth was so dry it was hard to speak. He managed to say, "Do you have liquid of any sort, please? I've had nothing for three days."

"Here's some hot chocolate my wife made, in a flask. Help yourself."

"Thanks.

He sipped the hot chocolate with untold gratitude, and tried to relax.

"That'll save my life."

He thought: This van has seen better days; it's sadly in need of new shock absorbers—but anything's better than walking.

Neil owed the driver an explanation. After a while, he tried again.

"Shipped out of Dunkirk about 24 hours ago on some paddle steamer. Jumped on the first troop train out of Dover. Crazy! Packed. No organization. Just a case of 'Get 'em out of here, away from the coast.' By my good fortune—the train came through Chesterfield. I'm parched—and famished—but that doesn't matter, I'll be home soon, thanks to you. I'm so grateful you stopped to pick me up."

Jeremy glanced at his weary passenger, unshaven and dirty, his uniform torn and worn, slouched beside him—and in severe need of a bath.

"Glad to be of help; I can see you've had a tough time."

He thought it was fortunate his young passenger was in uniform or he would not have stopped to give him a ride.

"Twenty miles inland from the French coast we were told to blow everything up. Leave nothing for the Germans, and walk to the beaches at Dunkirk. Nothing there but soldiers—endless troops. No food or water. No ocean transport. Then German Messerschmitt fighter planes strafed the beaches. Barely any cover, and no air support. But at night all these little pleasure boats defied the Channel currents; that's how many of us got back to England."

He paused, sipping the drink, recalling his anxiety:

"Wouldn't have been so bad trudging twenty miles but one of my boys broke his leg trapped between two vehicles and couldn't walk."

"That was a bit of bad luck. What did you do?"

"Heaved him up on my shoulder and carried him. I managed to find room for him on a boat about an hour before I got my ride, so he should be safe by now, in a hospital."

They traveled several miles in silence, each deep in thought. Neil's head drummed with unwanted recall of the horror on those beaches; he anticipated nightmares for weeks. *He could only discuss it with his fellows; they would understand. How long will it take to be normal?*

Then the driver said, "When did your parents last hear from you?"

They were grinding up a hill in low gear. Neil waited until they reached the top and the driver changed up, so he didn't have to shout over the noise.

"Nearly a year ago—and that was a printed Army post card. I had enlisted voluntarily, in January, part-time, after work, just for training, so I was sent with the first contingent after England declared war against Germany on the third of September, 1939."

"Bet they'll be surprised."

"I hope neither of them has a heart attack; they're not young, nor very healthy."

"Here we are. Good luck, son. Hope you'll soon be home for good."

"I doubt that. It looks as though it will be a long war. Thanks for everything."

The van driver dropped him off near the church in the center of the village. *He wondered whether Pops was still keeping the books and making sure all the accounts balanced? He said they were in a mess before he took over when they moved here from Manchester in 1927.*

Neil trudged the short distance up the hill and turned into the lane, thankful to reach level ground. Nothing had changed. The Derbyshire stone house with the lace curtains in the windows where the old spinster sisters lived was still there on the corner; and he could smell the vibrant blooms of the carefully pruned roses at the house next door...a few more strides and he would step up to walk along the old paved path... home at last.

Neil found the spare key in its usual hiding place and opened the door to the familiar house.

At that moment, his father, still clad warmly in his night attire, descended the final steps into the hallway which always displayed the "Peter and Paul" oak chairs from the chapel at Pops' big school in Manchester. He stood still in shock, or maybe fear, not knowing who might be entering at that early hour.

"Sorry, Pops, it's only me," said his son, breathless from the exertion of walking uphill and his overall fatigue, "ye gods, am I happy to be home? Never thought I'd make it!"

Overcome, but relieved that he appeared uninjured, his father held his arms wide and embraced his only son as though he'd never let him go. Then Neil rushed upstairs and knelt down to hug his frail mother so she need not get up from her bed that early in the morning.

His parents wept tears of joy amid disbelief. *Odd, Neil thought, how events trigger memories.* He recalled feeling very small and alone sitting beside his mature father on a bus taking him, for the first time, to his new elementary school in Bakewell, knowing nobody. Father looked down at him and, noticing the trembling lip, said, with the paternal expectation he felt for his little son,

"Young men don't cry; young men are always brave."

So now, to hide his overwhelming emotion, he said, "Food, a bath, and bed—in that order—I'll go and raid the kitchen. Eggs aren't rationed, are they? I'll try to answer all your questions tomorrow—if I wake up! My feather bed will reassure me I'm home—I can't wait for the feel of it!"

"Pops, in the meantime, look in my knapsack and you'll find a model German tank. I carried it back for you, together with my rifle."

CHAPTER 2

CONVERGENCE IN CONFLICT

Early in 1939, Jeannie's parents decided to take a cruise to the Outer Hebrides, entrusting the property to the care of the gardener and the house to the two maids. Ella had worked for them since she left school at fourteen, when Jeannie was two. Now, at sixteen, she felt safe left in Ella's care.

Jeannie's Dad loved Scotland: the open moors, the smell of gorse and heather, beautiful glens, tumbling rivers, and the pure history of the place appealed to his sense of adventure. Several times they had taken a car, to navigate narrow, steep dirt roads few would attempt other than possibly on foot. Often they took the caravan, parking it at a convenient farm, because there were so few places to stay in the North of Scotland, and the wilder the countryside, the happier her Dad would be.

This time would be different; he could sit back and let someone else be responsible for the navigation. It was to be their last vacation.

Jeannie was born in 1923, the same year that Adolph Hitler, the German Fuehrer, had other ideas—his own ideas—about the future of Europe; ideas that he was beginning to put in motion, changing the lives of children as young as Jeannie herself.

Jeannie's war began on September 3, 1939. She remembered the date and location for the rest of her life.

Often they took the caravan

"We'll listen to the news," her mother said, and switched on the radio in the little sitting room off the elegant entry to the large home her parents had built at Somerton Head, Devonshire, in southwest England.

The newscaster announced that Germany's Nazi Army had invaded Poland, following a similar intrusion of Czechoslovakia, at the demand of its Fascist Dictator, Adolph Hitler.

Anticipating Hitler's advancing armies across northern Europe, Neville Chamberlain, Great Britain's Prime Minister, declared war against Germany and later, its Fascist ally, Italy, ruled by its own Dictator, "Il Duce" Benito Mussolini, Premier since 1922.

Neville Chamberlain was a "gentleman's gentleman." Jeannie could see him now—top hat, bow tie, furled umbrella—who believed in diplomacy, but his diplomatic efforts were scorned by Hitler who, with mighty forces and egotistical will, believed Germany could become the flagship of the western world—with Hitler at its helm.

In a strange way, Jeannie was excited. She had grown tired of the news, with subtle threats of danger to her own country. Now, finally, something was going to happen. Winston Spencer Churchill, son of the Duke of Marlborough, and a military family, was elected by his peers to succeed Neville Chamberlain as Prime Minister. With Britain at war, there were no separate political parties bickering amongst themselves; he was free to select the best person for the job in hand. Churchill was in charge of decision-making. Undoubtedly predestined.

Jeannie had heard him speak. He was motivating and inspiring and sounded as though he would not put up with any nonsense. He had created a War Cabinet, and moved its personnel out of London to a fortified underground cellar for greater safety.

"I've got to get home by six," people said, "Churchill's speaking on the radio tonight!"

Her mother sensed her mood and was quick to respond to it.

"You have no idea what war means, dear. Your father and I lived through the Great War, when he was away in Europe for four long years," then reminiscing "and I was cutting pit props to hold up the trenches. There was rationing—meat, butter, cheese, sugar and clothes—and I gave all my gold rings, bracelets and brooches to aid the war effort and"—breaking into a smile—"I met Daddy in London prior to embarkation. He wore his Army uniform, but it didn't fit him. He looked awful—and you know how smart he always is. I bought some scissors, a thimble, and needles and thread and sat in our hotel room, sewing, while he lay in bed trying to get some sleep. In the morning he looked so well dressed because it fit, he picked me up and gave me a big hug."

Tears welled up in her eyes as she recalled the tender moment.

Jeannie said: "He came home, Mummy, and then you had me!"

"Yes, darling, about five years after the War ended. Your brother was born earlier, but he only lived for three days."

Jeannie knew that and felt sad; it merely reaffirmed that she was an only child. It would have been fun to have a big brother. Maybe? He might have been killed in this new, strange war.

British troops were sent to France immediately after WWII was declared, poorly prepared to combat Hitler's well-equipped forces which had been training since about 1923.

The winter of 1939/1940 was to be the coldest on record in Europe.

September 1939, two things happened to change Jeannie's life forever: Britain declared war against Germany on September 3, 1939; her father had low blood pressure, but suffered the first of five strokes, which ultimately paralyzed him.

Every day, a robin with a red breast came and sat on the top of the open casement window of his bedroom and chirped plaintively.

"Mum, why does the robin come and sit there? It sounds so sad."

"It knows your Daddy is dying, Jeannie. After he dies it will go away."

He died peacefully in his bed on January 22, 1940 at only 56 years of age, and they did not see or hear the robin again.

Jeannie commented, following his funeral that winter day, attended respectfully by many left in the village, "Daddy was so sick, he didn't really know what was going on this time, did he? He's been supplying cars, vans and trucks to important people and businesses in almost all the County since before the Great War, but I heard on the radio that all the engineering companies must build Spitfires and Hurricanes and Lancaster bombers. What's going to happen to Daddy's business?"

"Uncle will manage it; he's learned everything he knows from your father. He'll have to convert most of the building to a repair shop because there won't be any new vehicles to sell—but I'm sure there will be plenty to repair. They'll have to find second-hand spare parts."

She didn't like the idea of her father's business being left in the hands of her mother's brother; but there was really no other choice if her mother were to retain any financial interest.

"Can I leave school and look after Daddy's office? I can always go to College later, when war will have ended, and by that time I'll know what I want to do." She was thinking she could keep an eye on her uncle, and manage the accounts.

Little did she realize how much later College would be, or why.

"If you're sure that's what you want to do, dear. It would be a big help to your uncle and myself at the moment." She was obviously distressed, and probably not really capable of making logical decisions at that point, let alone on that day.

It would be years later that Jeannie recognized and appreciated how very brave and uncomplaining her mother was at the time of her father's premature death.

That July 1940, in spite of petrol rationing, Jeannie's widowed mother took Jeannie, and Jess, her close friend, to Minehead in North Somerset—"Lorna Doone" country—an adventure for them and a nostalgic trip for her; undoubtedly why she chose it.

The Battle of Britain also commenced in July 1940. Two of Jeannie's cousins joined the sparse ranks of "Spitfire" and "Hurricane" fighter pilots, defending the Dover coast and London against Hitler's waves of bombers. Cities were surrounded by a helium balloon-barrage suspending steel cables high in the air to obscure bomb accuracy.

Bombs struck East London—"Dockland." The depth of the River Thames made London a major inland port since time immemorial.

The many families whose homes were destroyed sought comparative safety in the depths of the subways, the rails for which and the stations, ran one above the other. Families took blankets down at night to the deepest platforms and lay like sardines in a can, sheltered from the "blitz"—a name soon to be added to the Oxford Dictionary.

The Battle of Britain fighter pilots, incredibly courageous in spite of being outnumbered, were deserving of Winston Churchill's praise:

"Never in the realm of human conflict has so much been owed by so many to so few."

"Wonder if we're going to be 'entertained' by 'Lord Haw-Haw' on the same wave-length as our favorite radio programs tonight?" Jeannie said to her mother.

It was the nickname of an Englishman with an exaggerated college-educated accent who had defected to the enemy and tried to unnerve everyone with his sarcastic lies and foreboding. In fact it had the opposite effect: Aggravation!

In 1945, the Nazi radio propagandist William Joyce, known as 'Lord Haw-Haw' was convicted of treason and sentenced to death by a British court.

A few days later Jeannie's mother said, "I had a 'phone call today. Homeowners with properties and spare bedrooms away from London and other large cities are asked to offer hospitality to those who are being evacuated. Since we have nine bedrooms, I thought we could offer six. The lady said there are some elderly retired people, so they would pay us for the accommodation. We still have the maids and the gardener; it would pay their wages. I understand that one of the ladies is Mrs. Gordon, widow of General Charles Gordon. She is traveling with her daughter and granddaughter."

Jeannie recalled having seen General Gordon's tomb in St. Paul's cathedral in London. He was killed at Khartoum, capital of Sudan, in 1878. Little did she then dream she would be playing card-games with his philosophical widow to relieve boredom in her late years. Or that she would conspire with his lively granddaughter to hide a couple of pet lizards under her coat collar, to peep out during the Vicar's sermon and alarm the righteous ladies in the pew behind . .

Penny was a little older than Jeannie but she had lost her father, her home and her friends and was resigned to spending time with her bereaved mother and very elderly grandmother for an indefinite period; an occasional spin in her sports car seemed to provide limited relief!

Completing the entourage was Charles—not Charley, Chas or Chuck—but Charles—so named in deference to the General—he would answer to nothing less. He was a magnificent, aristocratic tabby cat.

He didn't fight with the residents—Peter, Titsy and Dusky the dog—he merely regarded them with the utmost disdain. From the first day, Charles settled into his new abode—namely, the servants' quarters, ignoring his rightful owners—probably sensing that food was in the vicinity. Ella and Daisy always sat on a long antique stool at mealtimes, Charles regally between them. They didn't feed him at the table, but he was assured of being first in line.

Even domestic animals were subjected to some of the rigors of life imposed by war. Jeannie's former happy country life became restricted and vastly different.

Mother sounded relieved and quite thrilled with the entire arrangement so Jeannie hid her doubts; after all, they had the little bungalow in the grounds so there would be some privacy, and the war wouldn't go on forever.

Children were evacuated and sent to various areas of the country without their parents, to stay with those kind families who could look after them and to attend local country schools. Many had never seen a meadow or a cow in their young lives, so found it a very strange experience.

One such young evacuee asked Jeannie: "Ma'am, please can I have a job? I'm fourteen and I'm finishing school in June. If I can work part-time now I can learn a lot and work full-time then. Maybe I could learn how to use the petrol pumps and to mend some tires? My name's Louis; I'm staying at Mrs. Potter's. She can tell you all about me."

Louis was an enterprising "Cockney" evacuee, from Central London, and he was given the job.

It was not until after WWII that the Education Acts raised the school-leaving age in all County schools from fourteen to sixteen.

There was considerable troop movement in the normally quiet Devonshire countryside, following the return of the BEF—British Expeditionary Force—consisting primarily of young volunteers, who had received orders to blow up all vehicles and equipment and retreat to the Channel ports and beaches of France. It had been an ill-conceived notion to send them in the first place, poorly trained and under-equipped. Now, they had nothing but hand-held rifles with which to counter the Messerschmitt fighters splaying the beaches of Dunkirk with gunfire—back and forth, back and forth.

Jeannie heard the passionate message over the radio—to the following effect:

"This is to anyone who owns a seaworthy vessel anywhere along the south coast: Please sail for Dunkirk to bring back our boys from the beaches—tonight!"

Under cover of darkness, those who answered the call to cross the usually treacherous English Channel retrieved troops in varying stages of health or injury. A virtual armada of small boats—pleasure steamers and fishing boats accustomed to hugging the coastline—facilitated rescue at great risk of life and limb. Uniquely, that night was relatively calm. Commercial cruise ships and naval vessels followed in their wake; it took longer to get them organized. About four hundred little ships responded, of which a hundred were sunk by the Germans.

After three or four weeks' leave for those who had returned safely from conflict, instructions were transmitted by radio to the troops, scattered countrywide, to rejoin the original regiments at designated locations, and to proceed further as determined. Jeannie and her mother found that the local cider factory and the stables of various farms had been commandeered by the Army to house some of them. Military exercises were taking place in Devonshire, on Exmoor and Dartmoor.

The view from the house extended into the valley and hills eastward so the approaching convoys of trucks, with their motorcycle outriders assuring that none would be lost, could be seen and heard for a distance. To the two young maids, Ella and Daisy—to whom going "abroad" was visiting the next town—this was heart-throbbing excitement. Jeannie's mother urged them, "Load those two large trays with buns and biscuits and run across the lawn to hold them out to our boys as they pass."

Ella called to Daisy as they ran: "Let's run to the high banks at the end of the driveway by the main road. We'll be high enough to reach them in their cabs."

They needed no second bidding. There were whoops of delight from the young men—not only for the buns and biscuits, but also at seeing the pretty girls in their cute maids' uniforms!

Jeannie thought—Oh boy! Mum's managed to stretch the rations now that we have more people in the house—but all in a good cause.

the high banks at the end of the driveway by the main road.

She was not surprised—her mother's kindness and caring were well known. She remembered the old "tramps" pre-war who stumbled up the long driveway—homeless—they would shuffle from town to town or village to village, begging for sustenance, clothes or money. Mother always gave them a huge sandwich and filled their stained tin cans with steaming tea, telling Ella and Daisy,

"I will always give them food, but not money. It will be wasted on ale. You'll never die from starvation if you help others."

Her strict Victorian upbringing included compassion, so she bought hemp handmade exterior doormats and wooden clothes pegs from itinerant gypsies rather than from retailers.

Due to fear that German paratroopers would invade Britain, Army lookouts were stationed at many points of high ground inland from the southern coastline; there was one such lookout in the field adjacent, comprised of about a dozen soldiers, alternating duty.

In spite of the pitch darkness of enforced wartime blackout, Jeannie's mother made a huge flask of hot cocoa and delivered it nightly with some pies or pastries when she took her precious Dusky for his evening walk along the lane, aided by a shaded flashlight. Undeterred by the strict rationing of food, she invited each pair of guards for dinner once a week when the day shift came off duty.

One day, her mother called Jeannie at work: "Don't be late coming home tonight, dear. Such a nice young Scotsman stopped by today on a motorbike to thank me for my kindness to the boys in his charge, and I invited him back for dinner."

That evening Jeannie thought, I'm listening for a motorbike, but it is an army truck in low gear chugging up our long driveway and stopping outside the front entry door. Pity! He's not alone. He must have brought the exchange guards for the evening, and he'll be taking the other two back to camp after they've also enjoyed Mum's dinner. Of course, it's Saturday night; I'd quite forgotten.

"Good evening, please come in. If you just step inside I'll put the lights on as soon as I've closed the door." Ella greeted them at the front door with a flashlight, shining it on the step.

Since the dining room was the temporary domain of the retirees, Jeannie decided to sit at the foot of the refectory table in the large kitchen/breakfast room, and leave the rest to Mum. This was going to be interesting! She'd seen all of the boys who had been on guard duty in the field next door because Mum had invited them for dinner at the end of a week. They were young and missing home, grateful for her mother's care and concern. Mother had seemed really impressed with the young man in charge of them who was due to have dinner with them tonight. She could hear his step in the hallway.

He strode in with gracious confidence, in spite of being encumbered by military boots and uniform, his handsome face breaking into a captivating smile, illuminating Jeannie's world—just as though someone turned on a bright light bulb. His beautiful dark eyes looked straight into hers, and she thought: I know—I just know that I'm looking at the love of my life.

"Hello, I'm Neil. You must be Jeannie; your mother mentioned your name to me."

She shook his hand, thinking—Even his hands are perfect! They're pianists' hands—long, strong, fingers; beautiful nails; cool to touch; but capable of a firm grip.

She could barely hear Mum's voice suggesting Neil should sit at the head of the table—in Daddy's chair. Mother will sit at his left with the two, noticeably embarrassed, daytime guards, opposite her. She watched Neil standing by his chair, waiting for her mother to be seated, then quietly moving behind her, easing the chair in place as she sat down, and returning to his own place. She thought: He has a soft voice, he's courteous and cultivated, and he has such a charming smile; he's tall and more handsome than anyone I have ever met. He's gorgeous.

Jeannie was conscious of her heart pounding; and one of the guards monopolizing conversation in rather a loud voice, clattering his utensils on the china plate. Neil tried to respond to her mother in his soft tone, but Jeannie couldn't catch all his words. All she could do was look at his beautiful face with those incredible dark eyes—her heart melting when his glance turned towards her...

He looked at his wristwatch and indicated to the two guards that it was time they all got back to camp. She thought, I must catch mother's eye, and make sure she invites Neil to come back some other night when he is free—and that she gives him the phone number to call if he doesn't have a ride, because I can drive and pick him up. He can call from the post office.

Waiting seemed like an eternity, but after five days the 'phone rang and Jeannie picked it up—hoping, hoping?

"Hello, it's Neil," he said. "If it's still okay for me to come for supper again, I can get a ride with the truck bringing the guard change, but I have to be back in camp before dark."

"Of course, it's fine. We'll look forward to seeing you again, particularly on your own because it will be easier to talk."

The days are long in the summer months and it is usually light until 10:00 PM.

Neil didn't mention the army that evening, but began talking about his school days—Preparatory School in Edinburgh—and the fact that the very popular Principal there became the Principal of a boys' Public School in England, so the parents of the boys at the Preparatory School sent their sons—"the Scots contingent"—to the English Public School in Dorset when their Principal moved to it that September; the beginning of the school year.

"I was very happy there, and I still have friends among the staff; most of the boys of my year also volunteered for service."

Dorset is the County adjacent to Devonshire on its eastern boundary. Public Schools in Britain are all private boarding schools.

Neil pulled some small sepia photographs of the school and grounds out of his wallet. It was originally a beautiful private mansion, but the governors of many private schools in Britain at the time purchased these lovely old homes, being in need of the space for boarding accommodation and classrooms, with grounds sufficiently large for playing fields and further construction of laboratories and gymnasiums.

Most of them were conveniently located near a village whose occupants had worked for the original owner not only in the house and stables, but also on the surrounding land. Some of those same people were happy to continue their relationship with the property under its new management and needs. It represented work in the countryside for them. Stables were still useable, so riding was an additional sports activity.

Upon seeing the photos, Jeannie's mother said: "I recognize that property! I've been there—in fact, I stayed there with my husband. He was a distributor for several of the car companies since before the Great War, and I visited the homes of the purchasers, often to drive home in our own car after he had delivered the new vehicle. Sometimes, we had

It was originally a beautiful private mansion

to stay at a property for a few days to familiarize the chauffeur with the automobile."

It was a prestigious occupation at the time; vehicular transport of any description was still unique in the early part of the Twentieth Century.

Jeannie was feeling more and more close to Neil; they had much in common, and it seemed inevitable they should meet. Neil glanced at his watch, and thanked Jeannie's mother,

"I've enjoyed the evening so much. I'll walk back to the village while it is still light. I don't want Jeannie to waste petrol driving me back, because I know it's rationed."

Jeannie said, "The best way is through the lanes; it's shorter than the main road. But I had better walk with you part of the way so you don't take the wrong turning and get lost."

They chatted quietly, and she walked over a mile with him, down the hill, but when they came to the second junction she stopped, and said,

"You'll be all right from here. You'll come out at the end of the lane by the church. Turn left there and you'll be in the village."

He put his arms around her and held her tight, kissing her on the lips for a long moment.

"I'll come and see you again," he said, releasing her from the warmth of his strong body. And he walked around the corner, out of sight.

She skipped home—on air!

Neil came to see them several times, sometimes with the guard truck, sometimes on a motorbike. That last time he said,

"I have a week's leave, so I'm going home."

Jeannie, concerned, asked him,

"Please could you give me your address? I'd love to remain in touch. Who knows when, or where, you'll be sent next?"

There happened to be a large yellow legal-size lined writing pad next to the radio on top of the bureau in the breakfast room. Jeannie led the way across to it. Neil took a fountain pen out of the top pocket of his battledress jacket and wrote his name and the brief address diagonally across the lined paper, right in the middle of the first page:

Neil MacLeod, followed by the street name, and the name of the village: Baslow, Near Bakewell, Derbyshire.

CHAPTER 3

THE STEERING WHEEL—THE FORK IN THE ROAD DETERMINES THE LIFE TO BE LED

Jeannie walked in through the front entry door when she reached home after parting from Neil, and her eyes were drawn to the opposite wall. She remembered the old steering wheel from the earliest days, hanging on the wall as if to draw attention to itself, in the house where she was born—The Bungalow—now home to Grandma, Aunt Martha and Uncle Sid.

Jeannie and her parents had moved into The Big House, standing grandly about two miles away at Somerton Head, the top of a rise with views for miles across a fertile valley to a picturesque range of hills.

That's what she would call the house—"High Hills." She'd been eight at the time. The name stuck.

She remembered her father, that day. She'd been standing just inside the front entry door, like she was now.

"What are you doing, Jeannie?"

Her father's voice always had a little laugh in it. He was a trim, active man, with smiling blue eyes, clever, bright, and full of ideas. Jeannie turned to face him and he picked her up to give her a big hug before

The Bungalow

High Hills

putting her down to face the wheel, now hanging in the middle of the wall opposite the front entry door at the top of the wide steps.

The entry hall was an imposing room with an Indian rug on the polished floor, two antique log boxes, one brass and one copper, a round oak table against the left wall with one leaf up to support a beautiful antique copper tea kettle; narrow shelving at picture-rail level, wide enough to hold pewter pots and colorful china; and a large brass dinner gong near the door to the dining room.

Jeannie's mother had impeccable taste.

"There was a big war in Europe, lots of soldiers fighting, and the wheel was on the car which took me safely through many countries. When the war ended, I took the steering wheel off it as a memento, so I would never forget where I went and all the people I knew; some of them didn't come home."

"Why? Didn't they want to live in England any more?"

Daddy paused for a moment, then said: "You remember that sometimes I get your mother to drive her car with the soft top down so I can stand up on the passenger side?"

"Yes, so that the rabbits and hares all sit up on their haunches in the headlights—and you shoot them with your gun!"

"Well, that's what happened to lots of the soldiers."

"You mean someone shot them and they died and that's why they didn't come home to England?"

"Yes, but that is why I had that brass plate fixed to the steering wheel with each country engraved on it—so I wouldn't forget them—and so that people who see this wheel will never forget them either and maybe there will be no more wars."

"Have you seen Grandma and Aunt Martha?"

"Yes, but Uncle Sid isn't very happy about the move. Aunt Martha wants me to give him a job—I don't know what he could do with the new cars and trucks."

"Maybe he could wash them and keep them clean inside and polish the lights and brass door handles!"

"Kiddo, you're so bright! I hadn't thought of that! It's so difficult to find work for someone suffering from shellshock since the Boer War."

"I'm glad they came here to Devonshire. It was fun to go and stay at Grandma's Norfolk inn, but I'd rather live here."

Momentarily, her mind returned to the present. How she wished Daddy had lived to meet Neil; it had been an emotional day.

"I wanted to start a bus route to pick up people from the villages and take them to Norwich market but your mother didn't think that would work out." His normally energetic voice held a hint of sadness and defeat, which even Jeannie, at eight years old, recognized.

"That's when I decided to move to Devonshire and open a business, years ago."

" Mum told me that you wanted to sail half way around the world to a little island right in the middle of a big blue ocean, with a town called Honolulu; she pointed it out on the globe in the study. I thought that would be fun. Did you meet somebody during the Great War who had been to Honolulu? What a wonderful name. It sounds like a song!"

"No. It's just that your Mum said Grandma would be very sad because Uncle Fred already sailed away to New Zealand, and she's getting old so that would be like losing two of her children, and her grandchildren."

Jeannie remembered spending a long time trying to find New Zealand on the globe. It looked as though it was in the same ocean as Honolulu; anyway much closer than England.

Jeannie loved her Mum dearly; she was such an elegant lady. She wore beautiful silk dresses and looked like a princess. But Dad offered prospects of fun and adventure; life was never dull with him around. He was always inventing things, and he knew all about cars. He sold new cars for the manufacturers to the owners of the big country mansions—but nobody drove.

He had Jeannie and her Mum rocking with laughter as he described how he had been trying to teach the respected head coachman to drive the latest "horseless-carriage" and become a chauffeur, when the young groomsman—given the chance—would inevitably prove to be the better pupil. Jeannie still owned a valuable French glass and brass carriage clock given to her father by Lady Harrison in 1907, engraved with her name, in gratitude for his help and perseverance.

One Sunday he called—"Jeannie, tell Mum we're going for a picnic!"

It was always an adventure to go for a drive with her Dad. He loved to take them up Porlock Hill in North Devon. In those days—the late '20s—it was an unpaved road and had a notorious "S" bend at its steepest part. Just beyond the bend there was a grass verge on the left—in the U.K. you drive on the left because, years ago, when riding a horse, it left the sword-arm free. Reins are held in the left hand—and her father always pulled over at that particular point.

He sat in the car with his foot on the brake and his hand on the parking brake:

"Quick! Jump out and find rocks to put behind all four wheels."

Jeannie and her Mum got out of the car almost before he had finished speaking. The situation was urgent.

Jeannie always watched the car in trepidation, expecting it to run backwards, never to be seen in one piece again, but her Mum consoled her—"Don't worry dear, your father has put the car in first gear"—which didn't mean anything to Jeannie at her age. Daddy then got out, admired the ocean view, and took deep breaths of "fresh country air"—as though the rest of their lives were spent in a city.

The worst was still to come. Daddy was ready to go. He got in the car and started the engine—it was still in first gear—so he had to have one foot on the clutch, a foot on the brake, and a hand on the parking brake while they frantically removed rocks from behind the front wheels and jumped in with alacrity. Then came that terrifying moment when Dad's right foot moved to the accelerator while, simultaneously, his left foot released the clutch and—with wheels spinning on the steep grade—miraculously they took off amid a cloud of turf and dust!

He did it every time they went up that hill. The car was a Sizaire Berwick, a French body with an Austin engine; a large square blue box with solid leather seats and a split front windshield which one could open for air—its license plate: TA 8199.

The road ran between Lynmouth, on the coast, and Lynton, high up on the hill. It intrigued and delighted Jeannie to look at the ancient horse-drawn carriage, kept at Lynmouth as a showpiece. The attached brass plate explained that the carriage transported the Royal Mail. It must have taken at least three pairs of horses to drag it painfully up

Sizaire Berwick – TA 8199

that hill and to skid down again on the return journey with the two coachmen desperately hanging on to the brakes, which worked like clamps on the iron tread encircling each wooden wheel.

But all that was years ago. Jeannie touched the old steering wheel fondly, saying: "Goodnight, Daddy."

She switched off the hall light, went upstairs to bed, and lay there, dreaming as though it was all happening again.

When Jeannie's parents built "High Hills" it had a separate garage large enough for five cars and a stable for her pony. It was a corner property with two acres of land and a small, pretty copse of mature beech and oak trees with lots of wild flowers growing among them—primroses, violets, bluebells, pink campions and soft green moss. The birds built their nests there each Springtime—thrushes, blackbirds, robins, wrens—sometimes she'd even find a cuckoo's egg in with the others. Cuckoos were too lazy to build a nest of their own but they made plenty of noise about their intentions!

The back gate opened to a lane bordered by a wood filled with rhododendrons—another exciting place to play or ride her pony—or sometimes follow the foxhounds on foot if they chased a fox in there. It was easy to tell if there was a fox nearby because of its pungent odor!

Jeannie's "best friend" was the only young person living within ten minutes' walking distance of her home in the country in Devonshire, England. Jeannie met her through her mother's purposeful introduction when she was eight and Jess was six-and-a-half. Her father, a "gentleman farmer," had sufficient money never to have to work in all his life. They had horses, and cows, pigs and chicken for their own use, a wonderful apple orchard, fields with rabbits and hares, streams with tadpoles and frogs, and an exciting little woodland harboring primroses, violets, daffodils, bluebells and budding trees to announce each Spring's arrival.

They climbed trees with inviting branches, and each built a "house" under a chosen tree from willow stalks and ferns, but close enough to each other to share the day's secrets. They had no wristwatch to tell the time, but the familiar light of the sky and an occasional rumbling stomach let them know when the next meal was likely to be awaiting them. Often Jess' grandma baked some "treats"—tasty pastry filled with currants or sultanas and tied in a knot—which she threw from her bedroom window for them to catch below.

At weekends and during school holidays, they lived in the fresh air almost all year round; if not outside, in the hayloft searching for the latest litter of kittens. Or they saddled up two of the horses and rode them over the fields or around some of the many country lanes, which offered rides of varying length and interest. Devonshire lanes have high, mossy banks, covered with wild flowers. Or they rode to Aylesbeare Common or Woodbury Common to follow dirt tracks through the heather and to check out the latest gypsy encampment. Sometimes Jeannie asked the gypsies if they'd made any outdoor mats, which they'd then fetch from a caravan.

Jeannie knew her mother might want one, together with raffia place mats, string, and clothes pegs to hang sheets, towels and clothes from the washing line to dry. There were no washing machines or dryers when Jeannie was a young child—but her mother did have the maids—two fulltime and often two more part-time—for Monday's wash, Tuesday's ironing, and Wednesday's polishing of the copper and brass, and the tableware.

One day Jess told Jeannie that she, and her mother and father, were going to compete in a gymkhana at the local village. That name originated when India was a British Colony and the troops and aristocracy entertained themselves with various feats on horseback.

"I'm riding "Mystic Flight"—Mum's mare," she said, "and Dad's going to ride "Black Knight" because he's such a good jumper."

The occasion was the Silver Jubilee of King George V and Queen Mary in 1935, twenty-five years since they were crowned King and Queen. Each child was given a crock Jubilee Mug with a painting of the King and Queen on one side of it and an inscription on the other. Jeannie used hers and eventually it was broken. Today there are probably few still in existence.

The girls went to boarding school together in Exeter but made the journey daily on the old red country bus. That added about two hours to their day and they still had homework, but they preferred it to boarding. Besides, there were always the horses and the dogs and cats at home to look after, and the weekends to plan.

As a child, Jeannie took Titsy, the old tabby cat, to bed with her. Titsy lay with his head on the pillow and his body stretched down inside the bed, and Jeannie lay with her back to the purring cat—as close as she could to feel and hear the purr!

It was a precious childhood, and she treasured the memories.

CHAPTER 4

SURVIVAL

Jeannie questioned the sanity of her decision—to forego the final year of her education at a sophisticated English boarding school, for her humdrum existence in what had been her enterprising father's business, now changed beyond recognition by the war.

It was also an education of sorts: An education of life, and survival.

Jeannie was seventeen. If she volunteered to serve her country, rather than waiting to be conscripted upon reaching the age of eighteen, she stood a chance of entering the service of her own choice. In the meantime, she tried to benefit as much as possible from the effects of her current decision.

Now, she was a cross between an amateur secretary, an apprentice mechanic, a psychological assistant, and a chauffeur—the occupation of the moment varying beyond her control with day and time. Frequently, there were insufficient hours in the day. It was important to make the most of time. You didn't know whether you would be alive the next day. So she read, while waiting for others, and was seldom without a favorite book—and a writing pad and fountain pen.

Jeannie grew up fast.

Petrol was rationed, a coupon book supplied to each vehicle—one vehicle per family, more for businesses, upon application. Since the chauffeurs enlisted, many owners stored their vehicles under cover, raised on blocks to preserve the tires. To save petrol, Jeannie's mother bought her an "Autobike"—a motorized bicycle with a speed of about 20 MPH on the flat. It retained its pedals primarily for its rider's physical assistance to the engine going uphill. It had two forward gears, and neutral; a clutch operated by the left hand and a brake and accelerator by the right. It ran on a mixture of oil and petrol.

Jeannie first earned a license to drive a car when she was sixteen in February 1939. She was tested on a 1932 Two-seater Morris with a soft top and a rumble seat, three forward gears—without synchromesh—and reverse; a choke in the dashboard to pull up and reduce the air intake to the carburetor to make starting easier when the engine was cold; a shift and parking brake in the center front, and one driver's side mirror on the right.

She thought if she could drive that, she could drive almost anything.

She also drove a navy-blue Four-seater BSA with a "fluid flywheel," the forerunner of the synchromesh gearbox—nice to drive—and Jeannie found herself in demand by almost everyone without a car. Her mother had a Five-seater Austin Twelve—quite a large body for its time—so Jeannie alternated those three vehicles, depending upon the use required.

Life was a kaleidoscope of perpetual motion—cars, vans and trucks breaking down, having to be towed—Uncle towing, Jeannie, both literally and figuratively, "at the end of her rope." Searching for spare parts, mainly in junkyards, to get them on the road again. Pumping petrol, ordering fuel, filling out forms; typing bills, answering the telephone, changing tires when someone came in with a "flat"—there were no new tires, they were "retreads"—a rubber strip molded around the original tire. Fetching milk, bread, eggs, vegetables or fish from the village—all of which would have been delivered pre-war—taking them to her mother so that the new household could be fed. Starting the Petter engine to charge up the lights at the house; endlessly chauffeuring people from here to there and back again, sometimes waiting, other times dropping them off, collecting someone else, going back later for the others.

Shorthanded at the business with most able workers being enlisted, Jeannie felt like a breathless "jack-of-all-trades"—ready for a little relaxation with her girlfriends at a dance for troops in the village hall—to which she invariably chauffeured the girlfriends!

There was the constant duress of a threatened invasion, the daily anticipation of German parachutists, and compulsory removal of all signs of every description—from street signs to shop fronts. When day turned to night no light was seen anywhere; all windows blacked out, usually with separate drapes of blackout material; lights turned off when entering or leaving a building. Vehicle lights dimmed and shielded by a metal "cap" with a "peak" extending above the light so it could not be seen from above; rear lights a mere reflector. Some trucks, and all military vehicles, had the rear axle painted white, with a small light directed at it from below.

Throughout all this, wave after wave of German bombers decimated cities. Great Britain was preparing for all-out war. German U-boats sank supply ships. It was critical to grow food. Gone were the days when it was nearly all imported from the many Colonies—all a part of the then far-ranging British Empire—indicative of a mother country breeding adventurers, sailors, soldiers, engineers and civil servants. So, the Land Army—which included some prisoners of war—got to work and, according to post-war records, provided fifty-two per cent of the required food. Britain also fed increasing numbers of refugees. The rest came from America in the form of part of a "lease-lend" agreement—mainly Spam and canned fish, canned horsemeat, powdered eggs, powdered milk, powdered potatoes; the basic necessities of life.

But Britain and Europe needed physical and practical help.

On December 7, 1941 it seemed they might get it. Of all the unlikely things to happen, the Japanese bombed Pearl Harbor, a major American naval base on an island in the Pacific Ocean—Oahu, Hawaii. That brought America into the war on two fronts—the Pacific and Europe.

All troops in Britain were undergoing extreme training, including those from occupied European countries who had escaped and joined British forces. Neil's Company had been sent to Cornwall after a short stint in Exeter, when he was billeted in a three-story building on North Street. Jeannie seldom heard from him—until one day, he called:

"I'm in Penzance, but going on leave tomorrow after our overnight move. By the time I've dropped off my kit and the truck in Newton Abbot, about ten miles from Exeter, there's a train I can catch which gets in at 5:20 AM. I want to spend a few days with you on my way home to Derbyshire, if that's possible? I know it's early, but can you meet me?"

Like most trains, Neil's ran late. He traveled with a friend who was getting married the next day, so they dropped off the friend and Jeannie took Neil home. He sank onto a bed in the big house, Jeannie staying with him for about an hour until the beginning of her own frenetic day.

In early afternoon, when she managed to go home again, he was sitting on the lawn, clean and shaven, changed into long gray slacks, white shirt, a blue jacket, holding Dusky, momentarily a civilian once more—a stranger to Jeannie—a beautiful, elegant stranger. Noticing her hesitation, he jumped up, held her close, and kissed her, as if to reassure her. She could feel the warmth of his body through the soft, fine material, and his heart pounding as she pressed her face against him in the embrace. She closed her eyes. Don't ever leave me, she thought.

Instead of going into the house, she led the way up the few wooden steps into the bungalow in the garden.

Neil looked around at the neat little sitting room—an upright piano with a portable radio standing on it, a cabinet gramophone with a manual winder and built-in speaker, room to store records—modern and quite expensive for its day. Two soft armchairs with a small table between them below the window opening to a deck running the length of the building; there's another window higher up in the wall facing the house; and a freestanding electric fire.

He sat down in one of the chairs and pulled Jeannie down onto his lap.

She said, "You can always visualize me here. This is my favorite place to get away from everything and everybody. I can write letters to you when I'm sitting here, and I can dream about us."

"What do you dream about? You don't really know me. I've written a few letters but nothing really important."

She thought, I know that you are the sweetest, kindest, most adorable person I have ever met, and I never want to lose you.

She said, " I've met many people, but I've never met anyone else like you. Please promise me that you will stay in touch, because I know you will be sent abroad again and I won't know where you are."

He gave her a long kiss, and then tried to stretch.

Jeannie said, "I'm sorry there isn't a sofa in here. Am I cramping your legs?" And she got up, holding out her hand to him. "Let's go and lie on top of the bed in the other room; it will be more comfortable. I can put the radio on and see if there's some music if you like?"

"No, don't bother—it will be nice to lie down, though. I've been up for hours—driving all night—and I didn't sleep on the train. It's a waste of precious time to sleep in the daytime on leave."

They lay on the comfortable bed in each other's arms, trying to forget the war.

She said, "We'll have some supper about seven this evening, so then you can have an early night if you're tired."

He said, "In the meantime..." and pulled her close to kiss her. "I'm really glad to see you again. I missed you. I felt as though we were just getting to know each other when I was sent to Cornwall."

"Tell me about your parents. They'll be happy to see you when you arrive early Wednesday morning."

"Yes, I'm worried about Pops. He has angina and I'm afraid he may not live much longer. Mother is very frail. She has neuritis, and arthritis in her joints. She takes aspirin by the handful and has tried to get relief by going to the brine baths at Buxton whenever possible. She never complains about the pain. She has to go upstairs on hands and knees, but when I'm there I can carry her; she's not heavy.

"What a shame. What will they do if one of them dies?"

"What can they do? Whoever is left will stay on in the house. Mother's sister comes by bus from Sheffield most weekends to be with her and there's a local lady to keep it clean."

"I wanted to tell you," Jeannie said, "I'm going to volunteer for the Field Ambulance Nursing Yeomanry to drive ambulances and other vehicles. The F.A.N.Y.'s are a holdover from the Great War but they're being incorporated into the Auxiliary Territorial Service and I want to make sure I'm driving. I'm not interested in Signals, or anything like that. I've done so much driving this past year of all manner of vehicles, so I don't think they'd have a reason to turn me down."

"I don't want you to join the Army. What is your mother going to say? She'll be lonely without you. But I understand your reasons—the same reasons I volunteered, rather than just waiting for my name to be called, and dumped into some Company I didn't care for. What about all the work you're doing currently? How is your uncle going to manage?"

"One of the people staying in our house is a retiree. His wife died so he's on his own, and his son is an army doctor. Personally, I don't much care for the idea, but he wants something to do and he can take care of the office and I suppose he can drive the cars. In July, when school ends, Louis will be able to do some of the dirty work. He's so anxious to have a full-time job and he's too young to be called up yet. There's no choice, they'll have to manage, because I'd be enlisted anyway at eighteen."

"I went into the recruitment office in Exeter and told them what I wanted to do. They gave me a written test and a medical. I must have passed those all right because they told me I'd have to go to London for an Interview; they'll set up the appointment and let me know the date. In the meantime, I have to obtain three references from acceptable people—not relatives—and they gave me a list of items I could take with me. They told me it would probably be a couple of months after the interview before I would know the result. If they accept me I'll be sent straight to Camberley, in Surrey, not to an Initial Training Center. You'll remember—that's been a site for male officer training for years, but I'll be going on an Instructor Training course to teach others to drive ambulances and trucks. If I pass that I'll be posted either to Gresford, North Wales, or Dreghorn, near Edinburgh. What's happening to you? Do you have any idea?"

"You know what it's like," Neil said—she could sense the internal shrug of his shoulders—"all sorts of rumors float around, and even if we know we're not supposed to discuss it, but I'm afraid it may be somewhere like Burma—that's a British colony or protectorate or something, and it's been invaded by the Japanese. I doubt they'll keep us all hanging around here waiting for another opportunity to invade Europe. I'm afraid this war's going to drag on for years."

Neil then changed the subject.

"Since I finished school, I've completed one year of a five-year Bachelor of Science in Engineering Degree at university, coupled with a Management Apprenticeship at one of the major car companies in Birmingham. It wasn't my first choice—I wanted to be an oral surgeon—to rebuild a jaw after a bad accident, for example, but that would have meant it would take seven years before I could earn sufficient to be independent of my parents. As a student/apprentice, at least I get paid something for the actual hours that I work. It's all practical experience, and not such a drain on them."

Jeannie thought how kind and considerate he was to forego his personal ambition in the interest of his parents, so she asked, "Will you go back there after the war?"

"I expect so—as long as nothing has changed, and they still let me count my first year." He rolled across the bed, away from her, and sat facing the wall. They were quiet for several moments.

"I'll be here," she said. "I'll always be here; or Mum will tell you where I am."

He lay down and rolled back again. Then, leaning over her and stroking her hair away from her face, he said, gently, "You're so sweet. I want to make love to you—my body is aching for you—but only if you want me to; I'm not going to force myself upon you."

She could feel her nipples hardening and her body stirring with love for him. She wanted to wrap him in her arms and cross her legs over him, holding him tight, protecting him, but she said: "We don't know when we'll get the chance to see each other again. I want you to remember me and love me. I can't bear the thought of losing you. We're two lonely people, looking for comfort. Take care of yourself for me and write to me so that I know you're still alive."

"I promise," he said.

And he stroked her gently, so gently, with those beautiful hands, and brushed his lips against her lips, and kissed her neck under her ears, and down between her breasts...He raised himself above her and kissed her on the lips.

Whilst softly making love to her he whispered, "Tell me if I hurt you; I don't want to hurt you..."

"Oh, my god..." and he collapsed, with his arms around her, holding her tightly to him—she could feel his heart beating fast.

"I'm sorry, I'm sorry," he said, muffled, as he buried his face in her neck.

"What do you have to be sorry for?"

"I didn't give you time—time—for your enjoyment; for your experience. It was so overwhelming for me—I couldn't help it—I couldn't wait; you're so wonderful to me; so kind, and so...different."

"It doesn't matter. It's okay." She held him, and kissed him on the lips, seeing that his eyes were filling with tears from the emotion he felt.

"It matters to me," he said, softly. "It will always matter to me."

"We'd better freshen up in the bathroom; supper will be ready," she said. You'll be here another couple of days; we'll try to spend more time together. The minutes are precious, and I want you to be able to remember me—so you won't forget me."

"I'd thought of going home via Reading," he said, "so I could stop by to see Duncan's sisters. He shared my dorm at school, but he speaks Arabic fluently because he was born in Egypt when his father had a government post there, so now he's been posted there in the army. But I think I'll spend the extra day here with you, if you like?

"You know that any time with you is always precious," she said, catching his hand and leading him to the door. "Now let's go and eat; mother will be sending Ella to find us—it's time she was on her way home; she's probably busy lighting the carbide in her bicycle lamp. That's a horrid smell—like rotten eggs—and it's a poor enough light anyway, without having it shaded like a car light. It's a good thing she knows the lane home so well."

"Your mother's pretty tolerant to leave us alone like this," he said.

"She likes you. Besides, her sisters—my aunts—always said she was the "crazy one" who resisted their Victorian upbringing, even though certain facets were embedded in her, I suppose. I think that's what attracted my father to her. He was a confident, unique person, with a mind of his own—a true entrepreneur—and he respected that in other people, particularly of his day and age."

"I would always make sure no harm came to you," he said, "but now I know the traits you've inherited from both your parents!"

She gave him a playful slap and led the way into the house for supper.

CHAPTER 5

THE PARTINGS

Early in March 1942, Neil was still in the United Kingdom, but his company had been moved all over England, most recently to Lincolnshire on the east coast. He called Jeannie to say he was arriving by train at Exeter St. David's station to spend a few days with her, before spending the rest of his leave with his parents. His father was getting up for an hour a day but was still very sick. Neil's latest military move was going to be further away from his home in Derbyshire.

They both loved the countryside, so they took a flask of tea and a snack—and Dusky—and drove the Austin 12 through Ottery St. Mary and up over Chineway Head, where they could give Dusky a run while they enjoyed their impromptu meal and time together. They made plans to go to Neil's boarding school in Dorset the next day, working out the mileage on maps, ever mindful of petrol rationing.

With glorious weather and an undulating route, since the car had a stick shift they were able to "coast" for miles and save petrol. They turned in at the gates to Neil's school to make a nostalgic, unannounced, visit. Jeannie recognized the building from the photo Neil had shown her mother. He went in to see the Principal and his wife, temporarily leaving Jeannie in the car—and ran into a tea party. He was not long, but Jeannie was glad she had her inevitable book to pass the time so that he wouldn't feel guilty.

He took Jeannie around the extensive grounds, reminiscing about his senior years and how he'd organized his Scottish pals—most of whom were members of the then unbeaten 1937 Interscholastic Rugby Team—to dig a swimming pool for them all to enjoy that final summer. The project had prior approval from the Principal, who arranged for it to be suitably lined when the excavation was complete. They looked at the photos of the team, still displayed in the school hallway; some had not survived Dunkirk, or were killed in bomb attacks, or flying Spitfires. It was a very emotional moment.

"Let's explore the little village," said Neil, "I always enjoyed the traditional architecture of the old houses and stores and the one memorable inn. Then we can return to the school, because my Housemaster and his wife invited us to their apartment."

Jeannie was delighted finally to meet them; she'd heard so much about these two Scots who had treated Neil like the son they never had. He had been the House Prefect during his tenure, carrying all responsibility for the job of ensuring school discipline was respected, and no bullying occurred. His best friend, Duncan, with whom he shared a Study, would normally have shared the duties, but that year he was the school's Head Prefect, a post carrying its own responsibilities.

Dr. and Mrs. MacDougal obviously thought the world of him and were concerned for his welfare. Leaving them, and the school, was sad. Such momentous occasions were always accompanied by the fear that such a time may never occur again.

Two and a half hours later they arrived home; it was ten o'clock at night. Next day they drove into Exeter to ascertain the time of Neil's train. He was going to Derbyshire via Reading, this time, to see Duncan's sisters, and to find out whether his friend was still alive and well, in Egypt.

That evening, Jeannie wrote in her diary: It has rained ever since Neil left. He is my sunshine, and the sunbeams shine through all the clouds while he is here. When he is with me I feel so little can go wrong, and even if it does, it doesn't seem to matter—together we can put almost everything right.

Jeannie's grandmother, living with Aunt Martha and Uncle Sid, in the bungalow, had cancer. She had about a month to live. Jeannie's mother went to see her almost every day, and Jeannie, whose life was as hectic as ever, saw her most weekends. She was a dear old lady. Jeannie's aunt and uncle from Southend-on-Sea also came to see her.

Jeannie thought about the times she'd visited grandma as a child ... it all seemed so long ago ...

Jeannie's grandfather died but her grandmother and Aunt Martha—mother's elder sister—continued to live in the lovely old inn in Norfolk County, England, about six miles from Norwich, the County Town—not then large enough to be called a City but it was the center of commerce for the area.

Jeannie missed her grandfather.

"Hurry up, Jeannie," he said on Monday each week, "Misty is all harnessed up to the trap and ready to go. We've just got to stop by Mrs. Green's and the Farmers' and old Tom Smart's to see what they need from the market and then we'll be off."

She reached up to grasp his hand as he pulled her up to the seat beside him, and found a strap he put around her to make sure she would not fall. Grandpa always asked about the neighbors' needs because they didn't have a horse like Misty, and he returned with the trap laden with goods unobtainable in the small village. Jeannie knew Uncle Sid could handle Misty, but it wasn't the same. In any case Uncle Sid was a bit "odd" so she didn't want to ride to Norwich since Grandpa died.

But she loved Grandma's old inn—though sometimes it was rather frightening—after all, she was only six. It had a sign saying "The Green Man." There was a painting of him, looking like an elf from her storybook.

The village street was straight and wide in her eyes, with pavements for pedestrians on either side, and two-story immaculate brick homes interspersed with small shops—butcher, baker, greengrocer, fishmonger and the local post office which also sold the weekly newspaper, cigarettes and confectionary. The owners lived above their shops. Mrs. Green lived over the Post Office.

Grandma's "pub," as the public houses or inns were called, was an intriguing building for a kid. It was Tudor in style, older than the brick houses—a later addition to the village—and it faced directly onto the pavement, where there were two stone steps up to a heavy oak door to enter the pub from the street. It was three stories high, though the top story was just one large room, under the eaves, with two windows at the front and two at the back. Grandma called them "Dormer" windows because they were built out from the roof, she said, and each one had a little roof of its own. Jeannie thought it looked like her dolls' house from outside.

Jeannie never ventured up to the "Dormer Room" unless her grandma was there. For one thing, the door was always locked, but also each stairway had a door at the bottom and a door at the top and she was afraid she might be shut in there in the dark, with no candle, and nobody would know where to find her. Grandma kept the most wonderful collection of large tropical seashells—mother-of-pearl and conch shells—and she said: "Jeannie, hold them tight to your ear and you'll hear the sea. Can you hear the waves?"

And she could—though there was no sea in sight.

The old wood floors were uneven. There was shiny green patterned linoleum on the landings and stairs, with fluffy natural hides breaking the monotony of the linoleum. It was new to the stores in Norwich, though, and saved the labor of polishing all the wood.

At the back of the building was a big walled yard where chickens ran free, with stables down the side, a white-washed washhouse opposite, and a small bathroom adjacent to it, the natural wood toilet seat for which extended from wall to wall. Newspaper was cut into tidy squares and stacked neatly in a little box in one corner ready for use. Rolls of bath tissue did not exist in those days and paper was scarce.

There was no running water—just a pump with a long handle for drawing water from a well outside. Jeannie's mother, when describing a girl with thick, long hair, would often say it was "as straight as a yard of pump water." And that was true. But nobody knew what she meant unless they'd lived in Norfolk—the stream of water from the nozzle to the bucket on the ground would be about three feet—a yard.

A large jug of water always stood ready for use in the bathroom, which contained a washstand with a rail for a towel at each end, a bowl for the jug, and a soap-dish, so you could wash hands then tip the bowl of water down the toilet to flush it.

Bath-night was interesting. Grandma had a huge old portable hip bath in a large room next to the kitchen, both of which had red tiled floors. The hip bath—it had high sides and an even higher curved back but you could stretch your legs out in it—had to be partially filled with cold water, then boiling water was added from two enormous black kettles with brass handles which always occupied the top of the old coal-burning range. It never went out.

She also had a sausage machine, and all sorts of magnificent copper and brass pots and pans, stored handily on a rack hanging from an old oak beam in the kitchen. The house was spotless. It was furnished with fine old antiques, such as the oak dresser in the dining room displaying the blue and white dinner service, used daily. The house always smelled of polish. Jeannie had to wear large headphones to hear Grandma's scratchy radio!

Attached to it on one side was the "pub," consisting of two large rooms—the "Public Bar," "Bar room" or "Tavern" for men only—generally workmen—and the "Lounge" or "Lounge Bar" for "Gentlemen." Gentlewomen never considered entering the Lounge Bar without being accompanied.

In the poorer area of cities, it was common to see children dressed in rags sitting on the stone steps outside the Public Bar, awaiting their imbibing parent.

Jeannie was not allowed to go across the hallway into the inn, never mind into the Public Bar! However, child-like, she'd sneak in occasionally. The place reeked of ale. The old, whiskery men were always kind to a child. One day one of the "regulars" gave her a halfpenny, which she clutched in her little hand. Then he said: "Run down to the Post Office and ask Mrs. Green for a ha'pen'orth o' round squares. Be careful crossing the street."

All the whiskery old men in the Bar room laughed. Jeannie thought he was just being kind. A halfpenny bought a lot of little "sweets" in those days.

She pushed open the door of the Post Office and the old bell on its spring at the top of the door announced her entry. Mrs. Green was a cheery, plump lady. "Hello dearie," she said, "what can I get for you today?"

Jeannie held out the halfpenny on the palm of her hand, "Some round squares, please."

Mrs. Green smiled an extra big smile, saying, "Well, I don't have any round squares left, but perhaps these will do; I think you will enjoy them." And she deftly poured a mixture of tiny candies into a cone-shaped bag, folded over the top and handed it to Jeannie, telling her, "Wait a minute while I walk around the counter and I'll see you safely across the road. Does your auntie know you're out here by yourself?"

Jeannie thanked her and scampered back to the inn as fast as her little legs would carry her. She ran into the house and, crossing the forbidden hallway, opened the door to the Bar room a crack and waved the arm clutching the little bag, just inside.

There was a big laugh and lots of handclapping—but then a stern voice behind her said: "Shut the door! You know you are not allowed in there!"

The summer when Jeannie was eight was the last time she stayed at Grandma's inn. It was being sold, she was told, and Grandma, Aunt Martha, and Uncle Sid were moving to Devonshire to live in "The Bungalow." She heard Aunt Martha on the 'phone to her mother saying she'd be glad to leave the old inn because Uncle Sid spent too much time in the public bar and it was bad enough dealing with his shell-shock without that.

"Can I see the shells once more please, Grandma, before you pack them up?"

She held each of them to her ear, listening to the sea, then watched Grandma wrap each one carefully in tissue paper and pack it in a wooden box, each separated from the others by balls of newspaper.

That evening, Annie, the Gypsy Fortune-Teller came in. She always dressed in long skirts and colored blouses, with lots of strings of bright glass beads around her neck. Her long, dark hair was going a bit gray, and she always wore the same old flat slippers.

Annie was a well-known character in the village and, since Grandma was leaving, she wanted to be kind to Annie and to pay her for her trouble. Annie told the fortunes of Grandma and Aunt Martha and wrote everything down in pencil on a slab of paper.

"Can I have my fortune told, too, please?" Jeannie asked.

They laughed, and nodded to each other. "No harm," they said, "she's only a child."

Annie held Jeannie's palm open on her lap, and Jeannie listened intently, keeping her eyes on the glistening glass beads—too nervous to look at their owner.

" ... and you will be married to a tall, handsome man and you will have three children but one of them will leave you. Then you will travel a very long way from here, and you will live in the sunshine with lots of dark-skinned people. You will be very happy, and then—and then...I can't tell you any more..."

She put down the pencil, handed Jeannie the sheet of paper, got up and shuffled out of the room without saying goodbye. Jeannie thought she saw her wipe away a tear with the back of her hand. She folded the piece of paper into a tight square, put it carefully in the pocket of her dress, and kept it for a long, long time.

Although Neil's entire 48th Division had left the area long since, there were still lookouts stationed in the field adjacent to "High Hills" and Jeannie's mother continued her nightly vigil with the cocoa and whatever epicurean delights she could muster for "the boys," as she called them, with affection. By this time they were air force, not army. Louis, the little Cockney evacuee, who had asked for a job when he left school, was attending A.T.C. training some evenings, though he was still too young to be enlisted in the air force.

The evening of April 2, 1942, when Jeannie did the cocoa trek, she was told there was an "Alert" about enemy planes.

On April 23, 1942, the first air raid for some time hit the harmless hamlets at Exminster, Leighton Steers, Pinhoe and Exmouth. Jeannie's best friend, Jess, was on fire watch at the school she was soon to leave. Hitler's ***modus operandi*** at that time was dropping incendiary bombs.

The next day there was another raid on Exeter. Paris Street and Summerland Street were hit. Jeannie returned to the A.T.S. recruiting office in Exeter where she had been tested successfully, and was now given a London address to which to write for the specific interview at which, if she were subsequently approved, she would be guaranteed entry into her chosen army wartime career.

Phone calls anywhere, to anyone, were problematic. Lines were controlled when emergencies arose. That evening, a Friday, Neil was able to get through to her at about eleven-thirty at night to say he had been posted to Woodhall Spa, in Lincolnshire—then anticipated being shipped abroad. Jeannie told him she hoped to leave home on the following Wednesday, arriving on Thursday, April 30, 1942. She had to see him once again. Mother decided she would go with her because they would not be far from Spalding, where they could go and visit one of Jeannie's cousins. So mother called the hotel and arranged for two bedrooms.

On Sunday night, April 26, there was a terrific explosion: a German plane crashed with its load of bombs on Aylesbeare Common, about three miles away from "High Hills." No longer was the countryside safe.

Jeannie and her mother drove to Sidmouth Junction station on Thursday. Leaving the car there, they caught the train for London at 7:30 A.M.

It was the Southern line, running into Waterloo, so they took a taxi to King's Cross station for the journey north to Peterborough, changed again for Boston and again at Boston for Woodhall Junction, and from there to Woodhall Spa. A tedious journey; but it was 1942—and wartime.

Neil came to the hotel after dinner that evening. They went out for a walk—just to be together, and alone. There was a full moon. It was quiet and peaceful in the beautiful wooded park, lacking the tensions of war.

"What is the number for your bedroom?" Neil asked Jeannie, "And how do I find it? I'll try to slip away from the billets tonight."

It was risky, but it might be years until they were together again—if ever. She was concerned for him...then relieved when she heard the light tap at the door.

The only time Neil was free was in the evenings. Jeannie was quite glad her mother had accompanied her. On Saturday they decided to catch the train to Lincoln and visit the famous cathedral, where the Head Verger gave them a knowledgeable commentary on its history. He had a keen sense of humor and made the visit interesting,

Two days later, Neil reported sick to the M.O., who suspected scarlet fever. It was tonsillitis. He was taken to a hospital and Jeannie was unable to see him again. He left a message with one of his friends asking her to write to his parents to tell them what had happened and where he was. She did that right away, knowing he was very worried about his father. She was concerned for his health, and devastated over the brevity of their visit.

Jeannie and her mother decided to go to Spalding the next day, where Jeannie's cousin, Doris, met them at the station and took them for lunch at her mother's house. Doris had to work so they said they would look around Spalding and meet her for tea at 4:00 PM at a delightful café situated in some beautiful gardens. Lincolnshire was the source of many cut flowers and bulbs supplied wholesale to florists. After tea, they walked back with Doris to her mother's home. She was uncle's first wife. There were two cousins: the other was Martha, who served as a nurse during the war.

The next day was Doris' twenty-first birthday. That morning they toasted her with sherry, and ate delicious cake before catching the 11:00 AM train to Peterborough. It was coincidental that they had made the trip at all. It was the last time they saw Doris or her mother, who were killed shortly afterwards in an air raid.

At Peterborough they caught the train to London, King's Cross, and repeated their prior journey in reverse to Sidmouth Junction station; and the car.

Then there were repeated demands for Jeannie to drive someone somewhere. When she drove into Exeter she scarcely recognized the place. On Sunday night, May 3, 1942, while they were away, Exeter suffered the brunt of incendiary bombs, and many of the old historic buildings were destroyed, as were all the buildings on North Street, where Neil was billeted for several weeks en route to Cornwall. Shock at the destruction of North Street brought to mind an incident while Neil was there.

Jeannie never normally wore a hat. She didn't like hats—they squashed your hair down so when you took them off you looked as though you had just woken up. But this hat was different. She fell in love with it the minute she saw it, and the color was perfect with her new two-piece, on which she had used precious clothing coupons.

It was a "Marina Pom-Pom." Princess Marina possessed a refreshing sense of style in spite of the war. She was the popular, elegant Greek wife of King George V's son, third in line for the throne, younger brother of Edward and Albert. The "Pom-Pom" was like an inverted pot, with a flat top, and sometimes a short veil, ending in the most fetching way just below eye level, plus a ribbon or other decoration around the "pot." Jeannie's hat had two "pots," a pretty fur surrounding the upper one, which also concealed the manner in which the veil was held in place. She had to remember to duck when entering or leaving the car.

She saw him as she drove down Queen Street in Exeter, and pulled over to the left curb. Neil recognized the car and came over to the driver's window, leaning down to talk to her.

Another soldier saw him and made a caustic remark as he walked past. Neil drew in his breath but let it pass.

"In this life, you meet them all," he said to Jeannie. He made no comment about the hat, but she knew he would say something later.

Unfortunately, the Prince, Marina's husband, was shot down while flying over the west coast of France, and that royal love story ended in tragedy.

Now, today, Jeannie was searching the streets among the ruins. Some stores had moved to the outskirts, as had also some of the banks; it was a question of driving around to find them.

Jeannie was called at home to help out at various shelters, checking people in and attending to their needs. The Prime Minister, Winston Churchill, spoke on Sunday, May 10, 1942, and warned of the probability of attack by gas.

Grandmother bid her last farewell, dying in her sleep on May 21, 1942, following a painful illness. She was buried to join Daddy and his sister in the same village cemetery on a drenching afternoon four days later.

Jeannie had her pending interview in London on her mind, so she stopped at Strete Ralegh on her way home, to see Sir Henry Imbert-Terry, to obtain a written reference from him. Then she drove to Larkbeare to ask Captain Hunter for the same thing, which he said he was pleased to give. Now she only needed the third reference from the Rector, who had known her family for years. She was notified to attend her pending interview in London on Saturday, May 30, 1942, at 32 Grosvenor Gardens.

Ironically, Captain Hunter's funeral was scheduled for the same day; he died unexpectedly following an operation for a duodenal ulcer—but of course his written reference was already received.

Jeannie was interviewed by a F.A.N.Y. Captain, a lady who seemed to think she was "the type of presumptuous young person who would enjoy herself" in the Service of His Majesty, King George VI. "Presumptuous?" Nobody had ever accused her of that before. But the Captain smiled, shook her hand, congratulated her on the interview, and told her to expect a rail warrant in the mail, together with full instructions to enroll for the Course at Camberley.

At home, Jeannie researched the Oxford Dictionary definition for "presumptuous." "Readiness to presume in conduct or thought; impertinently bold; audacious; fresh; arrogant."

U-m-m? Maybe it was those letters of recommendation? What was she supposed to do? Devonshire was full of Army retirees and manor houses. She drove their owners all over the place since the chauffeurs enlisted. She had a good education, and her grammar passed muster. Oh well, time would tell.

She wrote to tell Neil all about it, and her apparent success at the interview. She knew he would laugh—and tease her, subsequently.

Jeannie's army papers arrived in June, telling her to go to Camberley on July 1, 1942. It was to be the first day of her four years in the Service of His Majesty.

On June 23, Ella awakened Jeannie early—Neil was in Exeter, at St. David's station. She drove in to pick him up. She took care of business in the morning, while Neil slept, following the long train journey from Lincolnshire. Then they had a special afternoon. They took tea and a sandwich with them and drove to Sidmouth for a swim. It was a glorious summer day. They lay on the smooth stones of the beach, had tea, and then drove via Sidbury to the Hare and Hounds, and down through Gittisham, stopping under the trees for an hour, where they walked up a high bank from the car, opened their eyes and arms to the view and each other, and planned to go to Dorset and the school the next day.

Jeannie's mother ran out to meet them when they reached home; they both sensed something was wrong. There was a telephone call for Neil to go home immediately since his father was critically ill.

The train was the 10:10 P.M. from St. David's Station, Exeter, and he changed at Shrewsbury for Chesterfield. That train seemed to be an integral part of their lives. Neil caught it so many times, traveling north, and Jeannie dreaded standing on the platform, waiting for it, when he left.

They spent the next few hours together in the bungalow in the garden, always to be remembered for its peace and music; but now, sadness. Neil loved his father but knew he had to face the fact that he would lose him. Six days passed before Jeannie received news from Neil. His father was still alive but the doctor did not expect him to last another week. At least Neil got home and was able to talk to him again.

Jeannie was already at Camberley when Neil wrote that his father died on July 22, 1942. He was very upset, but managed to get five days' leave to attend the funeral.

Jeannie thought, now we're both "only" children, each with a widowed mother; we cannot determine what the next hour will bring, let alone the next day.

CHAPTER 6

IN THE SERVICE OF HIS MAJESTY, KING GEORGE VI—CAMBERLEY

The car was a large Rover Staff car, sparkling clean and comfortable, transporting her from the train station. She felt isolated from the world seated alone on the luxurious back seat behind the uniformed F.A.N.Y. Sergeant.

Jeannie knew when she entered the training camp at Camberley, they were a "privileged" group to be there. Camberley was a renowned stomping ground for officer recruits for many years. Subsequently, Princess Elizabeth—elder daughter to King George VI, to become heir to the throne upon his death—received an introduction to army life there, taught to drive by their own Company Commander Wellesley, whom Jeannie remembered well as an expert horsewoman participating in horse shows and races in the West of England.

The grounds and buildings were immaculate. Her first impression of the F.A.N.Y. Sergeant was militarily smart but pleasant. She was admitted to "B" Squad, in Hut #7, with three Scottish girls and four others.

The curved metal hut, with some windows down the sides, held twenty wooden bed frames, opposite each other, each provided with its own mattress, consisting of three separate square "biscuits". Each bed was issued two blankets, a pillow, and a locker. A standard fixture in all army huts was a closed circular room heater, lit through a hole in the top, and ventilated by a stovepipe through the roof, which burned coke—all-important on cold winter nights.

When all twenty occupants arrived, the Sergeant returned to explain what was expected of them on a daily basis. There was a schedule—Orderly Duty—for cleanliness of the entire hut and responsibility for the room heater. Individually, every morning, they stacked the three "biscuits," folded the two blankets in an exact fashion, placed them on top of the "biscuits," with the pillow last. Any personal items and clothing went in the locker.

Showers, toilets and sinks were in a separate "Ablutions" hut; separate cubicles with a "stable door" for the toilets, but the showers varied from camp to camp, some in an open room with a tiled floor and walls. It didn't take long to get over any initial embarrassment—there was no choice. Later, Jeannie recalled one horrible night when, during an air raid, the lights went out in the ablutions; she was alone in pitch darkness, trying to find the exit door among the many "stable doors!"

They were warned to expect inspections—unannounced. Penalties ranged from a canceled "Pass" to additional Orderly Duty or preparing a vehicle for inspection.

"This is the Army, not a Holiday Camp," said their Sergeant—leaving no doubt in their minds—that first day.

No time was wasted. They received their kit the next morning.

Jeannie's feet were ruined at five years old from lying flat for so long, with no physical therapy, resulting in her having to wear Dr. Scholl's metal arch supports in lace-up shoes—most un-glamorous—until she was welcomed into His Majesty's forces when she volunteered at the age of eighteen, and was told: ***"You cannot wear those things!"*** She hastened to explain that she could not walk ***without*** them because her arches were too painful. His Majesty's doctor assured her, "We'll see about that!" He cut some thick felt with one adhesive side into the required shapes, pressing them into her shoes. Bye-bye Dr. Scholl! By the time she was released four years later she no longer needed arch supports of any description, and could wear all the glamorous shoes she'd been denied for so long..

They had a hygiene lecture after lunch; walked to the N.A.A.F.I. in the evening, where they could buy snacks, drinks, and personal supplies like pens, notepaper, envelopes and stamps.

The second day they had squad drill—and many days after that. Marching in step, turning, and still keeping in step, whilst looking easy enough, required a particular technique to avoid arousing the ire and sarcasm of the Drill Sergeant.

When told to drive an ambulance on the attractive route to Sunningdale and Windsor, Jeannie felt she could redeem herself from criticism. The need to "double de-clutch" to change gear was second nature after driving the old 1932 Two-seater Morris at home, and the butcher's vans, and most other well-worn vehicles which had come her way the past year.

The tall, rectangular, army ambulance was quite a luxury. It held problems for some short students. In the U.K., when reversing, one had to place the right hand on the floor and steer with the left in order to see under the spare wheel behind the driver's seat, protruding beyond the side of the vehicle. They were not permitted to rely on mirrors. Two students fell out, while the ambulance, in very low reverse gear, continued—the Instructor peering out on her side, not noticing on either occasion!

Back at camp, they had a lecture on mechanics and another on A.T.S. regulations before they were freed for the evening, which was a Saturday. Jeannie walked into Camberley with two new friends to see Bob Hope and Vera Zorina in "Louisiana Purchase."

The days soon became a routine of driving, manipulating different vehicles for various Instructors, daily maintenance—checking water, oil, brake fluid, tire pressures, cleaning windshields—getting underneath to change oil and clean for inspections, going to the N.A.A.F.I. in the evenings, writing letters, and often seeing a film in Camberley at weekends. They had a lecture about convoy driving, and were made aware of the concert they were expected to give at the end of the Course.

One day, Jeannie was out in the coal truck with another girl and the Instructor when they had carburetor trouble, so she found the tools, took it apart and cleaned it, as she had learned to do at home. Maybe that would chalk up a good mark for her?

Three weeks into the Course, Jeannie's Instructor said she put her name forward for a driving test. Joan and Effie joined her. They all were tested in the morning and were told at lunchtime the same day that all passed.

Jeannie received the dreaded letter from Neil on July 24, saying that his beloved father died on the twenty-second, so Neil must have written immediately. He was obviously devastated not to have been there with his mother, but attended the funeral. Jeannie wrote to him and mailed the letter to his home. On the positive side, it was fortunate he was still in England when it happened.

In the middle of the Course, the girls were given forty-eight hours' leave, with a special pass to leave the camp. Joan and Jeannie managed to call their respective parent.

The arrangement was that they all met in London, and stayed at the Park Lane hotel.

"We'll have an early evening meal," suggested Jeannie's mother, "and then we can walk in Hyde Park." She was quite familiar with London from much earlier days, having worked at Hayleybury College when she met Daddy. Also, they made several "long weekend" visits when Daddy was alive, generally to go to the theatre. Jeannie brought her mother up-to-date with everything at Camberley, and also told her about Neil's father's death.

Then it was Sunday morning. They were both tired and slept late.

"Let's have breakfast," said Mum, "and then we'll walk to Green Park Underground to catch a train out to Edmonton to see Mrs. Whitestone. It's a shame to be in London and not look her up."

Jeannie didn't mind. Mrs. Whitestone was the mother of an old summer vacation boyfriend, Eric, who had once broken her teenage heart by writing and telling her he was going out with the Head Prefect—a girl at school. She knew he was now in the Air Force and unlikely to be at home.

They found the house—with nobody home—so mother left a note expressing regret that the short visit to London did not permit an alternative day and time to meet.

Jeannie had no regrets. She thought of the escape she had from city surroundings like this at a time when Eric had seemed to be everything to her. There was nothing romantic any more about that summertime relationship. He'd been a nice enough guy, clever and musical, but not compared to Neil, with whom the future—although frustrating—promised excitement and adventure in its very mystery—and passionate love. How she longed to be with Neil again—just to hold him, and console him.

Mother interrupted her thoughts. "We'll take the tube back to Piccadilly and get some lunch, and then we can go back to the hotel until it is time to meet Joan and her mother at teatime, as we arranged." They lunched at the Monaco in Piccadilly.

Who should be sitting at the next table at teatime at the Park Lane hotel, but Will Hay, the hallowed comedian, recognizable anywhere, from stage and screen.

A taxi took Joan and Jeannie to catch the train back to Camberley and army life.

The more than one hundred girls in that particular Platoon at Camberley—all optimistically aiming to be driver-instructors—knew passing would give them their first stripe—the first "rung on the Army ladder." But, more importantly in their minds, success permitted them the distinction of wearing the strap of the cap across the top rather than around the front, ensuring instant recognition as a member of that elite group—no doubt a precept of the F.A.N.Y. regime and the Great War ambulance drivers.

Having wheels beneath them put them head and shoulders above the rest—at least in their own minds. Ripped from their homes and their diverse lives all over Britain, they formed a volunteer group with a common purpose, and unexpected friendships among differing personalities. There were mixed emotions when it came time to move on.

Company Commander Wellesley interviewed some students, but not all of them. Who would be posted to Gresford, North Wales or to Dreghorn, near Edinburgh, Scotland as Driver-Instructors?

There were additional tests to pass, such as map reading and convoy driving. Jeannie said to herself: They don't make me nervous; I don't expect to have a problem. Teaching our Instructors has been demanding, but fun. They just made life difficult on purpose, but we've had practice, so the test should not be too hard.

'Very demanding, but fun'—nothing compared to that which they had to face in the future.

The next day started with drill and then a gas lecture, followed by their general written examination: Maintenance, Map Reading, Gas and First Aid.

The day after, they had drill in the morning and an inspection by Company Commander Wellesley. This preceded their mechanics examination. After lunch, they walked up to Cordwalles for medical, including T.A.B. inoculations, and vaccination.

Over the weekend, the postings were up, and Jeannie found she was going to Gresford with six of her friends. Only thirty of the original one hundred or more qualified as Driver-Instructors. Jeannie was elated to be one of them.

I must write and tell Neil, she thought. He'll be so proud of me.

"End of Course" entertainment was scheduled for Monday night, August 3, 1942. They rehearsed singing as a group, and Mary had the voice for a couple of solos. It was a happy and successful conclusion to the concentrated training at Camberley.

What lay in store? Tuesday, August 4, 1942, was the date of the major move to North Wales. They traveled by train, with three changes en route, and a truck picked them up at Wrexham train station.

CHAPTER 7

IN THE SERVICE OF HIS MAJESTY, KING GEORGE VI—WALES

"I'm being posted to Gresford," Jeannie told her mother, over the phone.

"Really? Well done. I'll be very interested to hear how you get on, trying to teach all those 'would-be' drivers! By the way, I remember Gresford Colliery as being the site of one of the worst Welsh coal-mine disasters of all time, on September 22, 1934, when 266 men died; only eight bodies were recovered, all others were sealed in the pit. Coincidence you should be sent to that area."

No wonder she remembered it eight years later.

At Gresford Camp, the grounds were very different, larger and not as bright and attractive as Camberley, with its flower planters and green lawns—but it was a wartime location, not a permanent military headquarters.

"You'll be split between three different companies," they were told.

Their previously close-knit group felt dejected. The fourth company at Gresford was composed entirely of soldiers, mechanics and electricians, who manned Workshops, under Captain Winters, repairing vehicles to keep them on the road.

The feeling soon passed as they settled into their new routine. The future demanded attention. They had a job to do. All the new drivers they trained replaced men or girls who had been injured from bomb blasts or other accidents, or released them for action elsewhere.

Resident Staff escorted the new Instructors to familiarize them with four different routes for the learner-drivers. Each intake was on a Course lasting six weeks, learning to negotiate Routes A, B, B+ and C, each route increasing in difficulty. B+ Route explored the hills of North Wales, and was the scene of stopping and starting on steep hills, and changing gear going uphill and down, with no synchromesh or automatic drive to make it easy. C Route provided experience in town traffic in Wrexham and Chester. The Course was very concentrated, from eight in the morning until late afternoon on a standard day but late evening when it included day convoys into Wales, or night driving.

Vehicles ranged from small two-seater cars, through Jeeps to ambulances and three or four-ton trucks. The students learned to drive them all competently, and to tow and be towed. The Instructors also taught them maintenance, wheel changing, oil changing and minor mechanics. There was a trick to changing those huge, heavy, unwieldy wheels, making the seemingly impossible, appear easy. An accomplishment for the uninitiated!

Students, good, bad and indifferent, were spread randomly between the Instructors, so it was quite rare to be taught by the same Instructor more than twice. Some would never drive, no matter how hard the Instructors tried to teach them, and were a danger on the road. Jeannie had some students who had driven four weeks but were worse than those who had only driven one.

Aiming to encourage rather than criticize, she told them: "We can't all be good at everything—but most of us can be good at something. So, determine what that something is—and go for it."

"Unfortunately, driving cannot be one of the choices."

Life is what you make it, thought Jeannie, and it could be much worse than this. You had to like dealing with people and, in addition to expressing empathy for their various problems, to have the ability to instill confidence and to explain matters clearly and calmly. All in addition to having steel nerves when being driven by a novice day after day—regardless of the fact that the parking brake was within grabbing distance between them.

She found herself grabbing that in more than one crazy nightmare.

As in all facets of life, many of the students and staff had their own personal problems, and frequently these would disrupt progress in camp. Possibly, the most worthy of note was a girl who walked in her sleep on a number of occasions, to be quietly escorted back to her bed by whomever was on night duty. Although they tried to make light of the situation, it was "creepy" and they didn't enjoy having to deal with it. The poor girl, oblivious to the trouble she caused—walked around camp in the middle of the night—asleep with eyes wide open!

Jeannie was entitled to her first forty-eight hours' leave since Camberley, so she decided to make the trip to her home in Devonshire. She walked the two miles to Rossett station to catch the 6:36 PM train on a Friday evening to Shrewsbury, for the connection to Exeter. It should have got in to Shrewsbury at 9:25 PM but didn't arrive from Manchester until 11:00 PM. She traveled with some sailors on leave and nearly slept through Exeter St. David's station.

It was early on Saturday morning when she called her mother to drive the eight miles to pick her up, saying she'd walk up to Exeter Central station and meet her there. Fighting fatigue, she called around and visited various relatives and friends during the day.

That evening, Jeannie snuggled gratefully into her own bed—the first comfortable sleep since the brief break at the Park Lane hotel in London.

On Sunday, Jess, Jeannie's long-time girlfriend, made the ten-minute walk from her home to spend the afternoon with her and to catch up on all the news. Jeannie returned to St. David's station by car with her mother to catch the inevitable 10:10 PM train traveling north to Shrewsbury—though it was an hour late getting in. She arrived at Rossett on Monday at about 7:30 AM, where she found her bicycle, which mother had sent the previous week. The bike sped the last bit of her trip back to camp, where she dashed straight out with new students on "A" Route.

That whole experience was typical of any forty-eight hour wartime break—trying to make the most of every minute—whilst dealing with night trains running late, or "hitches" not happening. The girls usually "hitched" in pairs—for greater safety.

One Saturday, after doing maintenance all morning, Gwyneth, Effie and Jeannie cycled into Chester and had lunch at "Blossoms." Waves of beautiful music reached their ears as they walked by the cathedral. The Halle Orchestra was involved in practice, so they went inside to listen. Gwyneth had been a violinist with the Huddersfield Orchestra.

She said, " I know the First Violin, Lawrence Turner. I'll go and see him when the practice ends. I'll meet you here for the evening performance and get Lawrence to find you some seats, so don't be late." Effie and Jeannie shopped, had tea, and then met Gwyneth and Laurence, who had been rowing on the river. They'd found seats for the evening performance in the cathedral, Sir Malcolm Sargent conducting.

After the concert, Gwyneth suggested walking to the station with Lawrence. It was early for his train so they all had beer and sandwiches at the Station Hotel, then bid him farewell, afterwards walking back to the garage where they'd left their bikes. They cycled back to camp in misty rain—and found that one of the students' huts had burned down.

The students in that hut had to attend a Court of Inquiry about a week later.

One of the mixed blessings of the Gresford Camp was convoy driving—"mixed" due to the quality of driving by the students. Participation generated excitement. They took trucks and ambulances, no small vehicles. Two of the Sergeants rode motorbikes, to keep the convoy together and to mark the turn-offs or other junctions. They had maps but no road-signs. This time they were out on Day Convoy to Bala Lake.

Jeannie loved North Wales. The Welsh towns, many still drear and grimy from their traditional mining past, stand in stark contrast to the uplifting glory of the countryside.

Jeannie was with two students in a "Guy" open truck, whose lives were spent in a city. They were like school kids experiencing their first ride at a fair—a mixture of delight, excitement—and fear—when faced with the wild, open countryside.

She warned them: "Try to remember what you were taught. This road is narrow and winding, with sudden hills and blind corners. Remember to make use of your gears; don't rely solely on the brakes. I want you to enjoy the countryside, and we're lucky it's such a beautiful day, but don't let yourselves become mesmerized by it."

They were challenged to steer a heavy vehicle safely around the next blind corner, unable to see if the narrow road was clear, and awed by steep hillsides, and mountains rising against the blue sky set in high relief with white coronets of cloud. Sheep, cows and goats found any hole in the fence or rock wall, and a stationary large animal presented a formidable obstacle.

On that same road, a friend of Neil and Jeannie wrecked a Lamborghini, hitting a cow at four in the morning. The cow died. Fortunately, he lived to tell the tale.

The sunny day provided a scenic delight. Lakes of the deepest blue—shimmering jewels in valleys at the foot of the high mountains. Where was the war in this new world? They drove to Bala Lake. Just beyond that, up a hill, they parked and sat on soft grass to eat lunch brought with them in the large truck at the rear of the convoy. It was always a joke to make sure they didn't lose sight of the lunch truck! The break for lunch enabled the student-drivers to relax and express their emotions; most had never traveled into countryside like North Wales.

Then the convoy took the same route back to camp.

Jeannie congratulated her students on a day's good driving.

Thursday, September 3 1942, was the first day of the third year of war. Church Parade dominated the camp that evening. Jeannie received a letter from Neil, on a Course in Dorset. Jeannie suspected it was an Officers' Training Course and she had no doubt he would pass it with flying colors. She knew he would not accept any promotion unless in the Royal Engineers. The Army was not a career for him; he had no motivation just for the prestige or the money. He preferred to remain with those who experienced battle with him, and with whom there was a mutual loyalty.

Jeannie appreciated his feelings. She knew it was possible to become a very close group, where compassion exuded to defeat a problem.

Muriel was Jeannie's special friend at the Gresford Camp. Jeannie found more than once she gravitated towards the "black sheep" or "lame duck"—she just didn't like to see one person blatantly ignored, as had happened to Muriel. She felt the same way about the students and tried to ensure that each got the attention deserved. Muriel had a flamboyant personality and was a good Instructor.

The next Sunday Gwyneth cycled with them to Chester and lunch at the Y.W.C.A. Muriel found an available boat, so they spent the rest of the afternoon on the river, going to see Catherine Hepburn and Cary Grant in "Free to Live" in the evening, then cycling fast on the mostly flat road back to camp.

Another Sunday, when Jeannie had a free day with no duties, Betty asked her if she would like to go to Liverpool.

"Sure! I'd love to go." Jeannie jumped at the chance to see somewhere different. "I'll get a Day Pass." They awoke at 6:00 AM and tore up to the main Chester road, where they soon obtained a "hitch" in a furniture van as far as Chester station—not to catch a train, but to wait for the next "ride." Due to limited funds, they needed to take advantage of free transport whenever possible. They had an hour's wait before being offered a lift in a Gaumont film van, which took them through the Queensway Tunnel running under the wide River Mersey to Liverpool.

That was an experience in itself. The tunnel was built in 1934. All vehicles' shaded headlights were switched on even though the tunnel had lights in its roof. The damp walls, dripping in some places, made the road wet, causing an accident. They were delayed for about an hour while the river police sorted it out.

Eventually, they found somewhere for breakfast, then took a tram to meet Betty's two amazing old aunts in their junk shop—and to experience a lively introduction to their intriguing business! After catching another tram, they had a late canteen lunch, and walked to the ferry sailing back to Birkenhead—above the water this time—where they were able to get a bus into Chester. Not wanting to waste the evening, they had sandwiches and a drink at the Y.W.C.A., saw Cary Grant in "The Amazing Quest of Ernest Bliss" and caught a bus back to camp.

Jeannie felt her eyes had been opened that day! It's never too late to learn, she thought.

They worked hard and played hard, using any well-deserved free time to advantage. It wasn't all films and fun. A great deal had to be crammed into the students' six-week Course. They were teaching every day. One morning, Jeannie was battling Chester traffic on C route, and then, with different students, on B+ route in the afternoon—hills over the border in Wales—when she got stuck for petrol. The pipe switching the tank on one side of the ambulance over to the other side was choked. She tried to clear it, and by the time she'd finished she had a truck driver, two military police in a van, a farmer and his wife, and three children around her, all competing with suggestions. Eventually, it cleared.

Jeannie called her mother from Rossett. Mum had a message from Neil.

"He's starting ten days' leave on Sunday, October 4, 1942 and going straight to his home in Derbyshire. He wants you to join him there. Can you get leave?"

She applied for leave from October 6. She didn't think it would be denied; she'd had no leave for over three months

In the meantime, she and Gwyneth had to submit their respective vehicles to C.I.M.T. inspections in Workshops—major periodic inspections—so they spent over half a day cleaning the vehicles from the engine to the axles, the interior and the exterior. The inspections, next day, were concluded by 11:00 AM, but both checked V.O.R.—"vehicle off road"—Jeannie's for brakes, so they had the remainder of the day free.

Two odd things happened. They had a "hitch" into Chester with the truck driver who had stopped to help Jeannie with the blocked petrol pipe. The girls had tea at the Services' Club, going upstairs afterwards, because they heard superb music. The soldier at the piano lived at Exmouth, not far from Jeannie's home, and studied under Doctor Wilcock, the organist at Exeter Cathedral. Small world!

The Saturday before Jeannie left on leave the student-drivers had a map-reading competition. Instructors drove and students gave them directions by reading a map. It was good fun and excellent practice for the students. They reached their destination quickly.

"We're first!" Jeannie told her students. "I'm so proud of you."

She was instructing the morning of her leave but had a ride into Chester General Station in the afternoon. After obtaining a ticket to Exeter on her warrant, she walked to Chester Northgate to catch a train to Manchester and change there for Bakewell, Derbyshire. Neil met her at the station.

"I'm glad you could make it," he said. "I'm so happy to see you."

They walked to Bakewell Square to catch the bus to Baslow.

It was her first visit there.

CHAPTER 8

IN THE SERVICE OF HIS MAJESTY, KING GEORGE VI—AWAKENINGS

It was dark when the bus stopped in the middle of the village. Neil carried Jeannie's knapsack and held her hand to lead the way for the short walk up the hill. They turned into a lane on the left and continued to walk on the level until Neil said, "There's a step up onto the path, but it is narrow, so I'll go first—just follow me."

Then he turned back to her, laughing, and said, "There isn't room to swing a cat around here; take my hand again."

He opened the door and stood to one side for her to enter. He closed the door and switched on the hallway light, "Come in and meet my mother," he said, opening the door to a room off the hallway.

She held out her hand to the little lady with the welcoming smile, seated in a large armchair before a cheerful coal fire, "I'm Jeannie," she said. "It's so kind of you to let me come and stay for a few days."

"I'm pleased to meet you. Neil has told me so much about you. I've seen your photos because he stood them on top of the wireless, but that was several months ago—when his father was still alive."

"I was very sad about that. I lost my father too, in January 1940."

"Jeannie, I'll show you the bedroom and bathroom, and you can take your jacket off. Then we'll have supper, and we can all talk some more," said Neil.

He led the way and turned into a room at the top of the stairs. "You can sleep in my bed," he said. "I'll be right next door."

She noticed a large framed photograph of Myrna Loy hanging on the wall. "Do you like her films?"

"Yes. I broke my schoolboy heart over her!"

"Now I realize what I have to live up to. You should have warned me," said Jeannie.

He put his arms around her and held her close. "You're fine just the way you are," he said. "Don't ever change. Come down when you're ready. I'll go and see what there is to eat."

It was a big bed with a fluffy feather mattress. Jeannie thought, so this is what you came back to when you survived Dunkirk. No wonder you were happy to be home.

Neil explained previously about his mother's incapacity. It was difficult for her to get up and walk, but he said she never complained and always tried to be cheerful. She had been a teacher in a senior girls' school. Education was the connecting link for the family, and obviously the reason why the choice of school had been so important for Neil.

His mother was a crossword puzzle wizard but didn't have access to sufficient newspapers to keep her occupied. Jeannie vowed to remedy that.

They all talked for a long time that evening, until Jeannie said she was tired and needed to get some sleep. Shortly afterwards she heard Neil running the water for a bath; then he slid into the bed briefly and held her close.

In the morning he brought her breakfast on a tray. She dressed, and they walked down towards the village, but Neil turned into the driveway of a large house, explaining that the parents of a girl he knew lived there, and he wanted to introduce Jeannie. She thought them very kind and friendly. The wife joked that Neil, as a young boy, spent many hours talking to her in the kitchen while she baked. It was obvious they were very fond of him.

Then they continued down to the village and had coffee in a pretty little café before going to look at the church and his father's grave which, like Jeannie's father's, was dug sufficiently deep for mother as well, when the time came.

Jeannie thought how delightful it all was, from the stone bridge over the River Derwent, where they watched a gaggle of ducks paddling furiously against the current, to the lovely Derbyshire stone houses and the distant crags.

That evening they decided to catch the bus to Bakewell, where they had a drink at the famous Rutland Arms hotel and sat talking for a long time. Neil tried to explain his predicament, as it affected both of them.

"Even if I survive the war and continue with my management apprenticeship, and obtain a Bachelor of Science Degree in Engineering, it will be four years before I have a decent job, and I have no way of knowing what the condition of mother's health will be. I will be responsible for her. There's nobody else—and I can't commute to work from here."

Jeannie tried to console him.

"Always remember that I love you, darling. We have no way to foretell the future. All we can do is to make the best we can of the present, and deal with the future when it happens. We have each other; and we'll get through it somehow."

They went to the Forces' Canteen to eat, which saved preparing food from the sparse rations at home, and continued their conversation before returning on the bus.

That evening, Neil's mother was interested in everything Jeannie had to talk about, from her adventures working at her father's business to her decision to join the A.T.S. (MT) and her subsequent life in the forces. She wondered what Jeannie's plans were after the war, considering that her mother was widowed?

Jeannie avoided getting into details, saying that making plans was difficult for everyone without knowing the outcome of the war. She sensed that Neil's mother was trying to protect her son by ensuring nothing came between him and his future.

She went upstairs to have a bath; then snuggled into Neil's wonderfully comfy bed, when she heard him come upstairs. He bathed, then walked into her room, a naked Adonis silhouetted by the dim light from the stairway. How could she ever deny him anything? She loved him totally. He was kind and gentle and understanding in every way. His beautiful dark eyes encompassed her and lifted her onto an emotional pedestal.

Sometimes he seemed sad. The reason made itself apparent one day when he said,

"I've really led a very lonely life, you know."

She assured him, "You'll never be lonely any more. I love you, and I'll always love you." She thought about the lady's story regarding the talks in her kitchen. Maybe she had sensed his loneliness all those years ago? His parents were not young, and his mother spent many weeks away in the brine baths at Buxton. He appeared to have no men friends in the village, though there were three or four girls he knew—two of whose names precipitated prejudiced comments from his mother when they were mentioned!

They dressed and had breakfast the next morning, then went out and followed the street further up the hill where it disappeared into a dirt road alongside a forest in the Chatsworth Estate, owned by the Duke of Devonshire and his family for generations. The huge Manor House was expanded over the years. From the top of the hills they had the most magnificent views of the Derbyshire countryside. Neil told Jeannie legends about some of the landmarks and the history of the house.

"The first house to occupy the site was designed by Sir William Cavendish and his wife, Bess of Hardwick, and completed about 1555. The only reminders of its existence are the Hunting Tower and Queen Mary's Bower. Then, the house faced east. The first Duke of Devonshire erected the new building, started in 1687 and continued over the next 200 years by the family. It is designed to face west, standing on a rising slope above the River Derwent. The Royal Architect, William Talman, built the south and east wings; the west wing was added later by Thomas Archer. Then, Sir Jeffry Wyatville added the long north wing and that's as you see it today. Ten years later, the entire walled village of Edensor was moved to its present site within the grounds, but hidden from the residence. People often say that Chatsworth is England's finest house. I think it probably is. Anyway, it would take a lot of beating."

Jeannie loved the driveway through the property, with its view of the river, the magnificent house, the Hunting Tower half hidden in the trees above it, and sheep and lambs grazing peacefully in the parklands. Seen from her perspective, it was like a picture postcard.

They had supper at the Forces' Canteen in Bakewell again that evening. That night they lay again in each other's arms, aware that it could be the last time they would do so; Neil's deployment abroad again was imminent.

He thanked Jeannie for another wonderful day together to remember.

The next morning they wandered around the village and had coffee at the café once more. Jeannie sent a wire to her mother giving the potential time of arrival at Exeter St. David's station. Neil went with her to Chesterfield by bus in the afternoon, where they sat in a café drinking tea to pass the time until Jeannie's 3:30 P.M. train. She promised him she would split her leaves between his mother and her own when he was sent abroad.

"I want to be there," she said, "because I'll feel closer to you when I'm there. Also, we can see the same moon, even if not at the same time, and every time I look at it, I'll think of you, wherever you are. Come back safely to me, please."

He took her hands in his and squeezed them, saying, "It's time we were moving. You must not miss that train."

It took her right through to Bristol before she had to change. Her mother met her at St. David's station in Exeter. Jeannie drove home.

Jeannie's leave was a "busman's holiday." In a small country community news spreads fast. The next day the 'phone began to ring. Jeannie's "stand-in chauffeur" didn't like driving at night so she had to take the District Nurse to an appointment since her own car was "off road for repairs." The next morning Nurse had a "premature birth" to deal with, so Jeannie took Jess with her and they had a long chat. Jess needed to be back at College at 4:00 P.M. It had been evacuated from London to Crewkerne, in Dorset. Her father made the two-hour drive.

The next morning she drove Nurse again. In the afternoon she helped Mum clean out the stable. Her pony, Jerry, was found another home long since, but the stable was used for storing apples in racks.

Jeannie wanted to re-energize herself with the scents and sounds of Devonshire, the wild flowers and the mossy banks, the scurry of a rabbit and the calls of birds. Dusky was a willing companion for a long walk around the familiar country lanes.

The following morning she took Mrs. Stewart to the station in Exeter, where Jeannie then did various shopping for her mother, picked up some car batteries from Stanfield and White's for uncle, and had her hair washed. She gave an airman a ride from Honiton Clyst on the way home, knowing all too well what it was like waiting for a "hitch"—and a ride part of the way was better than no ride at all.

She longed to hear Neil's voice once more, but telephone calls were questionable as to quality, particularly over a long distance. She called Mrs. Potter at the local exchange—yes, the same Mrs. Potter at whose house Louis, the Cockney evacuee, lived—and told her she needed to make a long-distance call. Direct dialing didn't exist. Mrs. Potter called Exeter, who called Taunton, who called Bridgwater, who called Bristol, who called Birmingham, who called Derby, who called Matlock, who called Bakewell, who called the local exchange at Baslow, who called Neil's home.

Jeannie visualized the switchboard operators plugging wires into sockets at each exchange—it only took one to be pulled out en route and the call was lost. She heard the distant bell ringing, and he answered the 'phone. His beloved voice was fuzzy over the distance, but it was his voice—sending tingles up her spine. The feeling endured, particularly over the telephone. No matter the words—his voice made love over the wires. They'll burn up, she thought.

That last day of her leave, Jeannie and Bob—an airman manning the lookout post in the adjacent field—jacked up Mum's Austin car to scrape lumps of mud off and eventually hose it down with a stirrup pump. True to character, Bob dressed in old trousers, a short-sleeved pullover, tin hat and eye-shields. Jeannie wore Wellington boots over gray slacks, a jumper, overalls, and a scarf around her head. Her mother said all they needed was a camera.

Jeannie packed up her things, changed into khaki, had supper at home—and a piece of tooth broke. She drove to Exeter with her mother to catch the 10.10 PM train at St. David's station. She changed trains at Shrewsbury for Wrexham and "hitched" to the Gresford Camp, where she arrived at about 8:00 A.M. as required, and made an appointment with a dentist in Wrexham. He gave her an injection and extracted the tooth.

"Crowns" and "Root Canals" saved her teeth in the distant future—but not in the British Forces in 1942.

CHAPTER 9

IN THE SERVICE OF HIS MAJESTY, KING GEORGE VI—FRIENDS AND FRUSTRATIONS

Muriel and Jeannie stopped by the Office to see if there was any mail for either of them one late October afternoon. It was always placed in alphabetical order of the surname of the intended recipient, on a long table pushed against a wall. They carried their letters back to the hut before opening them.

"Mum says she wants to get away for a week or ten days, and she'd like to spend the time where she can see me sometimes. Problem is, the only decent hotels are in Chester, and that's too far away to be able stop by after duty," said Jeannie.

Muriel, ever the one with "bright ideas"—wise or otherwise—rose to the occasion.

"Let's go and check out the farms in the neighborhood; maybe there'll be one that's nice enough where they'd let her stay."

Jeannie was a little hesitant; her memories of farms were not all clean and pleasant, and also the request might be an imposition on farmers whose livelihood depended upon a daily routine.

"Come on," urged Muriel, "if we don't ask, we won't know."

And that was how they made the acquaintance of Mr. and Mrs. Jones and their two sons who helped them run the farm. Jeannie explained the situation, and Mrs. Jones said she'd be delighted to meet her mother. She had a spare bedroom with windows away from the farmyard and Jeannie's mother could come and go as she pleased, as long as she didn't need to be "entertained" and didn't mind joining the family for meals.

The boys—fifteen and seventeen—appeared to be excited at the prospect of seeing more of Muriel and Jeannie, and challenged them to a game of Pool on the spot:

"We have a full size Pool table in a room downstairs."

Their parents were obviously very proud of their fully mechanized dairy and offered to take the girls on a "grand tour"—including the bedroom for mother.

The entire place was spotless, and tastefully furnished. Jeannie knew Mum would be delighted to stay in a friendly, clean place like that, surrounded by fields and lovely views. She gave Mrs. Jones her mother's name and mailing address and asked her to write and let her know the cost of her stay, and the meals, because they would be taking her out sometimes. She would bring cash with her to save Mrs. Jones having to wait for a check to go through the bank.

Jeannie's mother was due to arrive on Wednesday, November 11 1942. Coincidentally, that was the date Armistice was declared at the end of the Great War, and Daddy returned.

It was nearly the end of October. Jeannie received letters from her mother, her friend, Jess, and her cousin Peter, stationed in Gibralter, but nothing from Neil.

On October 31 they all participated in a rehearsal for the Commandant's Parade the following weekend, then Jeannie did maintenance on an ambulance.

Muriel came by, saying, "Glad you've finished. Hurry, and get cleaned up. We'll skip lunch and get a hitch to Wolverhampton." By this time Jeannie was accustomed to Muriel's sometimes hair-brained ideas. They could be fun—most of the time. As it was, they first caught a bus to Chester. Then they were lucky enough to hitch a ride on a large "semi" to within ten miles of their destination. The driver told them the only reason he stopped was because they were two girls together; he wouldn't pick up a girl on her own:

"That can turn into a problem waiting to happen," he said, and went on to tell them the story of another driver who had been accused of molestation.

Jeannie said, "I've never thought about it from your point of view; we just hitch together because we feel safer; it's company; and more fun.

They thanked the driver when he dropped them off, and they were lucky that day to get another "hitch" for the ten miles into Wolverhampton; that driver told them he'd given a ride to London to two girls they knew at camp. In wartime, the long-distance truck drivers were the girls' best friends!

Muriel had relatives in Wolverhampton—an uncle, where they had high tea—in Britain that consists of a meal served at about five or six o'clock consisting of a light cooked first course—poached eggs or meat pie—followed by cake or some other dessert; they also saw Muriel's brother. Later, they went on to her grandmother's house where they were given a fantastic supper and sat up listening to dance music until midnight.

It was Saturday night. They shared a large feather bed and lay talking into the early hours.

Sunday seemed to consist of meals they only dreamed of. They then caught a "slow train," stopping at all stations en route, to Gresford, and walked from the station to camp.

Work, lectures, vehicle maintenance, duty ambulance, company office duty and evening German classes continued as usual, until Wednesday, November 11, when Jeannie's mother was scheduled to arrive. That day Jeannie was assigned to a convoy to Denbigh, in Wales, consisting of four ambulances. One of Jeannie's students managed to run into Gwyneth's ambulance, locking the two projecting spare wheels together, sending Gwyneth's ambulance careening downhill backwards. Luckily, Gwyneth was in the cab and grabbed the brake!

After returning to camp, Jeannie hitched into Chester to meet her mother off the train. Muriel had gone in ahead in case she was late. They met "Tiny" returning from leave, so they all had supper at the Queen's hotel and took a taxi back to camp and the farm. Jeannie discovered she was on an unexpected schedule the following day.

The Instructors and some of the better students were up at 6:00 AM for breakfast, after which they all climbed into the back of "Hellsapopin"—usually the lunch/breakdown truck—with a Sergeant driving—and eventually the students when it was light.

"Hellsapopin," appropriately named by the Sergeant in charge of it, registered the fact that she was far from lacking in a wicked sense of humor! It was a 3-ton truck with a soft roof, a short windshield and open sides; the only other protection from the elements was a large waterproof sheet to be rolled out from beneath the dashboard and fastened to the back wall of the cab, leaving holes for the driver's and passenger's arms and neck. By early afternoon, the Sergeant elected to choose a second student to drive in daylight. By this time it was raining—a steady, misty rain.

In any gathering, there is always someone who stands out, for some reason, good, bad, ebullient or reserved. Priscilla Hawthorne was undoubtedly beautiful; she would not have been out of place in a swimsuit contest. 'Scilla to her friends, Prissie, mostly behind her back—and she ignored it anyway. Jeannie could not recall ever having seen her beneath a truck or ambulance; she appeared to avoid doing the "dirty work." Nobody knew how she got away with it. Her beauty was always enhanced by extravagant makeup, and even in uniform she was very aware that she stood out in a crowd.

The sergeant told the first student driver to pull over to the side of the road, and to get in the back for a break. Then she jumped down and ran around to the back of the truck.

"Private Hawthorne, it's your turn at the wheel—now!"

Everyone knew she meant business. Priscilla got out with reluctance and climbed into the vacated driver's seat, lifting the wet sheet between finger and thumb to slide her legs beneath it. The Sergeant pulled the top of the sheet up without due ceremony and fastened it to the wall of the cab behind her shoulders.

They were scheduled to reach Darlington in Yorkshire to pick up some new Ford V-8 trucks, but it was already 6:00 PM and getting dark. "Hellsapopin" developed a leak in its exhaust so the girls, sitting in the back, were nearly gassed. Nobody was happy.

The unfortunate student-driver's black mascara ran down her cheeks—like makeup for a ghoul on Halloween! It provided plenty of levity to counteract the general misery—and Priscilla Hawthorne never wore heavy makeup again.

They waded through mud in the dark, picked up the new Ford V-8 trucks, and set off for York for the night. It was a miserable journey on icy roads through fog. The truck in front of Jeannie kept stalling, so she had to "nose it along" to get it started again. The lights were bad on the truck behind, so that girl followed Jeannie's "tail light"—a small bulb shining on a white axle.

The final indignity was reaching York at midnight and tumbling into bunks below strange females in a stuffy hut—only to be told in the morning that the F.A.N.Y.'s had prepared for them elsewhere but they'd arrived late and were misdirected. That did nothing to raise their self-esteem.

When the "residents" awoke the next morning—to find "strangers" encroaching upon their domain—and not just regular "strangers" but those "snooty drivers," all hell was let loose; the language would have done the back streets of New York proud! Jeannie then requested that the students should all have a chance to use clean ablutions and follow that with breakfast in the non-commissioned officers' mess—even though the drivers were privates!

"I think those girls in that hut are fighting a different war," she said.

But the problems didn't end there. They collected the Ford V-8 trucks to line up for petrol, when the nearside wheel of one of them came right off, stripped of the threads holding the nuts on. Eventually they left York at mid-day, driving through Darlington, Stockport, Leeds and Huddersfield before stopping at the "Floating Light" for food at 3:00 PM. They then got through Manchester together. Subsequently, there was a breakdown further down the line and they lost half the convoy—and "Hellsapopin."

Jeannie drove back to camp through fog in Chester, fortunately being familiar with the streets; parked the Ford truck at camp, then walked up to the farm—exhausted—to find Muriel there with her mother. Jeannie thanked her for being so caring.

Muriel looked glum. "I hope I've earned something for my good deeds because I've been told I won't get any pay next payday!"

"Why? What have you done now?" It wasn't exactly unusual news. With the best will in the world Muriel managed to do, or not do something between one payday and the next. This time she'd had her pay stopped for failing to drain a sump!

Jeannie had a pass to stay at the farm for the night, but she and Mum walked back to camp with Muriel, where Jeannie found mail waiting for her—a letter from Neil's mother saying he had been posted to a different section of his Company. Jeannie gave Muriel a hug when she said goodnight and told her not to worry, she and Mum would help her out!

To top it all, the Ford V-8 trucks were no use for instructing; the parking brake was not in the center! Who was going to get a black mark for that decision discrepancy? And why were they told to drive them all that way back anyway?

After breakfast, Jeannie and her mother walked past the camp, leaving a note for Muriel saying they would meet her at "Quaintways" in Chester at 3:45 PM. She didn't turn up, so they went to see a film before catching the bus back to the "Red Lion" in Rossett, from which they walked back to the farm for supper. Muriel stopped by at 10:00 PM to say she had just missed them everywhere in Chester—she had also lost her hat! She recalled later where she'd taken it off.

Jeannie's friends at camp were a caring crowd. If she was tied up with duty they made sure that her mother wasn't spending too much time alone. Muriel's mother, in a different Platoon, was returning home for two months' emergency leave, so that evening the four of them arranged to meet for dinner at "Bolland's" in Chester.

Jeannie was on a student convoy to Denbigh the next day. That evening she arranged to meet Muriel and Tiny in Wrexham, but instead they spent the evening at the farm playing billiards, and had supper there. Jeannie's mother made sure Mrs. Jones was suitably compensated for providing all the meals.

Jeannie received letters from Jess and her other friends—but still nothing from Neil.

Mother went home, and camp life returned to normal. One Sunday, Muriel and Jeannie missed their lunch but caught a bus into Chester and had an early tea at the Services' Club, where they bumped into Tiny and Trixie who said they had seats for "Gone With The Wind." Jeannie read the book three years earlier, and loved it, so they decided to see the film, too. They all had seats together, and enjoyed it.

Work continued as usual until Sunday, December 13 1942, when the Instructors rose early, had breakfast, collected rations for a Shrewsbury trip, and joined a convoy of evacuating vehicles—including the Fords brought from Yorkshire, useless for instructing. Ultimately, they dumped the vehicles in the muddiest place Jeannie had ever seen, but were taken elsewhere to collect the replacements. She drove back in a Bedford 30 cwt.

It was nearly Christmas. Muriel and Jeannie went to see Mrs. Jones at the farm, who gave them a welcome supper. Jeannie called Neil's mother because she hadn't heard from him. It was a bad line. His mother said she would write, but she knew he would not be home for Christmas.

Next day was a Saturday. Muriel and Jeannie caught a bus into Chester, where Jeannie ordered flowers to be sent to Neil's mother and her own mother for Christmas. She knew Neil would have wanted her to do that, so she sent the flowers from both of them.

Finally, like the best Christmas present ever, on December 23, 1942, Jeannie received a wonderful letter from Neil; he had mailed it from Loughborough but said he was returning to Woodhall Spa in Lincolnshire. His leave was due on December 29, 1942 for ten days, but he was trying to change it to Jeannie's date in mid-January.

On Christmas Day they awakened to a breakfast of bacon and egg in the Mess, followed by a Church Parade at Gresford. Later, they were given a real Christmas dinner in the Mess, including beer! Jeannie's mother had sent her a Christmas cake, so they made tea and ate cake in the hut. Then there was a Permanent Staff meeting in the Quiet Room, where they drank coffee and were given presents from America. Then they went to an ENSA show—Noel Coward's "Private Lives"—so Christmas could have been worse.

The next day life returned to "business as usual."

Selecting a bed in the hut under a window worked well for most of the year: more light, some sunbeams, fresh air as an option—until New Year's Eve.

An unusual noise outside elicited curiosity more than alarm.

Too late! Wet floor mops were thrust through windows secretly left ajar, right down the beds of unsuspecting occupants. By the time anyone could reach the door, the opportunists had fled—minus mops, of course.

Jeannie and Neil decided to spend the entire ten days of their leave in Baslow. It seemed only fair to Neil's mother. At least Jeannie's Mum had been able to travel to see her, and Jeannie was still going to be somewhere in the British Isles. Jeannie loved the place, anyway.

One afternoon Neil lit the fire in the sitting room, which was at the opposite end of the hallway from the room his mother used all the time. It contained a beautiful china cabinet at one end. Jeannie looked through the glass doors at the Royal Doulton and the Staffordshire china tea services and other individual jugs and teapots. She lived with antique furniture and lovely china all her life, so she was no stranger to its beauty. It was very gratifying that Neil had been exposed to it, too. The lovely old fireplace had a stone mantelpiece on which was displayed Jeannie's favorite tea service—hand-painted and signed Worcester in rich, glorious colors. It was a set, but each matching cup, saucer and tea plate was of a different china design, all individually painted, but using the same colors. It was unique and magnificent. The room had a large sofa opposite the fire, a bay window occupying all of an end wall, looking across the fields, and several delicate upright Edwardian chairs with padded seats and backs.

"I see you're approving of it all," said Neil, with a broad grin, "what about the fire? I lit it in here on purpose. Auntie Flo is coming over from Sheffield to be with Mum and I thought it would give us some time to ourselves without having to go and sit in a pub somewhere."

"Great thinking," she said. "I love you for it."

"We'll have an early supper and then go and have a bath ready for bed, but instead we'll come down here by the fire in our robes and make love in the firelight. What could be more romantic than that? It'll give me something to remember you by." He put his arms around her, gave her a big hug and a long kiss."

"You'll make me cry, thinking about it," she said. "I know you're going away."

"Please don't cry. I want to remember you filled with the glory and happiness of love in the firelight!"

And he laughed at the thought of it. It was a joke—but he wasn't joking. He was deadly serious—almost as though he had a premonition about his future. Jeannie told herself—don't keep imagining things. Make it a perfect evening for him. He has set the scene—now make it a beautiful picture.

And it was—very beautiful. And she saved her tears for later, when he had gone.

Neil left, in March, on a troopship—destination unknown

Jeannie made inquiries about going on a Course, with the object of obtaining further experience warranting promotion, but was told she would have to wait until she had been instructing for a full year—that meant August 1943. In July she was offered a "Squad Training Course" and could visualize the life she'd avoided by volunteering—"Boot Camp"—no amount of promotion could induce her to do that. A couple of weeks later she was told,

"There's an opportunity for you to go into Workshops on a Driver-Mechanic's Course, after which, if you pass, you will be posted to HQ at Ingatestone, Essex, until an opening comes up at an Outstation."

"Which Workshops?" Jeannie asked.

"Here, at Gresford Camp, under Captain Winters, but you'll be one of only two girls approved for it."

"Sounds like fun. Thanks. I'll take the opportunity," said Jeannie.

CHAPTER 10

UNDER THE HOOD

The first day was like all succeeding days: clean coveralls and caps and roll call with the men at 08.00 hours each morning.

Jeannie was moved to a room on the second floor in the house, with Muriel and three other girls. They were nothing to do with the Workshops Course but she supposed it was more appropriate than being in a large hut of Driver-Instructors. It was the opposite end of the camp from the Workshops Bays, so she had to get up earlier to be there for roll call.

As Jeannie walked through the camp, she thought of something Neil had said that last leave in January, which her present circumstances brought to mind:

"Uniform ensures commonality; it is only when you get to know the wearer individually that you appreciate what it conceals; often there is a large heart with concern for others, and a determination to succeed under the most dire circumstances; that same individual in street clothes would not have earned a second glance."

He mused, hesitant to continue, but then thought it important enough to express his feelings,

"You and I have been blessed with caring parents, lovely homes, and a privileged upbringing, none of which prepared us for encountering some of the people with whom we have to talk, eat, sleep and face unspeakable hardships and danger—in fact, people to whom we would never normally give a second glance. The army has taught me not to be judgmental; to give everyone a fair chance before I sift them out." He smiled and squeezed her hand when he said those last words—"before I sift them out."

She reached the Workshops Bays—the familiar high-roofed metal buildings with huge doors to accommodate the entry and exit of large vehicles, windows beyond reach in the rear walls, and a cold, uninviting concrete floor. The soldiers were wearing coveralls, like her own, increasing their anonymity—except a Sergeant, whom she saw when she entered. She saw the other girl, but did not know her; she was not from her Platoon, and they'd be working individually anyway.

The Sergeant called Jeannie over and then introduced them both—by their last names—to the men, explaining that they were attending a Driver-Mechanic's Course for the succeeding twelve weeks and that he expected the soldiers' full cooperation and assistance as far as supervising work on the vehicles was concerned. They were to undertake normal repairs, explaining what they were doing, and why, giving the girls the opportunity to do the same work as it became available.

There was a murmur, suggesting laughter, but it was suppressed when the Sergeant, said: "You had better grow up. Some of you may find yourselves at an Outstation where one or other of these young ladies is the Sergeant-in-Charge. They are taking their army life very seriously and with courage, or they would not be here."

Jeannie was allocated to one of the soldiers, about her height, and as Welsh as they come; she guessed he was probably thirty years old. Jeannie was quite happy about the situation because she loved the Welsh countryside and felt she'd have something to talk about to put both of them at ease and to show some camaraderie. She thought her new "boss" would probably be surprised at the familiarity she possessed regarding vehicles. Then she decided not to tell him; he'd find out eventually and it would be a surprise.

The second week into the course they had to work on a truck with a blown cylinder head gasket, which seals the joint between the cylinder head and the block housing the pistons and crankshaft. The soldier hadn't worked with a girl before and was obviously embarrassed, all of which was made much worse because he knew the others were watching him. Jeannie thought she had to put him more at ease.

"We'll have to remove the carburetor and the distributor and all the spark plugs, and the various hoses to get at it, won't we?" she said. "Has the water been drained out of the radiator? I guess that's one of the first jobs, isn't it?"

He stood there for a moment, nonplussed. "Have you done this before? I'll show you where all the tools are, but you must make sure they are all put back in the right place, otherwise it'll make life a mess when we need them again."

She had to listen hard because he spoke with such a strong Welsh accent.

"No, I haven't done the actual work, but I've watched others, and I was trained at Camberley as a Driver-Instructor, so we were made pretty familiar with all the parts of a vehicle. I suppose I know a bit more than most people regarding the names of tools, and spanner sizes, and what they're used for—things like that. If I don't know, you'll have to teach me; that's what I'm here for—and I have to take a practical and a written exam at the end of the Course, so don't be afraid to yell at me if I do something wrong!"

She laughed, and it broke the ice. He began treating her almost like "one of us," and they chatted while working. His name was Morgan Jenkins. She said, "Well, your name's Welsh, Morgan, and mine's Scots, so call me Jeannie."

They made good progress with the truck, dismantling everything necessary to access the cylinder head. Then it was time to grind in the new valves before replacing it. Morgan demonstrated, so she would understand what he was doing, but he then received a message to go to Captain Winter's office and to be prepared to be absent for an hour. Jeannie was left twiddling her thumbs. Then she thought, I'll grind in those valves myself. We can reassemble the cylinder head when Morgan comes back.

And that is what she did.

Morgan returned, apologized for his absence and asked Jeannie what she had been doing. She explained. He checked out the valve seatings, laughed, and called out loudly so everyone could hear: "You'll never believe it, my girl's ground in all the valves!"

Jeannie was "in like Flynn." – as the Irish saying goes.

She learned more than she needed for the Course she was on but, ever curious, she listened to whatever her little Welshman had to say—like a cat being proffered a saucer of less than fresh milk but thirsty enough to drink it.

Some of the conversations became almost like a debate. Morgan came from a coal-mining family in South Wales, living in a little village not far from Cardiff. His father no longer worked because he suffered from emphysema after years of breathing dust at the coalface. Morgan, his father and all their friends belonged to the Labor Party.

Morgan said, "I suppose, since your Dad had his own business, he voted Tory?

Partly to avoid confrontation, Jeannie told them all, "I was too young to vote before I joined up so I had not investigated politics much, but after the war I must show more interest."

"You don't know what work means to people like us," said Morgan, "long hours, low wages, no hospital or health coverage, poor schools—or no schools, not enough teachers: nowhere for the kids to play. And then, the one person who might have helped us, leaves the country."

"What do you mean? Whom are you talking about?" Jeannie asked.

"Edward, the Prince of Wales. He came down there by himself to see what was going on; he knew the conditions in the pits. He assured us he'd talk to the then Prime Minister, Mr. Baldwin, and get something done about it. But then he gets himself involved with that American lady, Mrs. Simpson, who's divorced, and the Archbishop of Canterbury reminds him that, as Heir to the Throne, he can't marry a divorcee, let alone the fact that she is a commoner. An English King has never married a commoner; that's why they're all intermarried with European Royalty.

"I know he abdicated, before he'd actually been crowned after his father, King George V died; I heard him on the radio, talking to all his people. He was very upset," said Jeannie. "He must have loved her enough to give up any right to the Throne."

"He loved her more than he loved his country, then," said Morgan, with some bitterness in his voice. "He was popular; the working people all loved him. He was the only person to take any interest in us. Now,

Albert is next in line, except they decided to use one of his other names because there's never been a King Albert, and he was crowned King George VI. He was already married to Elizabeth Bowes-Lyon and they had two girls, Elizabeth and Margaret, but no boys, and the throne has always gone to the eldest son. Don't know what they'll do about that when Albert dies?"

There wasn't a whole lot of dissention in Workshops. They'd all been laborers of some sort in "Civvy Street", convinced that Great Britain needed a Labor Government.

The day came for Jeannie to take her oral, written and practical exams, Captain Winters presiding. He would take into consideration the ongoing reports he had received from the Sergeant in charge of Workshops, and the verbal interview with Morgan.

She had to jack up and remove a wheel from an ambulance, change the brake pads, replace the wheel, check all the tire pressures, including the spare wheel, drain and refill the radiator, check all oil levels, including the gearbox, and add the correct oil where necessary, check the brake and steering fluids, water for the windshield wipers, and make sure they were working correctly and didn't need fresh blades. She changed the blades. Later, she was told to start the ambulance. It didn't start. She had to check it systematically to discover why? The wire to the distributor had been disconnected—on purpose, of course—but she found it and fixed it. Then, with Captain Winters as her passenger, she placed the vehicle as if she were going to pick up someone on a stretcher, as he commanded. Finally, she parked it in one of the bays. He asked her twenty questions orally, relating to the vehicles and any staff for whom she might be responsible, but he didn't indicate whether her answers were what he expected.

Captain Winters appeared pleased and told her to meet him in his office. The oral part turned out to be satisfying his curiosity about her life, more than anything else! He seemed to be intrigued, commenting,

"It appears to have prepared you well for handling responsibility in the Army."

She had little problem with the written paper.

Three days later, Captain Winters sent for her. He congratulated her on her prowess and awarded her a second stripe. Thenceforward, she was a full Corporal. She left for Headquarters at Ingatestone, Essex, promptly, and was issued a rail warrant.

I've done as Neil wished, she thought; that's the next rung up the ladder. I wonder what I have in store for me after Ingatestone?

The Ingatestone interlude was principally to familiarize her with responsibilities when in charge of an Outstation, regarding both vehicles and personnel. They didn't want her to feel "high and dry," and she could telephone the Section Headquarters at Bishop's Stortford if a situation arose too difficult to handle. A motorcycle was put at her disposal for personal contact with the Section HQ and the three separate areas of the Outstation. There was a male Officers' Training Substation in the vicinity where they arranged for her to take riding lessons on motorcycles. Pay for her drivers and herself was arranged with a Signals Company in Westcliff.

The Outstation on the Thames Estuary consisted of a CRS—Camp Reception Station/ Army Hospital—at Shoeburyness, including Thorpe Bay, the furthest point East; a CSD—Command Supply Depot in Southend-on-Sea—which had a mile-long pier reaching out into the shipping lane of the River Thames, where there was a steep drop-off into deep water—and Westcliff-on-Sea, with another CRS, which was to be Jeannie's own HQ, from which she worked.

She was posted to Westcliff-on-Sea on Christmas Eve, 1943.

CHAPTER 11

SOUTHEND-ON-SEA—MEMORIES

Jeannie had plenty of time alone in which to think when traveling by train from Ingatestone in Essex to Southend-on-Sea on Christmas Eve, 1943. Lots of memories!

"What's wrong with the little girl?" he said.

Auntie Audrey stood talking to The Man while Jeannie lay on her back in the long carriage Daddy had the carpenter make especially for her. Mum said she had to lie like that for a long time. Mum left her with Auntie, who lived in a town by the sea, where there were new things to look at and it was a change from lying looking at the trees and the sky at home.

She could see the window of the toyshop from where she was lying. Auntie wheeled her along to look at the dolls, but she wasn't close enough to see them properly. Jeannie wished The Man would go. Now, Auntie is wheeling her closer to the window, but The Man is still there.

The dolls have all got pretty china faces—like "Marjory" and "Ann," at home—but there is one, right in the middle. I'm five, and I've never seen one like that before, or the way she's dressed, Jeannie thought.

Then, The Man said: "Which doll would you like? I'm going to buy it for you."

Jeannie pointed to the doll in the middle with the black face.

"That's 'Oni,'" said The Man. "Her name is 'Wanted' in her African language. That's a good name for her. You'll remember it, won't you?"

Jeannie nodded her head.

The Man went into the shop, and came back with "Oni," the black doll, handing her to the little girl in the long carriage, who said, "Thank you," and held the doll tight.

When Jeannie was old enough to understand, her mother explained that she had tonsillitis, and was taken to the hospital in Exeter.

"The tonsils were taken out because they were infected and poison got into your blood stream, and I had to take you from Devonshire to London to see a specialist, who said you must lie flat for nine months."

But, years later, Jeannie's doctor said, when told:

"It was a pity you could not have waited for another thirteen years, when penicillin was discovered. It would have cured rheumatic fever, which is what you had all those years ago."

She supposed she was lucky to have lived this long and to have experienced such a diverse life.

At six she began to walk again, but her legs were weak and she tired easily; her feet hurt to walk far. Daddy drove her to the boarding school in Exeter every day. She didn't board. Girls in Kindergarton and First Year were in a much smaller building separate from the main school. She was admitted straight into First Year because she had learned so much by way of Miss Ferris, her Governess at home. She taught her little charge reading and writing—Jeannie had to sit up at a table for that, just for half an hour at a time—copying words in a book with lines just the right size for the letters to fit—"except for those with long tails and those which hold one arm in the air—like 'd', 'f'', 'h', 't' and 'l' and 'k'—you have to reach up and draw the arm first—and the same for the big letters, of course." And she learned all her math tables, and French. She knew the names of everything in the room and lots of things in the garden. Miss Ferris was nice and she was a good teacher, and she only had one little girl to teach.

The thing Jeannie remembered most about First Year was the bay-leaf hedge; the caterpillars loved it! She collected a few of the caterpillars, put them in a matchbox, took them home, kept them in a box with little holes in the lid, and brought them fresh bay leaves every day. Each of the caterpillars formed a chrysalis, stuck on the side of the box, so she took the box to school and gave it to her teacher who explained that a butterfly would eventually pop out of each chrysalis. They all watched that happen. Then they stood outside and admired the butterflies as they spread their wings and flew away.

She was soon moved into Second Year, and the Big School. The summer when she was seven, Mum said that Auntie Audrey had invited her for the summer holidays. She went by train to London, where Auntie met her at Waterloo station and carried her suitcase. They had lunch, and then caught the train to Southend-on-Sea, a "slow train" stopping at every station on the way. When she was older she understood that it was a "commuter" train because most of the travelers worked in the City of London and caught the train every day.

In July or August many people in London had a week's vacation from work and, of course, children were on two weeks' holiday from school, so there were day-trippers to the beaches and the carriages were full of children with buckets and spades. In many cases it was the only day they left the City to experience the seaside—because it was all their parents could afford, Auntie said.

Jeannie looked forward to the summer holidays. Her two boy cousins teased her but they played with Meccano, building bridges and towers for her with the metal pieces, and they had a wonderful stamp collection which belonged to their Dad, Jeannie's uncle, with the kind voice and gentle, soft hands. They had a whole set of "William" books which she read every time she stayed at their house.

It had high ceilings, and the stairway was steep, with high risers, the sturdy polished banister tempting for a rapid descent by her cousins. The bathroom was the most cold and intimidating room—especially the iron tub standing high off the floor on its four large claw feet, so she needed a little stool to get into it. Auntie told her to sit in the tub while she turned on the water, gushing out of two large taps—too distant for Jeannie to reach them, especially since there was a removable wooden rack across the tub to carry soap, flannels, shampoo and back brushes.

She sat, shivering, as remote from those taps as possible, terrified she'd float away under the rack and drown before Auntie came in to turn them off.

By comparison the ceramic sink was tiny, and the toilet, with its wood seat and rope flush pull, difficult for a child to deal with. She preferred the toilet by the kitchen, accessed from the yard—except when it was dark, or raining.

They had a piano, so Auntie made her practice her scales and pieces of music every day.

"We'll walk to the beach so you can paddle and play in the sand," said Auntie. "I've made sure it's high tide. It's the estuary of the River Thames, so the tide goes out nearly a mile, almost to the end of the pier, leaving mud flats nearly as far as the deep channel in the middle of the river which the ships sail up. When the tide is out, the stall owners near the water collect cockles, mussels, winkles and other small shellfish to sell."

Jeannie didn't mind looking at them but she didn't want to open the shells and eat the live creatures raw; and she didn't like the smell!

The days Jeannie walked along the pier with Auntie were fun. It was a mile, but they always caught the pier train coming back in the evening. There was a stage at the end where bands played and clowns and singers performed, and there were sticks of pink and white mint rock to eat, and hot sausages or toffee-apples on sticks, and there were machines that people put money in to play games—Auntie called them "one-arm bandits." Jeannie didn't know what that meant, but Auntie always held her hand and walked past them.

The paddle steamers crossed the river to and from Rochester, or Margate, in Kent. They moored against the end of the pier to let some of the passengers disembark, to catch the pier train to shore. Some passengers just came for the ride and sailed back to Rochester or Margate again.

At the shore end of the pier there were rows of empty deckchairs. Auntie would not let her sit on any of them. She said, "They are for the Jewish community who travel from London and want to sit together." Jeannie didn't understand that but she did as she was told.

Just up the main street from the pier was the Kursaal—all walled in so you had to pay at the entrance desk. It had bumper cars and all sorts of rides, some through scary, dark tunnels where ghouls popped out as you went past, and others behind rushing waterfalls or along steep cliffs or through colorful gardens—and, of course, there was the Big Dipper, which frightened Jeannie too much for her to enjoy the thrill of the ride.

Auntie trusted Jeannie's older cousin, eight years her senior, to take her to the cinema. He liked Laurel and Hardy so he always wanted to go and see them, but Jeannie thought they were stupid. He did take her to see "Snow-White and the Seven Dwarfs" which was a new film in color, and she loved that, but then he wanted to see "King Kong"—in black and white—which frightened Jeannie so much she couldn't sleep afterwards. She didn't go with him again after that.

Jeannie's uncle played cricket. She thought it such a slow game—only exciting when one of the fielders managed to hit the stumps with the ball before the cricketer running between them could get back to base. She didn't mind lying on the grass, waiting for it all to end, as long as she had a book to read—especially a "William" book. He was always involved in some escapade.

Every summer, Auntie Audrey made marmalade. That was the time when the special bitter oranges were in the stores. Auntie cleared the kitchen table and screwed a hand mincer onto it at one end. It was a special mincer, to be set either to dice food or slice it. Those oranges were sliced. Jeannie worked hard at rotating the handle but Auntie took a turn when she became tired. They measured out the sugar and water and put the entire concoction into a large shallow metal bowl to cook on the gas stove. Auntie set an alarm clock to time it. She then let it cool for a while before pouring it into jars and sealing it from the air with waxed paper circles and fine string. It made marmalade like jelly with orange peel floating in it.

She loved riding in the open upper level of the trams traversing the Boulevard—tracks running between lovely flowering trees and shrubs—all the way to Thorpe Bay. Beaches there had more sand than at Southend, and were better still at Shoeburyness, where the Thames Estuary was wide and opened to the sea. The tram turned at Thorpe Bay on its circular route and followed the River Thames back to Southend, so they had to walk over a mile to the beach hut Auntie's friends owned at Shoeburyness, where they kept a small Propane gas stove and some cooking pots, and beach chairs and towels and balls and buckets and spades, and there were always boys and girls to play with. Auntie's friends invited them for the summer holidays.

Jeannie, and all the other boys and girls, called Auntie's grownup friends Uncle Bob and Auntie Margaret. They were such kind people and they seemed to love having all the young kids around them. Auntie Margaret was deaf but she could talk all right; she had not always been deaf, they were told. She stood a small square box in the middle of the table and there was a wire from that to a sort of plug, which she put in her ear—then she told everyone that if they talked she could hear them—but they had to take turns and not all talk at once, so she told them to raise a hand if they wanted to talk, and she would choose who could go first. She said if they all talked at once the noise in her ear was like being in the Kursall in a bumper car with the music blaring.

That was where Jeannie first met Eric when she was thirteen. He stayed with his mother across the street from Auntie's house. His father was a jeweler in London who seldom got away from work. They were the same age, so after they met they went almost everywhere together, and wrote to each other to make sure they would be at Southend at the same time for at least two weeks of the summer holiday.

They walked to the beach at Southend together.

"There's the same old man on the street corner selling homemade ice cream from his bicycle cart," said Eric.

"Yes, it's a bit watery, but you can buy a cornet for a halfpenny or a penny; I feel sorry for the old man standing on the corner in the hot sun."

"Let's each give him a penny so he'll put a larger scoop of ice cream into a bigger cornet." They thanked the old man, and then ate the ice cream as they walked.

"I've almost finished—and there's the beach," said Eric.

"Let's go to Thorpe Bay on the tram tomorrow; we could then walk to Shoeburyness if all the friends at the hut are going to be there. Does your Mum know whether everyone's arrived yet?

"I don't know. I'll ask when we get back today. In any case you and I could go to the beach at Thorpe Bay for a change, and we could walk back from there over the Park. It's a fairly long way but it's nice walking on the grass—better than the hot pavements—and it saves a tram fare."

The highlight of the holiday was always the Carnival. Jeannie and her Auntie and Eric and his Mum caught the tram to Westcliff, where there was a park with lovely gardens, full of colorful flowers. They always found a front seat on their own big rug on the grass up above the road, where Auntie and Eric's Mum rented deckchairs, and they picnicked and saw the Carnival Queen and her Maids of Honor and all the decorated cars and trucks, and the clowns, and bands playing and marching down the street. It was a long procession. Every year, crowds of people arrived to watch.

Jeannie slept in the small third bedroom with a single bed under the window, but she liked it because she could look out at the quiet street lit by gas lamps at night. The gas lighter man came by each night and lit them individually. Jeannie watched a few night adventurers walk past. They couldn't see her looking at them from her darkened room, where she made up stories about them in her mind before going to sleep.

Auntie accompanied Jeannie to London on her return journey home, and made sure she was safely aboard the train for Devonshire—until next year.

The train was slowing down and the brakes squealing. Jeannie looked out and recognized the station as Southend, even though there were no signs. She got up and pulled her duffle bag and knapsack off the rack. She had to get up to Westcliff, so she hoped there'd be a truck from the C.S.D. to meet her. The Sergeant at Ingatestone had told her that had been arranged by 'phone—but she'd have to drag her stuff out of the station first.

That made her think about the little ponies which used to give kids rides on the beach… stop it, this is Christmas 1943, and there wouldn't be any ponies in the winter, and there won't be ponies anyway—just barbed wire—so you won't be able to swim either, even when the days get warmer…another life. This is wartime, and you've entered a Limited Access Zone, she told herself, because bad things can happen here. I guess I'll find out what those are, soon enough.

The train stopped, she dragged her duffle bag to the door and down onto the platform.

A young soldier said, "Hello. Welcome to the end of the line. Looks as though you need some help. You are the young lady I'm supposed to take to Westcliff, aren't you?"

It was easier than she thought it would be.

CHAPTER 12

SOUTHEND-ON-SEA—"DOODLEBUGS" AND OTHER THINGS

On Christmas Eve, 1943, Jeannie arrived at the Westcliff-on-Sea Camp Reception Station, and didn't have time to unpack her duffle bag before she was told a patient must be taken by ambulance to Banstead, in Surrey, south of London and the River Thames. It was very short notice for the four ambulance drivers, who had all made other plans for the evening, so Jeannie took pity on them and said she would undertake the trip.

The patient was in a straitjacket lying on a stretcher, waiting to be lifted into an ambulance; two male orderlies sat inside the ambulance with him and the third sat in the passenger seat next to Jeannie.

"Do you have a map?" she asked him.

"No. We don't need one; I've been there plenty of times."

Jeannie didn't feel very confident about that, but she didn't argue in spite of her achieved authority, thinking instead of the number of times she had been to North Wales but had always taken a map, just in case she had to take a different route for any reason—an accident or a cliff slide, for example—aware there would be no street signs.

And—it was Christmas Eve.

After nearly a two-hour drive, they arrived safely at the building in use as a Mental Hospital at Banstead, Surrey. Jeannie got out of the ambulance to stretch her legs and walked around to the back as the patient was being lifted out on the stretcher. He looked straight at her and winked, his mouth breaking into a slight grin.

She could scarcely believe her eyes, and she thought—probably a conscript, wriggling out of the Army, willing to put up with a mind-bending time in a mental hospital rather then face military duty—and there is Neil, who volunteered to serve his country, existing in some no-man's-land—and it's Christmas Eve.

The orderlies got back in the ambulance, and Jeannie turned for "home." They had only traveled a short distance when their route was diverted. On the outward journey they had to get off the highway to find the hospital, but there were no alternative directional signs when they tried to retrace their steps.

"Now, where is the map?" said Jeannie.

"Just stay on this road," said the orderly "and eventually we'll come to a main highway where we can turn off it."

They arrived at some hooded traffic lights, where their lane had to stop. A young soldier approached the vehicle, asking where they were going. The orderly sitting in front told him they had been diverted further back but needed to get to Westcliff.

The soldier said, "If you give me a ride I'll put you on the right route."

Jeannie told him, "We're not allowed to pick up passengers."

The orderly cut in, saying, "We're lost. If he knows where we have to turn, it's worth the risk of giving him a ride."

Reluctantly, Jeannie told the soldier, "All right, but you'll have to sit down on the floor between us." The floor was raised up about nine inches to support the seat on either side of the cab. He was hidden other than at close quarters.

They set off again, the soldier calling out directions as they came to various junctions. They crossed a Thames river bridge Jeannie did not recognize. It all seemed a long way, but eventually the soldier told them to stop and let him get off. "Carry straight on," he said, and turn right at the next lights. Happy Christmas!"—He jumped out and disappeared.

Jeannie felt concerned. At the next lights there was an elderly man waiting to cross. "Happy Christmas!" she shouted, "Please can you tell us where we are?"

"Outer Circle, North London."

At that moment Jeannie knew they had given the soldier a ride home.

Jeannie told the orderly, "We've come from south-west of London, and now we're north. We need to be going east. The only thing to be thankful for is we're the correct side of the Thames. If we follow the Outer Circle we'll eventually come to the main road just before the river and we can follow that out of London. If we have doubts about the road for the Outer Circle, we'll just have to ask someone—and you'd better hope there's someone to ask in the middle of the night on Christmas Eve."

They got back to the CRS—very late, but safe.

Jeannie told the orderly: "Never again do we leave without maps, I don't care what you say."

On Christmas morning she and her drivers were awakened by the scrawny cook's rasping voice at the door: "Wakey! Wakey! Merry Christmas 1943! Ham and eggs for breakfast! All ready and waiting in fifteen minutes! Don't let them get cold!"

They all dressed fast and walked downstairs to the Mess in the adjacent building, Jeannie introduced herself properly to her four drivers and told them about last night's episode, warning them never to give anyone a ride—in uniform or not—and never to venture beyond the local environs without a map; journeys were too unpredictable.

She was soon to find out how true those words would prove to be.

This part of the Thames Estuary, centered on Southend-on-Sea, was vastly different from the way Jeannie remembered it as a child. In wartime it was a Limited Access Zone. There was no freedom of movement in or out of the area. Those remaining had to have a reason to be there. Jeannie's aunt and uncle still lived in the familiar house on the same street, but he was Head Postmaster for the entire district. Her cousins were abroad in the Army. The Kursaal was boarded up—a silent cemetery of metal and faded paint. The only thing to be seen was the Big Dipper, where its track turned at the top of the highest rise.

Owners of many of the tall Victorian houses with high ceilings had left the area and soldiers were billeted in them. Jeannie's own headquarters—a large building—had been converted for use as an army hospital, with accommodation for nurses and orderlies, its grounds and drive-way large enough to park the ambulances and to provide space for those bringing patients from elsewhere. The Mess was on the ground floor, and serviced the hospital staff as well as Jeannie and her drivers. They slept, five to a large room, on the upper floor of an adjacent house.

There was a narrow wooden bunk in a big first floor room next to the Mess for use by the night ambulance duty driver. The room had a large bay with windows—there were five of them—two at each side, which opened, and a fixed one in the middle. They each had sash cords to pull them up or down, the bottom being no more than twelve inches off the ground. It was common practice to leave them half-open at the top and the bottom most of the year, so the fresh air could circulate.

There were less frequent trams than as Jeannie remembered, for public use, but many bicycles, and Army Staff cars. When off duty, Jeannie cycled everywhere—but she had to acquire the motorcycle maintained for her use in overseeing the sub-station in Shoeburyness and in Southend itself and to reach Section Headquarters at Bishop's Stortford—so she had to learn to ride the thing! A young army officer was assigned the task of teaching her.

She knew that the training ground for the men who learned to ride was a rough sand-dune area just outside town—steep slopes between hillocks covered with tufts of windblown grass—and she hoped she didn't have to display her incompetence to them. How embarrassing could that be? She had never really enjoyed riding a bicycle, never mind a motorbike. Then she thought about the girls she had taught who would never be drivers. I don't have the luxury of incompetence, she said to herself.

But Lieutenant Daniels seemed more nervous than she was. She recalled Morgan in Workshops and knew she had to be the one to make the first move.

"I've ridden horses, and bicycles and an Autobike, and I've fallen off all of them. I guess this will just add to my experience, so don't feel guilty if I fall off a motorbike and end up in the sand right in front of your eyes."

He laughed. "We'll start off on the flat. You'll have to learn to kick-start it without dropping the bike. It's quite heavy to hold up unless you get it balanced correctly. The right-hand grip is the accelerator. Twist it towards you when it fires, to rev it up."

"If I can't kick-start it, can I roll it down a hill in third gear, like a car, with the clutch disengaged, and let the clutch in to get it going? You'd better show me how to use the gears and the clutch," she said.

"It's important to be able to kick-start it. You might not be on a hill, and you don't want to be running with it to get it started until you are used to balancing it."

"All right, I'll do it your way," she said. "You've taught all those lads to ride so I'm sure you can teach me."

At least he was talking to her and she didn't mind seeming a bit silly if it encouraged him to do that. Men are strange when they're in uniform, she thought. They either attempt to exert their superiority to make you feel small, or they are embarrassed at having to deal with a woman; always remember that.

It was a 1943 Ariel and Jeannie always preferred it to the Royal Enfield, though the Matchless of the day was an acceptable alternative.

Jeannie wasn't obliged to do night ambulance duty because two drivers shared the responsibility for each ambulance and she scheduled their driving time, available for all to see on the Notice Board, but there was always the odd occasion when someone didn't feel well, and she stood in for them.

A slight noise disturbed her, not enough to awaken her fully. It was dark. There was no moon when she felt the surgically gloved hand across her mouth, and another hand pulling the blankets back. He was tall and strong, standing astride the narrow wooden bunk so close to the floor, well accustomed to lifting bodies much heavier than hers. He squatted down. She wriggled helplessly, trying to get away from him. She didn't need to question his name. She knew.

When he'd accomplished what he came for, he went out the way he came in.

Jeannie rushed to shut all the sash windows at the bottom, locked them in place, and vowed never to leave them open again. She ran into the bathroom to take a shower then remembered the emergency supply room used by the nurses, and found a syringe. But no amount of soap and water could wash away her fear and her memory. It would always be his word against hers, and he had plenty of male orderlies to back up anything he said.

The only person who would understand, and believe her, was Neil—and he was in a different place and time zone. She would write and tell him what happened.

The next time she awakened in the night was at hearing a loud droning outside. She didn't disturb the drivers, but got off her bunk quickly and ran across the room to look out of the window. The droning sound was low and close and very loud indeed—so great that they were all awake in seconds. It sounded like a monstrous bumblebee.

"Get away from the windows! Lie face down on the floor! Pull the "biscuits" and blankets over you, and cover your ears ***fast***," she yelled, as the adrenalin encompassed her entire body.

Momentarily, there was silence—then the sound of a huge explosion rocking the building and shattering glass—but nothing actually hit them.

The girls screamed. One of the drivers said, in awe, "What was ***that***?"

Jeannie told them, "It's a bomb, but it wasn't dropped by an aircraft, it must have been propelled here by some other means. Listen! There's another one—and another. They're self-propelled. We'll be okay as long as the engine doesn't cut out before it reaches us. I think they must be launched with no pilot in them and then when they run out of fuel, they just drop! Hard for them to be really accurate, but they can cause a huge amount of damage."

The next day their fears were confirmed—but by telephone messages from HQ, not on the radio. Presumably so that Hitler could not gloat about a successful mission—yet!

The bombings continued, mainly at night but also sometimes in daylight. It looked like a very small aircraft. In daylight it was less terrifying because you could see its direction and have some vague idea where it might come down when it ran out of fuel. Also it made a loud, wavering droning sound. They called it a "Doodlebug." Officially it was a "V-1—Pilot-less Aircraft."

The second pilot-less aircraft was launched several weeks later. That was worse—it gave no warning—just a searing rush of air before it hit the ground. This was known as a "V-2."

British Intelligence was aware of them. The difficulty was in determining the whereabouts of the launch site. When this was found, British soldiers fluent in German and working under-cover, managed to infiltrate underground caverns where the things were made and blow up the whole place. A fascinating film, post-war, showed how they did it.

Meantime, troops were building up in the area. They stood naked, nervous, and embarrassed, in the corridor of the CRS, awaiting various inoculations. The girls passed them but didn't pay any attention to them, other than to say, on occasion:

"Cheer up! It's not going to hurt and it's soon over."

Jeannie added, "Relax. That's the trick."

CHAPTER 13

THE THAMES ESTUARY

As time passed, Jeannie forgot the orderly's name. She didn't want to remember it, so she just called him "Jack"—Jack be nimble, Jack be quick, Jack jump over the Candlestick—like the nursery rhyme—that would do.

One Sunday, when she was off duty, Jack said, "Do you play tennis? I have a racquet, and the courts are open just down the road if you can find a racquet somewhere."

She wondered, privately, where he'd obtained a racquet?

He'd been plaguing her lately with this, and other seemingly innocuous questions—ever since "the night" in the dark, when she'd been convinced it was he who had climbed in one of the windows. Maybe he was seeking her company now to isolate himself from her suspicion... She didn't have any definitive proof... Maybe it was a form of "one-up-man-ship" as far as the other orderlies were concerned... Maybe he had a grandiose opinion of himself—or the opposite—an inferiority complex?

She couldn't hazard a guess, but somehow there was a little suspicious guy called "Doubt" hanging over one of her shoulders, and another little guy "Be fair," peeping relentlessly over the other.

She thought about Neil: "The army has taught me not to be judgmental—to give everyone a fair chance before I sift them out." He would have known exactly what to do—but he wasn't here.

"I'm sure one of my cousins would have left a racquet at my aunt's house," she said, "but I'd have to cycle over there to get it. She lives the other side of Southend."

"That's no problem. It's a pretty flat road all the way. It wouldn't take us long to go there and back to the tennis courts."

She had a nagging feeling of irritation at his assumption that he could accompany her, but it was a nice afternoon and what was he going to do while she went on her own?

"All right, I'll go and get it," she said.

"I'll meet you outside with my bike, then." It was a statement of fact, no hint of a question about it.

She groaned inwardly, and scolded herself: How could you fall into that trap?

He wasn't much good on the court, and Jeannie had not played since school, but she found herself enjoying the exercise.

Jack went with her to the N.A.A.F.I. sometimes, to get something to eat, and gradually he told her his life story—or a life story, anyway—he had lived in the East End of London, near the docks, where commercial shipping from all over the world came in to load and off-load goods which were stored in the huge Thames-side warehouses. His father had been a dockworker all his life. What chance was there for any of them to escape that environment?

The war offered him some opportunity. He was given training as a hospital orderly. Now, about half of Docklands was bombed, together with the row houses where all the workers lived. His parents died in one of the raids, but his sister was still alive. She went down into the deepest of the subways during the "blitz," which is why she survived. Many of the kids were evacuated to the country . . . Jeannie thought, I've heard it all before—except it was so much worse for the miners, they all worked underground, in the dark, and it was much more dangerous—and I've experienced the kids who were evacuated, and I know what it's like to be bombed.

She didn't enlighten him about her own experiences, but she began to be tired of his self-pity. So many people suffered in this war. He was no exception, and yet he spoke as though he was deserving of so much more empathy than any others.

About six weeks later, the little painting disappeared off the desk in the small room she used as her office. Had she forgotten to lock the door? Had someone taken her keys—she had a bunch of them, with spares for the vehicles—and made a copy? Mum gave her the painting—it was an original—of a little shepherd boy standing in a green meadow filled with daisies, and a blue sky in the background. It was a peaceful scene, and she loved it—apart from the fact that she knew the painting had some monetary value.

She made everyone aware of the fact that it was missing, but nobody admitted to seeing it. Jack expressed dismay and said that he, personally, questioned all the orderlies.

Time passed, and then the little portable wireless she had since Gresford days, disappeared—and finally—the tennis racquet, which didn't even belong to her. Anyone trading them would only get a few pounds. What was the point in stealing? Maybe, in some way, it was to convince the thief of superiority?

Who knew whatever the reasons were for dishonesty—to steal items of comparatively little value? Then she thought—Jealousy? Resentment? She had the benefit of a more satisfying life than many people?

She would probably never know the answer, but there were other, much more important, matters to be dealt with. Staying alive for Neil, for one thing.

For Jeannie, there would be another story about the old warehouses in Docklands. After the war, an enterprising young acquaintance of Neil from his boarding school days—now being a real estate broker—acquired the right to sell the old warehouses. He ran amusing and inspiring ads in newspapers of the day aimed at an ambitious, younger clientele, encouraging the purchase of an old building, or land left vacant by the "blitz," to be converted into a "Luxury Riverside Apartment, right in the City."

I wish I'd kept some of those ads, she thought.

So that is what can be witnessed today when cruising along the River Thames in East London.

CHAPTER 14

MEANS TO AN END

There was a great deal of activity, both within the Thames Estuary and on land. At night, Army trucks of various types were parked nose to tail in the side streets, and all the houses were packed with personnel.

On the morning of June 6 1944, Jeannie and the drivers awoke to discover they had all disappeared silently during the night.

The Thames was jammed with shipping, so it was little wonder that the Reich anticipated an Allied invasion by way of the Pas de Calais.

However, the Allies had other ideas. They studied maps of the North coast of France and the South coast of Britain, reaffirming the logic in moving the intended invasion from the Pas de Calais to the Normandy coast. The South coast of Britain offered many bays and inlets as well as substantial harbors in which to hide and amass seagoing forces, and room inland for the troops—a concentration of air, army and naval forces within a comparatively small area.

If invaded, two negative aspects presented themselves to the Reich: their forces spread thin defending the coast and inland areas from Scandinavia to Spain; and Normandy separated from the Reich by destroying the bridges of the River Seine.

With so many personnel in the area, Jeannie's ambulance drivers were kept busy night and day transporting troops sick, or injured from V-1 or V-2 attacks, to the CRS at Shoeburyness or Westcliff, or moving those more seriously ill further inland; and the truck drivers at the Command Supply Depot in Southend transported all manner of supplies throughout the region.

She anticipated meeting the pier train carrying injured personnel from the ships in the Thames—but it didn't happen. The Allies stationed an entire bogus invasion force, situated as though to invade Calais—shipping, disguised as destroyers and landing craft carrying inflatable tanks and trucks. All that was left was to determine the invasion date and to ensure supplies for the forces and gas for their vehicles—critical aspects, which received far less scrutiny in post-war reports of the entire enterprise. The concept was one thing; fact was a different matter.

The Allies knew that the Germans were in entrenched positions along the "Atlantic Wall." They could not count on using harbors like Cherbourg or Dieppe. Harbors were essential when crossing the English Channel, due to uncertain weather and exceptionally strong tides.

Harbors were needed quickly where none existed. They needed to be away from heavily defended ports but close to landing beaches.

How did they erect two harbors, each the size of Dover, in just a few days in wartime, when Dover took seven years in peacetime?

In 1941, a clever Welsh civil engineer, Hugh Iorys Hughes, had ideas about using flat-bottomed barges, or caissons, to form the bottom of an artificial harbor when lowered to the seabed and filled with sand—reportedly similar to an unused concept of Winston Churchill in 1917. Hughes had a brother who was a Commander in the Royal Navy who introduced the idea, which was subsequently coordinated with those of Professor J. D. Bernal, Brigadier Bruce White and Allan Beckett. The Allies met many times to discuss the options for sheltered harbors. One was constructed experimentally in the Clyde Estuary in Scotland—Gare Loch. There were many who doubted the feasibility of the Mulberry Harbours.

Admiral Mountbatten, uncle of Queen Elizabeth II, was on his way with his cohorts to meet the Americans in Quebec where the fate of the Mulberry Harbours would be decided. He called everyone into one of the bathrooms on the Queen Mary, where they apparently saw a partially filled bath, forty or so ships made out of newspaper and a Mae West lifebelt.

Half the "fleet" was placed in the bath and a young junior officer asked to make waves with the back of a brush. Of course the vessels sank. The demonstration was repeated with the "fleet" floating inside the Mae West and all the vessels survived!

Dare we think that the defeat of Germany in WWII was partially due to paper boats floating inside a Mae West in a bathtub?

In any event, the task of creating the Mulberry Harbours was given to Mountbatten's Combined Operations, for which they needed the resources of the War Department. Three designs were selected: (1) from the War Office; (2) from the Admiralty; and (3) from Iorys Hughes. "Test" beaches, similar to Omaha, were found at Wigtown Bay, in 1942, on the Scottish side of the Solway Firth, with its nearby Harbor of Garlieston.

The experimental Mulberry Harbours were still facing problems in 1943 and Churchill was getting increasingly irate at the lack of progress. Ultimately there were two Harbours, Mulberry A for the US beaches of Omaha and Utah, and Mulberry B for the British and Canadian beaches of Gold, Juno and Sword at Averanches. The designs would permit the floating caissons to be secured in place in four days. Each harbor would have a capacity of 7,000 tons of vehicles and supplies per day.

A final design was decided. Harbours were necessary due to heavy seas and unpredictable weather. There would be two—each comprising two breakwaters, offshore and flanking, made from hollow ferro-concrete caissons. To provide extra protection, seventy obsolete merchant and navy vessels—block-ships—would be sunk to fill the gaps in the protection provided by the caissons. Inside these protective cordons there would be pier-heads connected to the shore by Beckett's floating steel roadways. The English Channel is subject to very strong winds, currents and waves, necessitating harbor protection for vessels before and after crossing it.

The scale of the project was enormous—approximately 45,000 personnel; 212 caissons ranging from 1,672 tons to 6,044 tons; 23 pier-heads; 10 miles of floating roadway. Tugs were used to tow the caissons to within five miles of the French coast. The block-ships slipped their moorings in Poole harbor and sailed for France on their final voyages, where they were scuttled—or sunk opportunely by German bombardment!

Mulberry A was only used for about ten days due to the worst weather in forty years but Mulberry B was in use for five months, during which two million men, five hundred thousand vehicles and four million tons of supplies passed through the harbor.

It was a highly complex feat of engineering completed in just six months of manufacture by hundreds of contractors in many locations under wartime conditions and a shortage of skilled labor.

Americans landed personnel and supplies directly onto the beaches after Mulberry A was destroyed, suffering loss of life, time and material, and frustrated by the landing crafts' inability to offload closer to the beach, while being exposed to gunfire from the enemy's superior location high above them. This is illustrated only too well by the film: "Saving Private Ryan."

Imagine the vastness of the operation and the absolute necessity to move men, supplies, munitions and equipment to the right place at the right time.

It is probably best summed up by Albert Speer who gave the enemy perspective at the Nuremburg Trials.

Referring to the Atlantic Wall defenses, he said: "We had in two years used some 13 million cubic meters of concrete and 1.5 tons of steel. A fortnight—2 weeks—after the landings by the enemy, this costly effort was brought to nothing because of an idea of simple genius. As we now know, the invasion forces brought their own harbors, and built, at Arromanches and Omaha, on unprotected coast, the necessary landing ramps."

The Normandy Landings are documented in great detail. See Appendix under Mulberry Harbour—note spelling—for accounts accessible by Internet or in writing

But none of this solved the enormous problem of fuel for tanks and vehicles. Admiral Louis Mountbatten had the concept of pipelines under the ocean, which was developed by A. C. Hartley, Chief Engineer with the Anglo-Iranian Oil Company—Operation P.L.U.T.O.

Pipelines relieved dependence on oil tankers, which were susceptible to bad weather and German submarines, and at this time were also needed by the U.S. in the Pacific Campaign. The first line was laid from the Isle of Wight to Cherbourg—over 70 nautical miles (130 km), prototypes having been tested across the River Medway and the Firth of Clyde in Scotland.

The P.L.U.T.O. pipelines were linked to pump stations on the English coast, hidden in cottages and garages, which were supplied by a 1,000-mile network of lines from ports as far away as Liverpool and Bristol. In Europe, the pipelines were extended as the troops moved forward, eventually reaching as far as the Rhine in Germany.

By VE Day in June 1945, over 172 million gallons of fuel had been pumped to the Allied Forces in Europe.

Jeannie remembered, one day she drove a VIP—Very Important Person—to Tilbury docks on the Thames, nearer to London. She noticed some monstrous spools on the dock—a bit like those which carry electric cables—only huge. They were spools carrying P.L.U.T.O., except that she did not know it at the time.

A few years later, Jeannie experienced a close-up account of work on the Mulberry Harbours and P.L.U.TO. One of Neil's cousins was a civil engineer working for a firm closely associated with both. He ultimately went on to be a Professor at a famous British University, only to die later of Altzheimer's.

Life can be cruel to the best people sometimes.

CHAPTER 15

A NEW COMPANY, A PARROT, A GOOSE, A TELEGRAM AND A STRANGER

A couple of months after the Allied Invasion of France and the movement of so many troops away from the Thames Estuary, Jeannie was sent to a new Company stationed at Newmarket, Suffolk, and awarded her third stripe. Parachute companies were in the neighborhood and the majority of vehicles were Staff cars, though there were some ambulances and trucks.

At least she didn't anticipate being bombed any more.

She was assigned a room in a house with a tall, willowy corporal from a well-known aristocratic family in southwest Ireland. They were to become close friends. Her family also knew Boyd Rochford, the Queen's horse Trainer, who had stables at Newmarket.

Jeannie found the old wardrobe in their room more than half full of elegant, if dated, civilian clothes, a careful selection of which Brighid ("pronounced 'Bride' but just call me 'Biddy'") took with her, even for a 24-hour Pass. Jeannie could not be bothered with that; in fact, she found that uniform, particularly for women, carried certain automatic privileges in wartime. Biddy, in her mind, clung tenaciously to her youthful past in the mountains of southwest Ireland. Who could really blame her?

The paved yard with covered parking bays all down one side of it, may have been used originally by the adjacent old inn, which had a side door opening onto it. The innkeeper had a talkative parrot sitting on a swing just outside the door. It was friendly, and they all spoke to it. Consequently, it learned a whole new vocabulary, in many different voices—to the ultimate dismay of more than one driver.

The girls assisted each other when backing into or out of the bays: "You're okay. Come on, come on, right hand down, straighten up. Okay,"—or some such instructions.

The moment a vehicle began to move in or out of the bays the parrot started his commands—in the voice of the moment. Unfortunately, he rarely said, "Stop!" or, if he did, it was at the wrong time. More than once the girls backed into the wall of the inn.

However, one never-to-be-forgotten night, the innkeeper's wife left an electric iron switched on, standing flat on the ironing-board, and he earned his Medal of Honor, screeching as the room filled with smoke—until someone came to his rescue!

It was a nice posting. On free mornings, Jeannie and Biddy walked up to watch the racehorses being exercised, or if they had a free afternoon they hitched into Cambridge and spent a peaceful time paddling on the river.

There were plenty of depressing days, too, when they received news of the war in Europe, or the number of planes missing—when the planes should have been returning from discharging the parachutists—and they'd chatted to the crew in the canteen only the day before.

Jeannie received a one-page letter from Neil. He had cut out her paragraph about the rape, cut out the same amount of space on the blank sheet, stuck the two together, put the new "sheet" in an envelope, and sent it back. He made no comment. The ocean travel all took weeks. All correspondence was scrutinized or partially obliterated. She didn't know where he was. He was alive. But had she lost him?

It had been nearly a year since she had any leave, so she applied for ten days over Christmas, 1944, caught a train to London and another to her home in Devonshire. She needed to go home.

In England, during WWII, there was food, gas and clothes rationing and a general shortage of everything else, with nothing being any longer imported from the colonies. Jeannie spent four years in the Army. This was the one time she managed to get back to her mother's house on leave at Christmas.

The original evacuees had all gone. The widower who helped out at Jeannie's father's office was still around.

Jeannie's mother had two geese and a number of chickens in a shady fenced corner of the large yard. They became like pets, but Mum hardened her heart and decided that one of the geese would make a good Christmas dinner, particularly since she had Senior Citizen evacuees staying in six of the bedrooms. He duly showed up in grand style on the large oak table in the dining room—but nobody could eat him.

Jeannie and her mother took him to the local Church Hall, complete with all the trimmings, where the hungry poor had no such misgivings—and he received a blessing from the Rector. Everyone at home ate poached eggs that Christmas.

It wasn't really peaceful at Mum's; there were too many people around. But, when she wasn't driving someone somewhere, she spent time in the little bungalow in the garden and dreamed dreams of when Neil was there with her. She wondered whether she had lost him due to that stupid letter—she was only looking for comfort. Then she thought how he must have felt, receiving it, trapped and helpless, unable to do anything for her. She should not have bothered him with it.

Also, she had promised him she would split her leave between her Mum and his mother in Baslow so, on the fifth night, she caught the 10:10 P.M. train from Exeter St. David's and made the overnight trip to Chesterfield, where she waited for a morning bus to complete her journey.

Neil's mother was very happy to see her, and since his Auntie Flo was there, too, they had plenty of questions for her. The next day Jeannie and Auntie Flo walked up the dirt road on the Chatsworth Estate where Neil had taken her, and she relived that other day. The weather was chilly so they did not walk as far, and soon returned to a cheerful coal fire. I've kept my promise, she thought—it's the only opportunity I've had to do so.

She told Neil's mother that she had heard nothing from Neil.

"He's depressed," his mother told her, "and concerned about the future, and how much work and study he'll have to do before he achieves anything, and how long it will be before he's home. He's thinking about how much of his life has been wasted—but he hasn't mentioned any problems to cause him not to write, and I'd just hoped things would go along happily until he is back and settled. Don't be upset, dear. He just isn't in the mood to write."

She was always very sweet to Jeannie, who felt guilty about bothering her, and even more guilty about that letter to Neil.

She went back to Newmarket, where life resumed as usual. Then one day when Jeannie was having dinner in the Mess, someone handed her a telegram. She read the few words over and over again—they couldn't be true—"Home at last. Will call tonight." No name. No signature. No need. No supper—she was too excited and disbelieving to eat. She sat on the stairs for at least two hours, waiting for the precious call. It was June 1 1945.

When finally she heard his voice he said he arrived home too late yesterday to call. He wanted her to try to get leave as soon as possible and he would meet her in London to make the trip to Devonshire, after which he planned to take her home with him to Baslow.

Gradually the truth sank in—he loves me, he loves me, the first thing he wants to do is to see me...oh my darling, I'd be on that train tonight if it were possible..."I'll call you at home as soon as I can arrange the dates for my leave," she said, "I love you. Take care of yourself and give my love to your mother, too. She's been wonderful at trying to keep my spirits up—I want her to know how grateful I am for that."

Two or three days later, she was walking down the street towards the Downs, with three of her friends. A tall civilian coming towards them said, unexpectedly, "Hello, Jeannie."

She felt the girls draw closer to her, protectively, at the arrogant sound of his voice. He had his back to the sun, so she could not see him properly until they were closer, but she knew that voice. She thought, what is ***he*** doing here? She felt her heart pounding nervously and the use leaving her legs. This can't be happening, she thought. Nobody's going to believe it. Things like this only happen in a two-penny comic. But it ***was*** happening—and she had to deal with it.

She pulled herself together, and said to the girls, "It's all right. He was a hospital orderly at Southend. I'll meet you back at the bays."

They walked on, leaving her to face him. She turned back the way she had come, feeling it would be safer, knowing there would be more people in the town than further out.

With deep sarcasm in his voice, he said,

"What could be more opportune? I didn't have to chase you down."

"I don't know what you want," she said, "but whatever it is you're not going to get it. I don't know what you think you're doing, deliberately pursuing me like this?"

He must have made all sorts of inquiries to track her down. And why was he not in uniform any more?

She was taking in his appearance—no wonder the girls were defensive. A cheap old brown suit which had seen better days, frayed at the wrists and bottoms of the legs—a bit short for his tall frame; worn black lace-up shoes and a slouch hat worn over his eyes.

"Some money would come in handy," he said, "I'm sure your mother and your boyfriend would be interested to know how you spend your time in the Army. I had a nasty operation, and I've got a plate in my head; that's why I'm wearing a hat—until the hair grows. It will leave a scar."

She knew him too well to be taken in entirely by his story. Truth? Had someone finally got tired of his boorish behavior so they'd got in a fight? She'd probably never know, but whatever it was, he'd obviously been discharged from service—a dishonorable discharge?

And Neil had just arrived home—she had to get rid of him—somehow?

She felt her anger rising.

"How dare you threaten me? Get out of my sight or I'll report you and have you arrested if I see you around here one more time. I know you stole my painting and wireless and even my cousin's tennis racquet. You think you can domineer everybody with your height and your attitude. It's not going to work. I'm warning you! Get out of my sight or I'll walk right into the police station just down the street—and if you try to stop me you'll be arrested anyway. You've got a nerve to follow me like this. I have three witnesses that you're in town, who have had a good look at you. Goodbye—and good riddance.

They had walked back to the entrance to the yard and she knew he would not dare go any further since he was not in any type of uniform. She walked in, leaving him in the street.

Days passed. She was constantly on the lookout for him, but she did not see him again.

She tried to put him out of her mind, but he was a constant nagging anxiety. It didn't leave her for years. The fear was always present. Would he show up again to disrupt her life?

Biddy had ten days' leave and was meeting her fiancé in London—a regular army captain, back from abroad. She was packing an extraordinarily large square bottle of "Chanel" perfume into her knapsack, when she dropped it, and the bottle broke on the wood floor of their billet. Frantically, she scooped up a short fur coat, which she kept for special occasions and threw it into the perfume.

"At least it won't be totally wasted," she said, her face glum at the expensive loss.

Jeannie said, "He'll smell you coming! That perfume will permeate the room like a beauty parlor for days—and that's putting it mildly!" They both laughed.

Some time later in June, Jeannie received an official invitation to Biddy's wedding. Her many relatives sailed from Ireland for the occasion—held at the King's Chapel of the Savoy, in London—looking as though they had stepped straight out of an Edwardian novel.

Biddy walked happily back up the aisle in her slinky gold dress, on the arm of her military captain.

Jeannie couldn't help visualizing the same occasion in Ireland, where she was sure Biddy's father would have been much more in character arriving on a black stallion, with his wife riding traditional side-saddle on a roan mare, and the happy couple leaving a cathedral in their carriage with a coachman in top hat controlling the prancing steeds!

She joined the attendees in chauffeured limousines to the reception.

CHAPTER 16

CLOSE ENCOUNTER ON THE SUBWAY

The automatic doors clanged shut and the London underground train sped to its next stop—closer to her—Neil thought, to my lover—to be my wife—how strange it seemed to be able to think that—after another three seemingly endless years abroad during World War II. He was on a precious twenty-eight days' leave, still in uniform, unsure where he would be sent at the end of the four weeks.

Jeannie waited for him at King's Cross station, ready for the train journey together to her mother's home in Devonshire for a few days, then they would leave for Derbyshire, up north, catching the 10:10 P.M. at St. David's for a brief visit with his mother to the end of his leave, as he had done several times before that deployment—traveling, traveling—but at least they would be together this time—both only children, each with a widowed mother.

How are we to determine our own future? He still pondered that question. How much longer would Jeannie wait for him? He anticipated at least four years' hard study prior to obtaining a remunerative job.

Then Neil noticed the teenager sitting across from him in the "tube" where seats ran parallel with each wall. The familiar school uniform gave him an emotional jolt—some of the best years of my life, he thought.

Neil said, "That's 'Winterbourne' uniform, isn't it? That was my school, too."

"Great school," the boy smiled and his eyes lit up, "I'm having the time of my life. They're still giving us preliminary training for the armed services, too. What's your name?"

"Neil MacLeod."

"Guess what?"—The boy leaned forward excitedly—"I've got your rugger shorts! Your name is still up on a gold plate in the entry hallway; that rugby team held the title for the Inter-Scholastic League in 1937 with an unbroken winner's record, didn't it? Imagine playing at the White City!"

Neil smiled at his enthusiasm. "Good luck," he said, getting up as the tube train braked to a halt at King's Cross, "take care of those shorts; they may become valuable relics in the school sports world!"

He jumped out as the doors opened, thinking he had to remember to tell Jeannie that story; the school meant so much to him and the encounter with the boy would never have happened but for wartime clothes rationing and the fact that most British Boarding Schools appealed to past scholars for their uniforms because of it!

She stood up eagerly as he entered the main waiting room at King's Cross. The welcoming smile dispelled any fears or doubts he may have had; he just wished they could have met somewhere less public. But it was wartime and everyone was used to witnessing emotional meetings and farewells.

He was wearing a bush hat and a smart new uniform, shorts and puttees, having just returned from Burma or West Africa—where protection from snakes was paramount—she had no real knowledge as to where he had been; it was just guesswork from prior conversations. He was as handsome as ever—but so thin!

It was early June, but on the 'phone he had complained about being cold—having returned from the humid heat of the tropics after over three years at what was supposed to be a one-year deployment. But Jeannie knew he was fortunate to be alive. Her first and only indication that Neil was back on British soil had been that telegram: "Home at last. Will call tonight." How on earth had he discovered the 'phone number to call?

"He was wearing a bush hat and a smart new uniform"

She sat for hours on the stairway leading to the Mess waiting for the precious call to come through on the one and only 'phone, in between outbound calls being made by others in her unit…

Their eyes met as he strode into the waiting room, tall and confident, his normally tanned skin slightly yellow from months of cholera shots and malaria pills.

"Hello darling, let's get out of here," he said, as casually as though he'd seen her yesterday, belying his aching anticipation.

"Let's go and get some lunch," she said, "I know a nice Greek restaurant off Leicester Square, and it's a while before our connection from Waterloo to Exeter."

The tube train came in as they reached the platform. They sat together and the train moved off.

Neil stood up to get off at the first station.

Jeannie said, "We're not there yet …

Neil told her, as he stepped out of the door—"We'll be a long time getting there going that way; we're going North when we should be going South…" and he led the way confidently to the platform for the train running in the opposite direction.

She said, "You're such a rotten tease. I haven't seen you for three years and you just let me do that without saying anything."

He laughed. Neil looked at her with those gorgeous dark eyes which had stolen her heart all those years ago, but said seriously, "I'm back now, so you don't have to worry any longer about who has to wear the pants in this outfit. Come along, here's the train… " And he held out his hand to help her board. She knew she no longer had to worry—he would look after her for the rest of his life.

On Christmas Eve 1943 she had been posted to Westcliff-on-Sea on the estuary of the River Thames. She had survived Hitler's V-1 and V-2 unmanned rockets, and the trauma of working all hours of the day and night, supplying and caring for troops assembled for the next move against the enemy—to be D-day, June 6 1944.

Now it was June 1945. Jeannie's Company HQ relocated her in September 1944 to Newmarket, Suffolk, northeast of London, famous in peacetime for its horse races and Boyd-Rochford's stables. He was the Queen's horse Trainer. She was Sergeant in charge of Staff cars and their drivers for the company stationed in the area.

Jeannie had a problem getting leave at such short notice. Her last leave in almost a year was at Christmas 1944, which she split between her own mother and Neil's mother. It seemed like a dream to be looking at Neil in the flesh again; she valued every precious minute. They settled into the train on the Southern line for the West Country, thankful to find two seats together. Neil held her close and whispered—she could feel his warm breath on her cheek—"You don't know how I've longed to be with you; I thought the day would never come. I had such a lonely life until I met you and I've been so afraid of losing you."

She said, "I thought I lost you when you sent my cut-out paragraph back to me. Why didn't you write and say something?"

"I had to do something to prevent you from sending me stuff like that. You have no idea what it did to me. I couldn't stand it. I couldn't do anything about it in a lousy third-world country."

She snuggled into his shoulder, grateful for the semi-privacy of belated wartime blackout afforded by the still dimly lit carriage.

"I'm so sorry, darling. It was selfish of me. At the time I just wanted some comfort."

She thought, it's really a lesson learned—for anyone.

Relaxing to the click-clack of the old steam train crossing the sleepers, she smelled the aftershave and the masculine strength of him as she closed her eyes to savor the memory of those precious moments. Click-clack!

She thought, I've slept on so many different guys' shoulders. Train journeys going on leave were so slow, in darkness, stopping at every station en route, traveling at night to make the most of every minute. Click-clack!

But World War II brought everyone closer together. It was happening in your own backyard and you had no way of knowing whether that day might be your last. Refugees from France, Belgium, Poland and Czechoslovakia joined British Forces or worked in the Land Army. Click-clack! Canadians, New Zealanders and Australians enlisted to support the Homeland.

Following the Japanese attack on Pearl Harbor on December 7 1941, Britain welcomed the support of the United States, ill-prepared for war as it was, and weary of its stance, like "David," since September 3, 1939, against the German "Goliath." Click-clack!

At almost every pause at each train station, its name obliterated to confuse anticipated enemy parachutists, the Women's Voluntary Services provided with compassion, tasteless, half-cold, bottled coffee–normally used for cake flavoring–no matter the time in a 24-hour day... plump matrons, whose husbands, no doubt, had served their country during the Great War. Click-clack!

I should not complain, she thought; I don't believe I was ever expected to pay for a single cup of that coffee and I made a number of close wartime friends—Dutch, Polish, British... Click-clack!

"Would you like some coffee?" Startled, she trembled disbelievingly at the sound of the sweetly romantic voice disturbing her reverie—"I just recognized this as Salisbury and we're about half-way there. I used to have to change trains here for Shaftesbury when going back to school."

He leaned out of the carriage window, reaching for the brown, tepid drink.

He thought of the many years they had been at school in adjoining Counties before the War had brought them together. He sat down and, leaning close to her, told Jeannie about his encounter with the teenager on the subway.

Then, he drifted into memories flooding his mind, which changed his life, until the click-clack ceased and the brakes squealed to announce the destination of that night's journey.

Jeannie had a momentary "flashback" as Neil handed her the backpack from the rack: Nineteen forty-two, Muriel, the old Roman town of Chester, the film version of Margaret Mitchell's "Gone With The Wind," the very first film to have an Intermission, due to its length. Like life, she thought.

Leaving the train with Neil, she recalled Scarlett's final words: "After all, tomorrow is another day."

CHAPTER 17

"CIVVY STREET"

World War II, between the Axis—Germany, Italy and Japan; and the Allies—Britain, the United States and latterly, Russia—commenced with Germany's invasion of Poland on September 1, 1939. On September 3, 1939, Great Britain declared war against Germany, deciding Germany had already invaded sufficient countries in Europe, and ended with the surrender of Germany on May 8, 1945 and of Japan on August 14, 1945.

Everyone went crazy in Newmarket on May 8, 1945—VE-Day—Victory in Europe Day.

A couple of gunners from a nearby company drove a gun-carriage down the street and into the yard, where two of Jeannie's drivers jumped up on the sides of it, waving black-out drapes torn from the office windows, while the soldiers in the gun-carriage drove it fast up the street and round and round the 1914-1918 War Memorial at the end. There were drums beating and whistles blowing and the parrot, on his usual swing outside, screeched at all the noise and chaos. The inn did good business that day, regardless of licensing hours' restrictions!

Neil was discharged from military service, but into the Reserve, in June 1946, over a month earlier than Jeannie but a whole year after he returned from abroad for the second time, following a three-year stint.

That year dragged. He was concerned that he might very well be sent back into the war zone in spite of the six years he had already served.

Jeannie was sent on a "Pre-release Course." Since she ran her deceased father's office with no prior experience, she decided to benefit from the opportunity, however brief, afforded by the Army, to learn the requisite skills. That was how she arrived at Luton Hoo, a grand old mansion with extensive grounds, at Luton, just north of London.

She was always interested in her "Family Tree" and the manner in which the various branches converged. Her father, his two brothers and a sister, all died very young. Her father lived the longest—to barely fifty-six. Conversely, her mother's side of the family all lived into their eighties and nineties. Jeannie stayed in touch with their children all her life; it seemed important to do so for their own children's sake, because she and Neil had neither brothers nor sisters, which made second cousins and close friends additionally important.

When she discovered that one of her father's cousins and his family lived in Luton, she looked them up. Their two sons had been Battle of Britain Spitfire and Hurricane pilots in 1940—fortunate to survive. She was interested to meet them, finally. The elder of the two boys married a girl from the Isle of Guernsey, in the English Channel, which was Nazi-occupied throughout the war. Jeannie lost touch with them, subsequently.

She was discharged from military service whilst at Luton.

For the first time in her life, Jeannie felt alone—and lonely. It was wonderful to be home, but—what an anti-climax after visualizing freedom for so long! She missed the daily routine and the thrill and excitement of Army life—and, most of all—she missed her friends. Jess, her lifelong friend since she was eight and Jess was six, no longer lived in the neighborhood, either. She completed Secretarial College, enabling her to obtain a job in London working for a Catholic magazine. She was not Catholic but she had the requisite skills for the job.

Jeannie told herself that it would all be different in peacetime anyway, and that she had to look upon her new life as just another adventure—which is exactly what it turned out to be.

One day Neil called Jeannie out of the blue:

"You know that thing you wear on your left hand? Mail it to me."

No other comment or explanation. Jeannie felt naked without the green stone ring she wore since he bought it for her when they were together in Woodhall Spa just before he went abroad again.

"That's just to help keep the boys away until I get back," he said.

Now, a couple of weeks after his call, he was spending the weekend in Devonshire with her and, as usual, they were listening to music in the little bungalow in the garden at Jeannie's mother's house. He sat in one of the comfy chairs and pulled her down onto his lap when she finished adjusting the automatic feed to a selection of records on the gramophone. It was playing "My Very Good Friend the Milkman," with Fats Waller singing the lyrics in his own unmistakable fashion—she knew Neil loved Fats Waller. The record ended and clicked onto the next one while Neil reached into his pocket and brought out a little leather box, which he opened—inside was a glistening diamond ring.

He let Jeannie admire it for a moment, then took it out, held her left hand, and put it on the third finger.

"Good. It fits, doesn't it? The old stone ring didn't lie, even after all this time." He held her face in his hands and kissed her gently on the lips…

"They'll never believe me, they'll never believe me, that from this great big world you've chosen me…"

The ring sealed the fact that Neil and Jeannie were engaged to be married rather than just having an "understanding." It opened up a whole new transparency between them and almost daily correspondence with passionate love flowing from each side, expressing frustration at their continued separation. Their families and friends were generous in their congratulations and good wishes for their future happiness.

They had each other—but not together—and each had the responsibility of a widowed mother, living independently, alone—about seven hours' driving distance apart, which did nothing to ease the situation. Neil was accepted back into his pre-war university education combined with a management apprenticeship at one of the major motorcar companies in Birmingham, centrally placed in England, but a closer traveling distance to Neil's home in Derbyshire than to Jeannie's in Devonshire—each of which he had to access by train.

In the unenviable position of renting a shared room with a fellow student and continually eating out, there was nobody and nowhere to prepare meals. His living situation, on top of work and study, was more like an endurance test than a life. He was ultimately released from the Army into a potential career.

Now Neil was back at work, and study, the only free time he had were sporadic weekends, "Bank Holidays" at Easter, Whitsun, Christmas and New Year when the Works—and most other businesses in the Midlands—closed, plus two weeks' annual vacation, taken when the Works, and pretty well everything else, shut down in the industrial center of England.

"Stay at your mother's place in Devonshire," said Neil. "You don't want to be living under the conditions I'm experiencing. Until I have a real job we can't afford to live anywhere decent. Renting is just throwing money down the drain. I want us to start our life in our own home. I'll come and see you whenever I can."

Jeannie's heart sank, but she knew he was right and that it was the best thing for them to do.

Jeannie's mother bought Neil an "Indian" motorbike. She knew nothing about bikes, but she said it "looked good. It has a nice big shiny tank."

It was a typically kind gesture, but Jeannie wished she had consulted Neil first—even if she had put a limit on the amount she was prepared to spend. What could he say? It was a gift.

He said, "A bike? That's so kind and generous of you. Thank you so much."

He rode it three or four times—somewhat precariously—between Birmingham and Devonshire. The last time he took Jeannie into Exeter to look at a brand new Triumph 350cc in a showroom, and asked whether he could take it or a demonstration model for a test run?

He had a Triumph pre-war, his last year at school, and he rode it all the way from Dorset to Edinburgh, in Scotland, but that one year he worked and studied in Birmingham he exchanged it for a little two-seater Austin Seven Sports car. He had to sell the car, reluctantly, when sent abroad in the Army in September 1939.

"It's a much better bike, Jeannie, and I'll feel so much safer riding that when I come to see you. I'd like to get it if they'll take the Indian for a down payment. Do you think your Mum will mind? I don't want to hurt her feelings."

And that was the beginning of the saga of the Triumphs.

Jeannie signed up for a Course at a noted Secretarial College in Exeter. She wanted to be qualified to get a good job. The College guaranteed finding her appropriate work if she passed the requisite exams at the end of the Course. She felt that the Course would serve a dual purpose: alternative companionship and a practical stepping-stone into the future.

Jeannie and another girl were the competitive but equal "stars" of the Course that year, and had their names in the local paper—undoubtedly a recommendation for the teaching success of the College, which found Jeannie a good job with the Chairman of an ecclesiastical manufacturing company, selling garments and other fabric requisites to Roman Catholic churches, mainly in England, Ireland and France. She had not only to learn the names of all the clothing and articles, but also to brush up her French in translating the written or typed requirements arriving from abroad. Fortunately, the typewriter provided by her employer did not have the requisite keys for a reply in French.

"They can get it translated," she told her boss. "After all, they write to us in French and expect us to deal with that."

He was quite a character, hard for some to get along with, but she didn't dislike him. He approved of her work and appreciated her sense of humor.

Jeannie worked there for a year. Neil made the trip from Birmingham about once a month, arriving late on Friday evening in all weathers, leaving at about 4:00 P.M. on Sunday for the return trip. There were no freeways in those days and it took about four and a half hours each way—in good weather.

Early in August 1947, he called, very distressed. His mother was dying. Her heart was giving out, finally—probably caused very largely by all the aspirin and other medication prescribed for the extreme pain she suffered. Jeannie said she would explain the situation at work, and leave the following day to be with him.

Neil said Auntie Flo was there, sleeping in his bed, no longer able to share the bed with her sister, but he said the old spinster sisters a couple of houses away, in the house with the lace curtains in the windows, had said Jeannie could stay with them. They provided her with a huge

Victorian mahogany bed, and a light breakfast each morning. They were sweet and caring—having known Neil and his parents since 1927. Jeannie told Neil she would borrow Mum's car and drive straight there—anticipating a seven-hour trip—largely due to having to circumnavigate the City of Birmingham.

Neil and Jeannie went in to see his mother together.

"Give me a hand each, my darlings," she said, with difficulty breathing, "care for each other and make each other happy. Jeannie, I am glad my son will have such a good wife. Neil will give you my gold watch and pearl pendant with its gold chain. They were a wedding present to me from his father. I'm tired. I can't talk any more. Goodbye, dear. Don't cry."

It was so sad, but she died in her sleep peacefully on August 12, 1947, finally relieved of all pain, to be buried in the grave with her husband, as they planned. Neil arranged for her name to be added to the tombstone.

They had little time to make arrangements about the house because he had to get back to work.

"We can't keep the house because it's too far from my work," said Neil," and it's unrealistic for you to live here; that would be a worse arrangement than we have now. We'll have the furniture held in storage in Birmingham. I looked at a modern furniture display in Leeds but the post-war quality was terrible. We'd be much better off to keep what we have. Mum left the Crown Derby tea service to Auntie Flo, but the Royal Doulton and the remainder of the china to me. I think we should pack it carefully so you can take it in the car to your mother's house in Exeter until we have a home of our own. It will be safe there."

And that is what they did. But there was another little body to be cared for, and that was "Tammy," the little feisty brindle Scottish terrier he bought as a companion for his mother. Jeannie took him to her mother's house, where he tried to drive her own dog nuts. Dusky soon put him in his place, and all was well.

With the house empty, Neil arranged for it to be cleaned. He "camped" in it one weekend when he also had to see the attorneys in Sheffield. The following weekend he rode his bike to Exeter to see Jeannie—with his precious hands bandaged.

"What on earth have you done to your hands?" she said.

"Thereby hangs a tale! I got some oil and dirt on my gray pants and I had an appointment with the attorneys the next day, so I put a little petrol in a basin in the kitchen sink and was going to sponge the marks off...but I forgot I'd had the burner on the electric cooker turned on. It was off already but the glowing ring ignited the petrol in the basin; my pants were lying in the sink beside it and they went up in flames. I managed to get them out of the sink and onto the concrete floor but I was frantically trying to push them outside around the back door, which opens inwards, to finish burning before they set the whole house on fire! I burned my hands in the process. Had to go and see the doctor, and the attorneys, dressed in my fur-lined flying suit pants which I always wear on the bike—I didn't have any other clothes at the house."

"And then you rode all the way down to Exeter this weekend to see me!" said Jeannie.

"Well, my hands are getting better. Besides, I didn't want to disappoint you; I knew you'd be expecting me."

"And you've been at work all the week?"

"Yes. I guess I was an object of considerable curiosity for several days. But we've got a buyer for the house, and it didn't burn down. That's the main thing."

A couple of weeks later he called to tell Jeannie not to send any more mail to the street address where he was renting a room with another student, "When I got back there today after work I discovered my landlady had left her husband for the milkman and she'd stripped the house of everything in it, right down to the light bulbs. All she left was my own bed, with my clothes from the wardrobe and in a chest of drawers, piled on it."

"What are you going to do?"

"For the time being I'm going to Alcester, near Stratford-upon-Avon. The secretary to the Head of Department, where I'm working at the moment, lives there with her parents and her sister. The neighbors have said I can have a bedroom. I can eat with the sisters; that'll be better than eating junk food all the time, as I've had to do. I'll ride into work on my bike."

In the meantime, Mum sold "High Hills." She didn't want the responsibility of it any more, but the buyer virtually stole it from her, cutting down the price asked and telling her he wanted it sold with the antiques, many of which were priceless, including a dining table and a full set of Chippendale chairs, a collection of original "Cries of London" paintings, three mahogany Georgian card tables, a huge Indian silk carpet, Wedgwood china, pewter, copper and brass pots, and sets of brass fire irons and brass candlesticks.

In retrospect, Jeannie often wondered what her mother was thinking in relinquishing all her lovely antiques like that? She had nobody with whom to share the responsibility; she had no room for them herself; she was so accustomed to living with such furniture that the intrinsic value escaped her; Jeannie did not yet have a home of her own, and in any case she and Neil had antiques in storage in Birmingham. Years later, Jeannie felt sick at the loss, but circumstances often determine actions.

Mother kept sufficient to use in the three-bedroom home she bought on the outskirts of Exeter, with front and rear fenced yards, to become showplaces under the care of her "green thumb."

There were two superior women's clothing stores in Exeter at that time and Jeannie walked into one of them intent on buying a "girdle" or "suspender belt." "Panty hose" had not yet been invented and underwear, generally, was practical rather than romantic; therefore rather an embarrassing purchase. She recognized the girl who selected several garments—and showed her the way to the dressing room—though Jeannie did not give any indication of that fact at that moment. Her mind flashed back to Southend-on-Sea.

Since her Headquarters was not in the immediate neighborhood, arrangements were made with the Captain in charge of a Signals Company for Jeannie and all her drivers to receive their pay through the Signals Company. Their practical daily clothing for driving trucks and ambulances consisted of boots and long trousers, a shirt and tie and a battledress top. However, for the privilege of collecting their somewhat meager pay, they were expected to appear in shoes, skirts, a shirt and tie, covered by a tunic with shining, polished buttons—and the girl now selling undergarments in a clothing store had been known for throwing her weight about as a Signals Staff-Sergeant ensuring those orders were carried out!

At the time, Jeannie and her drivers worked under pressure ***and*** under the threat of V-I and V-II pilot-less aircraft, so polished buttons for the interruption of collecting a pay envelope with a smart salute seemed more suited to "boot-camp" than active duty. Jeannie protested the "illogical" order on those grounds. The Staff Sergeant accused her of being "insubordinate" so she made her plea directly to the Captain, and won her case. Now, as she paid for her purchase, she looked approvingly around the elegant store and commented, "Um-m! Bit of a change from the Army, isn't it?" And, with a smile to her erstwhile antagonist, she walked out.

Several months later Neil called Jeannie to say he'd been investigating the housing market and was disgusted with the condition of all the pre-war homes for sale and the amount of work they needed—"But I saw some land," he said.

Jeannie anticipated another year before they had a house, if they bought land, even if there was a permit to build. Permits were hard to obtain after the war. Wood for roofs, doors, floors and structure, was rationed.

But Neil already thought about the answer to that problem. "We'll buy a caravan," he said, "a big one, and we'll live in that on our own land while the house is being built—I've already been to see an architect—he's well-known and I've looked at some of the houses he's designed; they're Tudor-style, and beautiful. I've seen pictures of a suitable caravan and I'm getting it towed to and sited on our land in September 1948. We'll get married that September and I'll carry you across the threshold… well, not quite, because the entrance door won't be wide enough…but you know what I mean, and we'll get married on September 4, 1948."

"Why September? Why not in the Springtime? That's six months away anyway."

"Because then we can go to the Isle of Man for our honeymoon—to see the motorcycle races, for the first time since the war. They are held on the regular roads, which are closed to traffic for two days for the races, but first we can drive all round the course and decide on an exciting viewing point. Petrol is still rationed, but we should be able to save up enough between now and then. At least it's somewhere we haven't been. In regard to the dates, I have to fit in with my Course at the University. I'll be back there after the two weeks we're away."

"All right," she said, "I had to get a different job after your mother died because of being off work so long. You'd better look in the papers nearer the time and see what's available as close to our land as possible so I can go to work there when we get back from our honeymoon! You've organized everything else; maybe you can find my job for me!" She was laughing at him, knowing he was perfectly capable of doing that, too.

She always knew life would be exciting with Neil, but she couldn't help wondering how many wives-to-be would agree, not only to the location of their new home, but to the house to be built upon it, and the intended abode in the meantime—the caravan—without even having seen a photo of any of it? And what was she about to promise him…"to love and obey, for richer, for poorer, in sickness and in health, as long as you both shall live?"

She knew it would be fine—as long as they were together.

Although it was months away, she started to organize the wedding. It would be relatively quiet because both his parents died and he had no brothers or sisters; she just had Mother. They each had cousins, and friends, but many lived a distance away or had families they could not leave. She arranged for their banns to be called at the local church they attended on the outskirts of Exeter, where her mother frequently arranged flowers from her own lovely garden. Jess was happy to be her bridesmaid, Mum agreed to lend them her car for their honeymoon, Neil made all the arrangements for the ferry from Liverpool to the Isle of Man, and for the hotel, Jeannie arranged for a photographer and the flowers, and the first overnight stay at the Rutland Arms, Bakewell, Derbyshire. They mutually agreed about two new suits for Neil, pants, shirts and a sports jacket, all of which were to be made or purchased in Exeter.

Jeannie, Mum, and Jess spent two days shopping for clothes and hats for themselves. Jeannie selected invitations. Mum said she would make the three-tier wedding cake and get it professionally decorated. She arranged for the reception at her house, to be professionally catered as soon as she knew the numbers of people attending.

Neil phoned, worried that he could not find a nice gold wedding ring to match her engagement ring.

"They are all only 15 karat," he said, "and your ring is 18 karat."

When Mum learned the problem, she said, "Tell him to get the ring for me, and you can have mine; that way it will stay in the family."

Jeannie couldn't believe it. Her parents married in 1910—on the same day as her ultimate birthday thirteen years later—"You were our wedding present," Mum said—"and the ring is 22 karat gold. It will be 100 years old in 2010."

So, they exchanged rings, and had the old gold ring polished up like new for the occasion. Jeannie thought—she's amazing. I couldn't do that under the same circumstances; I would have to be dying before I would part with it.

Then, one evening, Jeannie and Neil were discussing cameras to take with them on their honeymoon. Jeannie had a little old square Brownie box camera. Mum said, "I'll go and find Daddy's telescopic camera, and you can borrow that. It's a good camera."

Neil examined it with interest, to see how it worked. Then he said, "There's a film in it, I'll take it out carefully so you can get it developed. We'll get some new films to take with us." Mum was intrigued. She couldn't think what the film might be? The camera was unused for so long.

When the prints came back they were of the very last vacation Mum and Daddy took to the Outer Hebrides in the Spring of 1939, before war was declared that September 3, 1939, and before Daddy died the following January, and before Neil came back from Dunkirk and they met that summer. It was now nine years later and the film had been in the camera all that time, the camera having been unused.

Jeannie said, "What a good thing you noticed, and opened it so carefully, Neil. Those are precious photos for all of us."

He just smiled. He was always careful, handling anything. But he told Jeannie later that he was thinking—nine years, and seven of those years I've spent in the army.

She said, "Yes, but now the world is our oyster; all we have to do is crack it open—and enjoy it."

He put his arms around her and held her tightly to him. "Thank you for still being here for me," he said, and kissed her. "I know we're going to be very happy together."

CHAPTER 18

AN EXTRA PASSENGER—AND A HONEYMOON

The weeks dragged along until Neil and Jeannie's "Big Day." Her anticipation was high; the weekends when he managed to make the trip from Birmingham, occupied partially by suits and the new sports jacket and pants fittings, all of which made him look ever more attractive and elegant in her eyes. They bought shoes and socks to go with everything, shirts, his father's gold cufflinks, and—Jeannie's specialty to "set everything off"—beautiful silk ties. Neil actually hated wearing a collar—held in place by gold studs at the back and front, plus a tie—so, a few years later, when shirts with attached collars became the fashion, she bought him elegant silk cravats for evening wear. He could pull them off—without looking effeminate.

When Jeannie drove back from Baslow to Exeter with the china after Neil's mother's funeral, she took the little feisty brindle Scottish terrier Neil had bought for his mother to keep her company. He said that Pops had always had a Scottish terrier. There was never any doubt as to "Tammy's" real owner. He bounced around in circles upon hearing the bike climbing the driveway to Mum's house, and he jumped straight into Neil's arms the minute he stepped off it.

Jeannie's mother took both dogs for a walk on leashes, Dusky walking politely at heel, ignoring everything in his path, leaving no doubt that he was Mum's dog; Tammy, always looking for trouble, dashing from side to side. Mum carried a whip to rescue him on more than one occasion from the jaws of an otherwise harmless monster he harassed.

He was a picture of dejection if they left him behind when going for a ride on the bike. Jeannie carried him between them, on her lap, but it was uncomfortable because it pushed her too far back on the seat.

"Let's get some panniers," she suggested to Neil, "so he can sit in the one nearest the curb."

They consisted of a firm metal frame, supporting a bag on either side of the bike, made of a strong woven waterproof fabric, like an army kitbag, one corner of which they folded back so he could sit with his head sticking out. Add to that some goggles to protect his eyes, a small child's sweater, and he was all set for the longest journey. He was also the source of much attention and amusement as they traveled the countryside. A little horror on the sidewalk but a model of obedience on the bike!

Neil seemed happier with his rental arrangements at Alcester, though Jeannie was a bit disturbed at receiving a letter from his mother a couple of months before she died, asking,

"Who's the blonde? Neil arrived with her riding pillion last weekend."

Jeannie explained the circumstances, but she knew by the tone of the letter that his mother wasn't very happy. For her part, Jeannie thought, how could he do that? She'd be sleeping in our bed, and he'd be introducing her to places special just to the two of us—almost sacred in Jeannie's eyes—due to the association of time and place in wartime.

She didn't question him. She waited to see whether he would tell her. He didn't mention it.

Jeannie was busy the day before the wedding, collecting Auntie Flo from Exeter St. David's station, who traveled from Sheffield, and her younger cousin from Southend, at Exeter Central, who accompanied his brother's wife and young son. They couldn't all come but were representative of that family. She also met Neil's "Best Man" whom he knew from school days—though not really well. He was vacationing with his sister in Penzance, Cornwall. Everyone else lived locally.

A friend from Jeannie's school was at the station, doing the same thing—and getting married the same day. Aunt Martha drove in from her home at the bungalow, ready to accompany the bridegroom back there for the night. Tradition and superstition stipulated that the bride and groom not meet on their wedding day until they were before the altar!

They all chatted rather awkwardly in the sitting room of Mum's house, awaiting Neil's late arrival from Birmingham on his motorbike. He arrived, tired and wet, at about 11:15 P.M. Jeannie went out to meet him and they entered the house through the back door, opening to the kitchen. She took his wet outer clothes, hung them up and explained that Neil was expected to go and sleep at Auntie's house for the night. She told him his clothes, ready for tomorrow, were in her car.

"Oh god, I'm tired," he said, "do I really have to go out there?"

"She'll make you comfortable. You can have a hot bath and some soup, which will go down all right at this late hour," said Jeannie. "Trouble is, we've got all these visitors to accommodate somewhere, and we've figured that out, so I'm afraid you'll need to go and stay at Auntie's." She felt sorry for him after the long, miserable trip in the rain.

"Okay, then. I've got a couple of things here that I brought with me, which they gave me at Alcester."

He opened a package containing a beautiful, finely knitted pale yellow vest. "This is to wear under my suit jacket tomorrow," he said. "Don't you think it will look really smart? Dana knitted it for me. And she gave me this gold watch as a wedding present."

Jeannie examined the watch. On the back was inscribed: "To Neil, with love and best wishes, Dana. September 4 1948."

She said, "It's a nice watch, but a bit strange for a wedding present. I always thought wedding gifts were for the couple, not individuals. You'd better come in and see everybody and then get on your way. It's getting late.

That's what happened. Then everybody left except those who were staying at Mum's house.

Jeannie thought: This is our wedding. This is what we have promised ourselves over and over. It's what we have waited for all these years. How did she have the gall to ruin it for us—for me? What has been going on?

What is Neil hiding from me? For the first time ever—on our wedding eve—he didn't even hug me, or kiss me.

The day was fine and sunny. The little, familiar church decked with Mum's flowers—she must have worked hard on that yesterday. Uncle waited, with his arm crooked, ready to lead her down the aisle—where Neil and his Best Man awaited her. He looked tall and handsome as ever, refreshed from a night's sleep, wearing the tailor made suit they had chosen for the wedding. She could see the pale yellow vest peeping under the jacket, and the gold watch on his left wrist.

They looked at each other as they said their vows. Neil slipped Mum's lovely old ring on her finger. As the Vicar pronounced them Man and Wife, Jeannie could no longer hold back her tears. It wasn't supposed to be like this, she thought. Neil squeezed her hand tightly, probably perplexed at her tears. They turned to face the Vicar, who was blessing them and offering his words of wisdom, then entered the little room at the side of the altar and signed the Register, with Mum and Auntie Flo as witnesses. Jeannie managed to regain her composure and to smile as she walked back up the aisle on her husband's arm.

The photographer took photos, friends showered them with confetti, and the whole wedding party rode to Mum's house in beribboned vehicles. Only then, seated in the back alone, did Neil put his arms around her and kiss her. "Hello, Mrs. MacLeod," he said.

The caterers did their work. Jess stepped up with little stories about Jeannie and Neil, standing in for a non-existent brother. Jeannie's cousin toasted the bride and groom. Jeannie changed into her "going-away" outfit, Jess took some photos, they waved goodbye to about thirty guests, and left in Mum's car on their honeymoon—first stop scheduled to be the Rutland Arms Hotel, Bakewell.

It was early evening as they approached Birmingham, so they decided to drive through the city rather than around it, and Neil said he wanted to stop and see a friend he knew in the army.

"Don't forget we have to make it to the Rutland Arms at Bakewell, tonight," Jeannie reminded him.

They were longer than she hoped, and after they'd driven a few more miles they ran out of petrol on the outskirts of Birmingham on one of the main roads running into the city.

Jess took some photos

Neil said, “The only open petrol station is right in the center of town. I’ll borrow a petrol can from them and get that filled up. Then we’ll have to drive in there to fill up the car’s tank. Can you stand in the road and flag somebody down for me? They’re more likely to stop for a girl.”

Jeannie did that successfully, and watched him being driven off. She noticed a telephone booth and decided to call the Rutland Arms Hotel to explain that they would be late—otherwise she could see spending the first night of their honeymoon in the car. She was standing in the ’phone booth waiting to be put through by the operator when she felt something crawling up the back of her leg. She brushed at it—and was promptly stung on her butt by a wasp!

Eventually, Neil returned with the can of petrol. They tipped it into the tank, drove into town, returned the can, filled the car’s tank and arrived at the hotel—very late, hungry, tired—and frustrated to find they’d been given single beds!

Forget dreams and romance. That would have to wait until tomorrow. Besides, her butt was swollen and it hurt.

They ate breakfast, and went to see the Ramseys the next morning. He was the Manager of the Bakewell branch of a chain of local grocery stores; Neil was very fond of his daughter, who had been at elementary school with him, now to be married to a mild-mannered, kind fiancé—ex-air force. For some reason, Neil’s mother had not encouraged that relationship. Jeannie thought them all very kind and friendly.

They drove to Baslow to visit the neighbors who had been so kind when Neil’s mother died, then returned, lunched at the Rutland Arms, and set off for Liverpool—after filling the car with petrol—not risking that tragedy again. They checked into a hotel convenient for the ferry. That evening they visited Neil’s aunt—his late father’s sister—and family, whom Neil had not seen for years. Jeannie realized how much Neil valued relationships of family and friends and that he was proud to introduce her as his wife.

The crossing was without trauma, considering the reputation of the Irish Channel, and they arrived safely at the port of Douglas, Isle of Man, checked in at the hotel at the far end of the bay, with nice views and remote from the general chaos of the races.

They explored the Course, and their chosen location, for the next day's race—which was subsequently canceled, due to fog. They looked around town, and played table tennis at the hotel in the evening. There was still a little chill between them, which wasn't warmed when Neil tried to make a 'phone call to Alcester "to thank Dana for the gifts."

Why can't that wait until we get back, like everybody else? Thought Jeannie.

Wednesday was glorious—and fun. They went to Ramsey Hairpin and the Waterworks Turn and spent time with a visiting couple, riding a pre-war Triumph. The husband was with a Petrol Company attached to the 48th Division in 1940, billeted at the same cider factory in Devon, where Neil had been. What a coincidence!

After the race, they looked around Peel. Jeannie photographed Neil sitting on a rail overlooking the beach. They drove back to the hotel to freshen up, and drove out to Laxey in the evening for supper with a couple they'd met on the boat.

Thursday was an exciting day, the principal race of the week being won by a rider from Ramsey on a Triumph!

Neil and Jeannie then drove to Point of Ayre, down the coast to Glen Hellen, and back along the Course. They were due to leave the island the following Monday but there was still plenty to explore. From high ground, when it was sunny and clear, they could see Cumberland and Scotland.

They missed the morning ferry but spent the time looking in stores for mementoes. Neil bought a brooch for Jeannie—a large and a smaller spider joined by a gold chain. She found him two Scottie dogs, sitting and looking at each other. They caught the ferry at 4:00 P.M. and the Irish Sea lived up to its reputation; they had a really rough crossing. They drove to Auntie Sissy's in Manchester for the night, as arranged. She and her husband were Neil's parents' friends who had been very kind to both Jeannie and Neil during the war when either was within traveling distance for a twenty-four or forty-eight hour Pass.

Inevitably, when Jeannie thought of them, she remembered the one weekend they managed to stay at the house together after Neil returned from abroad the second time. Neil accompanied her to the train station—another goodbye—would it be the last goodbye?

"We'll find a quiet corner outside," he said, after one glance at the crowded, smoke-filled waiting room.

It was dark, with only dim reflected light from the old, roofed structure. A cold wind blew, carrying with it the dank, musty smell of a city steam train station. He drew her into a corner by a shuttered news stand and stood in front of her to protect her further from the wind, holding her close within his Army greatcoat, both his strong arms behind her back, all the while whispering consoling words into her ear.

Suddenly, they were disturbed by the harsh voice of a Military Policeman:

"Stop that! Move along there! Split up, or do you want to be arrested?"

She felt like a prostitute, with a one-night-stand—out for a quick fix.

Neil said, "I'd better go; you'll be able to board now—the train's just steamed in." And he was gone, their love for each other lying shattered in the grime.

She thought, when will this war end? Jeannie never forgot that experience.

The next day of their honeymoon, they went to see Auntie Nancy and Uncle John (sister and brother) and Lisa, who looked after the house and the three of them. Uncle John was Neil's Godfather. He was a History teacher at Pops' school in Manchester. Neil showed Jeannie an illustrated book describing his career, including stories about his magic lantern shows, with the lantern lit by a gas light, where the boys took delight in squeezing the rubber gas pipe to put the light out during the show!

When Uncle John died, his Obituary was published in the Manchester Guardian, written by a famous and well-liked British film actor who had been a pupil; he also attended the funeral. He based the character of one of his most famous films on that of Neil's Godfather. It was a striking likeness, both in appearance and mannerisms. Neil loved and respected his Godfather and was very sad at his passing. They went over to Baslow and Bakewell and said goodbye to various friends, then set off for Birmingham, where they stayed with Jeannie's cousin in Quinton.

Jeannie took Neil to work that Thursday morning and again on Friday, in the car. They were still essentially on their honeymoon, with a necessary interruption for Neil to sign on again at the University, having acquired a free place for passing all his prior exams with distinction, and at work for a continuation of the Management Apprenticeship.

Then, on Friday evening, September 17, 1948, they stayed at the elegant Brimpton Grange Hotel off the High Wyckham road, on the way to Oxford. That night, feeling comfortable, secure and happy in a beautiful bed in luxurious surroundings, the "ice" broke between them, and it was like it always used to be in the little bungalow in the garden at "High Hills."

Jeannie thought philosophically, if he found someone else, at least for a while, she could not blame him. He was young, and handsome, and full of longings—as was she. Jeannie didn't mention her feelings and Neil didn't volunteer any comments, so she let it ride. Why spoil a wonderful night when her lover had returned to her? If he'd ever been away?

Saturday was another fun day, making their way south to Reading to see Duncan's sisters and mother, after which they had lunch in Reading. Then they drove over to Shalbourne to see Neil's ex-Housemaster and his wife—now retired from school in Dorset, and finally on to his boarding school. That day, Jeannie recognized the photo of a nurse in uniform on the stone mantelpiece in the now Headmaster's Study; he was a prior teacher. She was his sister, now Matron at the school. She was at the Army C.R.S. where Jeannie was stationed at Westcliff-on-Sea in 1944.

They arrived at Mum's house in Exeter at about 8:30 P.M.

Neil left for Birmingham, and work and study, on the bike after lunch the next day.

Jeannie put the emotional problems of the wedding behind her. She didn't really care any more. They had a wonderful honeymoon in spite of continuing wartime restrictions of fuel and food rationing. She married the greatest guy in the world who was so obviously loved by all his long-time friends and family, and she was optimistic that everything would work out just fine. She loved him totally.

CHAPTER 19

WHEN A SENSE OF HUMOR HELPS THE DAYS GO BY

Neil left Jeannie in Exeter at her mother's house because they needed to take the car back there—and Neil had to return to work, so he rode his Triumph 350cc motorbike back to Alcester.

Jeannie worked for a retired army officer and his son, raising money for a national campaign, based locally, but with national headquarters in London, after she left her job with the ecclesiastical tailors when Neil's mother died. As 1948 was drawing to a close, her employers were planning a move to Chilcompton, in Somerset—too far away for Jeannie to commute—but opportune as far as her ability to join Neil in Warwickshire. She went to Chilcompton for a couple of freezing cold days, to introduce the new secretary to her work, and was glad to leave, already feeling chilblains on the backs of her fingers and her heels. There was no central heating and the rooms of the old stone building were drafty and damp. Her employers gave her some beautiful solid silver spoons for a wedding present, though.

Then, she received a letter from Neil enclosing a newspaper cutting: "Answer this," he wrote, "if you can get this job it's only ten minutes' walk from our place, at the top of the hill to the right at the fork, coming up, and you'd be working for the Chief Scientist, who's second in charge." Apart from the possibility of the job, the best part was the confirmation that he really did want her there with him.

Correspondence ensued, within which Jeannie explained briefly about her wartime experience and the course at Luton Hoo, her successes at the Secretarial College and the two jobs—from which she received good references, and that she would be ready to start work on Monday, October 4, 1948, since she was moving to Warwickshire on Friday, October 1. She enclosed copies of the references, certificates for her secretarial successes, and her army discharge papers, which also included references.

She received a response to the effect that the job would be held for her, subject to approval at an interview on October 4, 1948 at 9:00 A.M.

Mum and Jeannie packed the car with bedding—the caravan slept four—pots and pans and dishes, cleaning materials, utensils, mugs and glasses, clothes, and Tammy's bed. Dusky was going as well, but returning in the car with Mum next day. They arrived as Neil finished work, so he met them there. He went to considerable trouble explaining things about the caravan, saying to Jeannie,

"I hope you like it because it's going to be our home for a year or so. I was amazed at the hidden storage space, but you don't have to examine it minutely tonight; you must be tired after the trip?"

He picked up Tammy and said: "I'm going to show his lordship to the folks at Alcester. I'll be back here first thing in the morning."

He put the little dog in his pannier, waved goodbye, and was gone.

Jeannie was shattered, though she tried not to show it, saying to Mum, "I guess he thinks three's a crowd, and if he stays in Alcester for the night it will save opening up the other bed fully; it can be used as a single bed. Let's go down to the village. Neil said the shop there has a fantastic reputation for fish and chips, and I really don't feel like cooking tonight."

Suddenly, realization hit home!

Cooking, she thought? What's that? I've never even learned to boil an egg, what with the maids, and Mum when I was at work.

Neil arrived at about eight o'clock on Saturday morning, suggesting they'd go out and get some breakfast so that Mum could be on her way and, since the trip might take her nearly five hours, she'd arrive home before it got dark. He said he wanted to show Jeannie the neighborhood, so she wouldn't feel so lost, and they'd ride into Redditch if there were other things they needed; they had the other pannier to carry stuff in. He was tactful, but Jeannie could tell he wanted to spend the weekend with her on her own.

They returned from breakfast, Jeannie gave Mum a hug and thanked her for everything. She left for the long trip back to Devonshire, with Dusky. Jeannie's last words were, "Mum, please could you send me that recipe book of yours?"

Tammy ran around outside and rushed up and down the acre of land. He didn't care where he was as long as Neil was there, too.

Neil said, "Let's investigate our "house" and make up the bed so it's as comfortable as possible—we don't want to be having to experiment with that tonight." They would be sleeping across the width of the caravan, and he was nearly 6 feet 3 inches tall.

Jeannie said, "I think we'll have to leave the cupboards over the wheel arch open so that you can stretch your legs into it, and we can push the pillows into the other one for our heads. Lie down and try it out. I'll put cushions inside to make them comfortable."

She was right! He needed every inch of the space to lie comfortably. It was a neat arrangement. The table, which seated five—including a stool for the end—dropped down to form the base of the bed, together with the built-in seats; and the seat cushions were the "mattress." Jeannie had the foresight to bring pillows and cushions from home.

"Reminds me of 'biscuits' in the army," said Jeannie—"except they're thicker, and we don't have to stack them every morning." She laughed at the thought.

"I'm not waiting until tonight," said Neil, pulling her sweater off over her head, and stepping out of his pants, "I've been waiting all my life for my own place to call 'home.' Let's celebrate. Dreaming of this is what kept me alive when I was abroad, except I didn't know it would be in a caravan—but who cares?"

He removed the rest of her clothes gently, and pulled her down on top of him.

The land was out in the country in a small hamlet right at the top of a hill with one small general store and an even smaller post office where the houses ended, but it had views to the Malvern Hills on a clear day, and to the Lickey Hills on the outskirts of the City of Birmingham, with open fields in between, and the occasional farm or pub. Neil discovered that the owner of the land was subdividing it into six separate acres—over 43,560 square feet each—whereas a normal house-lot was usually not more than 8,000 square feet. They were fortunate to find it so near to a city where Neil had to work. Maybe his decision to build rather than buy was a good one, after all?

There was only one gateway at the far end of what had been a six-acre field. Neil said, when the caravan arrived, it had to be towed across three other properties to reach theirs. Neil was able to ride the bike over the bank beside the oak tree, but Mum's car had to be driven in the same way as the caravan for them to unload it. The seller didn't fence the properties in any fashion; he only had property pins installed at the front and the back. So the first thing Neil and Jeannie did was to buy some wire and iron posts to delineate their boundaries from their neighbors'—it wasn't pretty but it worked.

On Monday, Neil left early for work and Jeannie prepared for her appointment at the property just down the lane. She had only seen the entrance, since it was all you could see from the road, but it looked like the entrance to a country estate with graceful old trees, rather like the Chatsworth Estate but not nearly as large and elaborate; she was not surprised to see the old manor house which had been converted for use as a research association by her potential employers.

She was interviewed by the Secretary to the "Top Gun" who left no doubt that she was "in charge" and expected everything to be done one way—her way, especially as far as the display of correspondence being dispatched from the establishment was concerned. Jeannie thought the layout old-fashioned but kept her opinion to herself. After all, her acceptance for employment depended upon cooperation and first impressions. She was taken around the establishment and introduced to the men in charge of the various departments, including her potential "boss," Doctor Ainsley, whose secretary she would be replacing in a couple of weeks. He was a genial man and she felt an instant empathy.

After talking with her for several minutes, Doctor Ainsley led the way to another room just down the corridor where its sole occupant looked up from his desk and stood to greet them.

"This is Mr. Winters. I may ask you to help him out sometimes, since he doesn't have a permanent secretary of his own," he said. The young man looked slightly embarrassed, but Jeannie held out her hand, "Remember me?" she said, "Workshops at Gresford Camp. You awarded me my second stripe!"

She must have been considered suitable for the job because she was asked to show up for work the following Monday week—the first day of what was to be four years' enjoyable employment in that establishment.

But there was to be an adventure at the end of the current week. It began with Neil's arrival on a brand new Triumph 500cc on Friday. She heard the purr of the twin-cylinder engine as he came up the lane, then he changed down to ride it up and over the bank to the caravan. She rushed out to welcome him—her handsome laird with his emotional voice, making her heart quicken every time she heard it! She was so proud to be the wife of Neil MacLeod but sometimes had little nagging doubts over her suitability as his lifetime partner. What did he see in her, she wondered.

It was Friday evening and he got home a little later than usual. He explained in his unpretentious way that when he went to Coventry to pick up the new bike, the Production Manager, John Blair, with whom he had become friendly, explained that this new model was specially equipped with a "spring wheel." It was not yet available on the open market. It consisted of a very large hub for the rear wheel containing springs—to facilitate a more comfortable ride. Discovering that Neil made long trips quite frequently, John wanted Neil to keep records of mileage covered, together with weather and road conditions, gas consumption, and his personal experience relating to performance, to provide the company with a buyer's practical comments as opposed to "test-bed records." Neil was very upbeat at being asked for his cooperation.

Jeannie noticed that the frame for the panniers and the panniers themselves had been transferred from the Triumph 350cc.

"Where's the other bike?" She asked.

"John's going to ride it home—he lives up on the Lickeys—so we can fetch it from there and you can ride it back here," Neil told her.

"Put Tammy in his pannier and jump on the back and we'll go and fetch it."

So off they went. Jeannie hadn't ridden a bike by herself since Southend days, but it's not really something you forget and the Triumph 350cc was much nicer than the old 1943 Ariel.

Neil introduced Jeannie to John and his wife, and thanked him for bringing the bike home. He apologized for the fact that they could not stay and chat since they were off to Devonshire that evening, because he'd thought it a good opportunity to try out the spring wheel.

Jeannie laughed and said, "That's news to me—but where he goes, I guess I go, too—and the dog! Did you notice?"

John kindly kick-started the Triumph 350cc for her, and she rode it home—even up and over the bank. Neil parked it under a cover behind the caravan while Jeannie threw a few things into the other pannier for the weekend, put Tammy's sweater and goggles on him for the long ride, dressed in her own leather fur-lined flying suit and leather helmet, and jumped up happily behind Neil on the new 500cc Triumph.

"We'd better call Mum when we reach Bridgwater," she said, "we don't want to be locked out when we get to Exeter."

Luckily, it was a fine night, but the ride still took them over four hours. Mum was happy to know she would see them again so soon and said she'd have supper ready for them when they arrived.

Neil carried Tammy through the house and out to the fenced back yard, where he tried to get Dusky to chase him—in vain.

"He doesn't change, does he?" said Mum. "I've never known such a perky little dog—but I suppose most small dogs are like that, trying to show off their ego!"

They had hot baths and snuggled up in Jeannie's bed after the long trip.

"Thank you for being such a good sport at short notice," said Neil. "We'll have fun riding over Woodbury Common and down to the beach tomorrow. Tammy will enjoy the sand and the water. I thought the more powerful bike would be a more comfortable ride for you; that's why I bought it."

On Sunday, the time came to depart for Birmingham. Jeannie loved riding pillion with Neil; it was so much more exhilarating to experience the handling of an expert. The road led up over the Bristol Downs with breathtaking views of the City below and the Severn Estuary in the distance.

Suddenly, there was an ominous grating sound. Neil stopped abruptly. Something had broken in the spring wheel. However, Jeannie anticipated that Neil would be resourceful under difficulties.

"I'll have to push it," he said, "so can you manage to walk the three miles to the train station carrying our leather pants? It's all down hill. We'll leave Tammy in the pannier and I'll push him as well."

Jeannie said, "Of course." And she threw the heavy fur-lined ex-RAF leather pants over each shoulder.

Exhausted, they finally arrived and arranged for the bike to be loaded into the luggage compartment of the train. Neil found a pay-phone and called a friend with a truck to meet them in Birmingham. He took them out to their land and the caravan.

The next day Neil left work early and came back on the Triumph 350cc to pick up Jeannie, saying, "We'll take the spring wheel to the Triumph factory at Coventry; it's about ten miles."

Visualize a motorcycle rear wheel. Now, visualize that same wheel with an oversize hub. Don't overlook the large, flat metal bracket to hold the hub to the frame.

"Sit on the bike but put your feet on the ground to steady it and I'll lift up the spring wheel," said Neil.

Jeannie sat obediently as far back on the little seat as she could—the weight of the spring wheel would be better served by the seat than her own legs—and she clung to the wheel saying urgently, "Get on and let's go; I can't support the bike as well!"

They dropped off the wheel at the Triumph Works and Jeannie asked Neil, "What happens now?"

"We're going home," he said. "It will be ready some time tomorrow."

They discussed the situation that evening.

Jeannie said, "Presumably they'll call you at work to let you know when the wheel's ready, but by the time you get home the Triumph factory will be closed."

He said, "I'd thought about that. Perhaps you could go over on the bus and pick it up. Someone from the works will load it onto the bus for you to come back."

"Then what am I going to do with it? I can scarcely lift it, let alone carry it up this hill. I've got a better idea. Run me down to the pay-phone at the end of the village and I'll call my cousin at Quinton. If I can take it there on the City bus, you can come there after work and pick me up with it. I'll leave Tammy on a leash under the caravan. He won't like it, but there's no choice."

And that's what happened—more or less. Jeannie rode into work with Neil in the morning and caught a City bus into the center and then a No. 9 bus from there to Quinton, where she spent the morning with her cousin's wife, waiting for Neil's call.

The familiar, beloved voice said, "It's ready to be picked up. They'll help you get it on the bus, as I said."

So, she caught the City bus into the center of Birmingham and then the bus to Coventry.

The problem arose at the bus depot in Birmingham on her return journey. The spring wheel had been off-loaded by the sturdy conductor onto the sidewalk. Jeannie tried wheeling it—but remember the large, flat metal bracket? It wheeled a half-turn, but then she had to lift it past the bracket and wheel it another half-turn—up hill.

A deep voice out of nowhere asked, "You got a problem, Ma'am? Where you wanna go?"

Jeannie turned to face the owner of the voice. A strong pitch-black angel had been sent straight from heaven to help her in her time of need.

"To the No. 9 bus stop, please," she told him.

The angel picked up the spring wheel and put it on his shoulder as though it was a sack of potatoes. Jeannie followed him—thinking—"Man Friday?"

Unfortunately, it was about 500 yards to Jeannie's cousin's house from where the No. 9 bus stopped in Quinton, but it was "all down hill"—sound familiar? She had to "wheel it a half turn and lift, wheel it a half-turn and lift" all the way.

Subsequently, Neil arrived from work on the Triumph 350cc.

"Oh, you made it!" he said. "I knew you would. Thanks!"

Jeannie said, wryly, “I don’t know what you would have done if I’d been one of those dependent ‘helpless’ types!”

Neil considered that comment for a long moment, and then he said, gently, “My dear, I would not have married you if you’d been like that.”

CHAPTER 20

DISCOVERIES

One of the things Jeannie would never forget was the "dawn chorus." Living in a caravan in England out in the lush countryside was about as close to nature as you were likely to get—other than sleeping in a tent, and she would do plenty of that, too. But now, she was content to open wide the large window beside them, extending right across the end of the caravan and opening up and out to let in the air, and the sounds, to their bed.

Sometimes they would be fortunate enough to hear the nightingale warbling in the moonlight, and invariably the old barn owl perched up in the oak tree by the road and added its hoot to the night-time rustles and scurries, but it was when the first signs of dawn were visible that it started. One bird, just one bird, sounded its musical trill with slight hesitance—a pause—and then a repetition, and then another, until perhaps, there were three or four birds—usually a blackbird or a thrush, then a robin and a wren, even the chirp of a sparrow or a starling, numerous little birds awakening to contribute to a cacophony of sound—the dawn chorus—mystical and beautiful—hundreds of little throats celebrating the dawn of a new day.

Neil was always the first to arise. For one thing, he lay on the access side of the bed, but Jeannie soon learned it was really for that first cup of tea. For the rest of his life he brought her a cup of tea before she arose in the morning. It was made traditionally, by first warming the pot, either on a stove—as in the old days—or with hot water, then placing loose Indian tea in the pot—"one teaspoonful per cup and one for the pot"—allowing it to "brew" for 3-5 minutes, then pouring it into a cup through a tea-strainer, to catch any stray tealeaves, adding milk, plus one or two sugar lumps to taste. Jeannie didn't take sugar and she preferred the milk to be placed in the cup first, so that the quantity could be judged more accurately. It was the best cup of tea of the day, and she always raised the cup, like a toast, to him.

"We really need a shed or a garage," she said one day to Neil. "The bike needs to be under cover, particularly if you have to work on it, and I don't want to be out in the open, washing clothes in a tub, using an old-fashioned "dolly," like the maids. I don't mind doing it because there's no alternative at the moment, but not visibly!"

What with that, and having to learn to cook, married life was kind of a chore. Then she thought, no, the real problem is—I was a spoiled child—or maybe I was born too early, at the time of maids and gardeners and chauffeurs and such? No matter what, she wanted some sort of additional building.

Within a week, she had it—a large metal building with windows and doors at each end, and now she could even install a washing line to dry the clothes and it didn't matter if it rained. Neil had to get a County permit for it—but he did that "after the fact."

Jeannie learned two things: it was possible both to bathe yourself and wash laundry in ***cold*** water; and a ***Pressure Cooker*** was one of the most wonderful things ever invented for someone who couldn't cook—it had its own recipe book because those who could cook had to learn how to use it, too!

"We need a pressure cooker," she told Neil, "because the regular cooker in the caravan isn't large enough to be able to use all the pots and pans to cook a decent meal."

He came home with a really great pressure cooker—better than she would buy.

The first time they had any kind of an argument was when he came home with almost half a young pig. Apart from pork not really being Jeannie's first choice as far as meat was concerned, and the fact that her knowledge of how to prepare it lacked variety, they didn't have a refrigerator, and she could visualize living on pork for eternity so it

We really need a shed or a garage

would not be wasted. The mere sight of it almost put her off pork for life.

"Don't be ungrateful," said her ever-practical husband, inwardly upset at her lack of enthusiasm for his enterprising venture, "you know meat is still rationed. Jeffrey raised the pig but decided to kill it while it was still young and small so the meat would be good and it would be easier to share among friends."

"Well, you can cut it up; I can't bear to touch all that raw meat." Jeannie screwed up her face in disgust.

He threw the bag just inside the door of the caravan, jumped on his motorbike, and rode off.

You know what it's like when you're young and in love and inexperienced and are sure the world will come to an end because of half a raw pig? Jeannie burst into tears and turned her back on the bag full of pork.

Then she remembered what his Mum had written to her one day: "Scotsmen—bless them!—are difficult—they want to succeed off their own bat…I would suggest, let him alone for a while…" She did—all her life—and it always worked. He would return, and carry on as though nothing had happened between them.

She searched around for somewhere cool to keep the pork—the shed was no good, rats and mice might get at it. Eventually, she found two secret metal storage spaces, ventilated by small holes, hanging under the floor of the caravan—perfect. They had little trapdoors in the floor for access. She picked up the bag and put it on the counter, and was busy reading Mum's recipe book when he returned.

She smiled, and said, as though he hadn't been away, "All we need is to go to the store and get some waxed paper and tinfoil; I've found a couple of wonderful storage spaces under the floor which will stay really cool."

"Okay! Jump on the bike," he said—"Oh, don't forget the dog."

By the time they got to the end of the pork, she'd served it from chops to curry and discovered there were many ways of diversifying the flavor and appearance. She'd learn to cook if she died in the attempt! But she was still thankful when it was all gone.

CHAPTER 21

TALES OF TRIUMPH

Jeannie had only been working at the research association for a few days when she realized that, far from brushing up her French, as had been the case for the ecclesiastical tailors, she now needed to delve into the far forgotten past of chemistry, with words such as molybdenum occurring in her shorthand notes with terrifying frequency; it was easier to write in shorthand than to try to remember the scientific abbreviation of many such words. However, "practice makes perfect" as the saying goes, and she certainly didn't lack practice.

Dr. Ainsley had no complaints, and she enjoyed working with him, taking notes at his lectures, transcribing long Reports for publication, transcribing his responses to inquiries about changes to applications of a variety of chemicals for numerous processes. She became so familiar with his work that often she already knew what his chemical responses would be.

Many of the young chemists working at the establishment had gone straight from school to university and from university to this—their first job. They had no practical experience of commerce, so when they visited factories to give advice regarding a process, the advice related solely to the chemical aspect of the change and they were not aware of any possible effect it may have regarding the lives of those employed there.

Neil expressed his frustration to her many times in dealing with similar problems, resulting in discussions with the unions due to inevitable improvements causing lay-offs for workers and certain operations. This illustrated the marked awareness derived from his management training in conjunction with separate university instruction for his degree, obtained under such exhausting circumstances. He had to deal with similar youngsters straight out of college with no practical experience, expecting to be paid top dollar for their services. Here he was, playing "catch-up" having lost seven years of his life to the war, while those who had stayed at the factories making munitions had leapt into available promotions. There were others in similar circumstances. It was hard for many of them to deal with.

Jeannie did her best to boost his morale, whilst understanding fully his frustration in coping with circumstances beyond his control. His brilliant mind, which dealt with mounting problems with little effort, was in danger of not being sufficiently exploited or rewarded.

The weekends were theirs to enjoy, so she tried to make certain they would do something to take his mind off work.

Then Triumph brought out another "hotted up" version of the 500cc motorbike—known as the "Tiger Twin" which also had a spring wheel. Neil said, "I'll sell the 350cc and buy that, then we can ride the two 500cc bikes together." Secretly, Jeannie would have preferred to ride pillion.

One weekend John, at Triumph, called Neil at work, saying, "My wife, Kirstie, and I, are going to stay at our cottage at Llangwnnadl on the Lleyn Promontory, North Wales. Would you and Jeannie like to join us there?"

Jeannie was thrilled at the opportunity. They rode the Tiger Twin with Neil in command and Tammy in the pannier, cruising through glorious countryside down the winding road between lakes and mountains, until they could see the Irish Sea, after which they followed the south coast to Pwhelli, then forking right to the north coast almost to the end of the Promontory, where it narrowed and they turned down a lane on the right towards the north shore and their destination. The lane ran straight through a farmyard which lay on both sides of the road, so chicken and ducks flapped around in alarm

Tiger Twin

at the intrusion and Jeannie held her breath—"Fresh country smells!" she yelled in Neil's ear.

So this was Llangwnnadl—a tiny hamlet with scattered cottages and farms. They were to meet Mr. and Mrs. Jones, who lived in the white cottage on the lane near the entrance to John and Kirstie's property—better known as "Jones the Post" and his wife, Cainwen. They cared for the property in John and Kirstie's absence, and delivered mail to the local households. The majority of Welsh held the last name of Jones, closely followed by Smith, Williams, or Jenkins—so, for ease in identification—the occupation was often tacked on as a matter of course. Mr. and Mrs. Jones the Post were like family, and welcomed any friends of John and Kirstie like family, too.

Neil looked out for the "white cottage" and turned up the grass driveway just beyond it. There was a boathouse/garage on the left and a wooden cottage at the far end of the half-acre, surrounded by open fields and with an ocean view. They were to discover that lighting and cooking were by means of Propane gas, and there was no hot water—unless the old enclosed coal range in the corner of the living room was lit to warm the room—and that was by means of a water tank surrounding the chimney; the tank had a tap, from which to convey the hot water by means of a jug. Dishes, pots and pans, towels, clothes—and bodies—were all washed in the kitchen sink. The back door led outside. There was a small room which housed the chemical toilet—"home from home" thought Neil and Jeannie, being accustomed to a similar arrangement for their caravan, except that they had permanent heating and hot water by way of an enclosed stove burning anthracite which heated water the same way. No different was the need to dig a deep hole in the ground periodically to dispose of the contents of the toilet!

John and Kirstie owned a boat which, that weekend, was anchored just offshore with an outboard motor attached.

"We use it for fishing, and for cruising up and down the coast to remote bays, and also to bait lobster pots," John explained. "We'll all go out in the boat and see if we can catch our supper. Kirstie and I normally only buy bread, and sometimes fruit and vegetables from the store. We get most things fresh from the farms so they charge very little. I'll take you up the coast; it's the easiest way to see the beaches."

They left the bay where the boat had been anchored and turned right around the first headland—and the beach stretched before their eyes.

"It must be over a half-mile long," said Jeannie, "and there's another bay just beyond that rocky point."

"Yes, it's wonderful," said Kirstie, but you need to make sure you're not around that rocky point at high tide or you'll be cut off; there's no way of getting up that cliff."

They were trolling for fish, and she called out to John when she noticed the line tighten, so she began to reel in and Neil jumped up to help her, his strong arms and wrists making sure the line did not slacken. With a practiced motion, Kirstie removed the hook from the mouth of the fish, dropped it into the ice bag in the bottom of the boat, then renewed the bait on the hook and threw it back in the water.

Jeannie clapped her hands. The calculated movements were worthy of applause! They stayed out until they had enough fish for supper and then sped back to the bay.

"That was fun," said Neil.

"Yes. That is why we enjoy our trips here," said John. "It's very peaceful—like another world. You can leave all that behind and forget it."

Neil nodded in agreement and Jeannie noticed that the stress had left his face—for the moment.

"Tammy will be glad to see us back," she said. "I left him in the boathouse, but I hope he hasn't been kicking up too much of a row."

The little dog flung himself up at Neil as soon as the door was opened to let him out—a wriggling mass of affection and excitement—or maybe relief that Neil had returned.

It was still light, so John suggested they ride up the steep cliff just above Aberdaron, the little town near the end of the Lleyn Promontory. He had a sidecar on his bike, which was a Triumph Thunderbird 650cc, and Kirstie sat in that. Road access up the steep cliff consisted of two strips of concrete. He rode the bike up one of them but poor Kirstie was left to bump up the rocky portion between the strips, which were set a suitable distance apart for car tires but not for a bike and sidecar. He did it on purpose and thought it hilarious. Kirstie yelled at him but took it all in good part. They were such a fun couple to be around.

The cliff was the furthest point west, where the sun set on the horizon, across the Irish Sea. Local ancients, for years, had climbed down the ocean side of the cliff and lowered deceased loved ones, encased in a wood coffin, into the waves on their final journey to where the sun set. Superstition compounded their beliefs.

On Sunday, Neil and Jeannie changed into swimsuits and, carrying towels, followed a track across a couple of fields and climbed down to the huge sand beach they had seen from the boat. John said he didn't swim, so going to the beach held no attraction for him; he preferred to climb along the rocks in the other direction, looking for hidden bays he could access in the boat—currents permitting. They walked all the way along the beach, Tammy scurrying in every direction and digging frantically when he saw an unwary crab emerge briefly, only to disappear upon sensing danger. They walked around the far rocky headland, where there was not a soul in sight, and plunged into the water. It was much colder than the south coast of Devonshire, to which Jeannie had been accustomed, but refreshing and stimulating. Neil ran back up the beach and threw down one of the towels on the sand.

"You're not getting away with this weekend as easily as you think," he said, putting his arms around her so they fell onto the towel together.

"I love you," she said, "I'll always love you."

They all left together for the journey back to Birmingham. In spite of the encumbrance of the sidecar, John flew along the narrow road and Neil had quite a job to keep up with him. They'd had a wonderful weekend and enjoyed every minute of it. Neil relayed an account of it to friends at work—and came home with the following poem to show to Jeannie:

A Thunderbird without a chair swiftly flits from here to there;
When fitted with a large two-seater—surprisingly—the thing's much fleeter.
With Neil MacLeod upon its tail this outfit shot o'er hill and dale,
Performance such as rarely seen according to his loyal Jean
Who, in the slipstream, pale with fright, fought to keep Thunderbird in sight.
Neil's trusty Tiger's speedo went right round until the needle bent,
While Thunderbird just wuffled gently in second gear, like ancient Bentley;
And when its driver changed to third, took flight and soared just like a bird.
In short, if you believe this story, it was a most amazing quarry.
But, as with all good yarns, a snag appears just as it's in the bag.
For 'tis well known, the Triumph folks possess some wizard tuning blokes
Who don't use Engine Testing Beds, but use their skill on Speedo Heads,

Thereby inducing owner's pride without a strain on bike's inside,
And those who ride these gaudy buckers are just a simple lot of suckers,
Who, one day will wake up to that, when an Autocycle leaves them flat.

However, Neil had more than one unanticipated adventure with the Triumph 500cc bikes. On one occasion, he and Jeannie borrowed Jimmy's car to drive to Oxford for a christening, at which Neil would be Godfather. It was to be a somewhat momentous occasion so they didn't want to arrive on one of the Triumphs. Jimmy had remained quite closely in touch with Neil over the years, being, in his mind, forever indebted to Neil for saving his life by carrying him twenty miles to safety at Dunkirk when he had a broken leg. They exchanged modes of transport because Jimmy was headed to Cornwall on vacation and Neil and Jeannie were driving on to her mother's home in Exeter after the christening.

The next day, everything having worked out according to plan, Neil said he had to drive to Cornwall with the car to drop it off with Jimmy and recover the Triumph 500cc, which was normally Jeannie's ride. He was on the return trip, following a bus, thinking he'd overtake it on a straight stretch of road when, with no warning, the bus took a turning to the right…in Britain, both the bus and Neil were traveling on the left side of the road, so the bus was swerving in front of him. With instantaneous reaction, Neil braked, laid the bike down, and stepped off it whilst it slid under the bus. The driver may have seen him at the last moment, because he stopped.

Jeannie was becoming concerned when it was getting dark but Neil hadn't returned. Eventually she heard the bike coming up the steep driveway. Moments later, he walked into the house. He apologized for being late, saying it took him longer than he anticipated.

Next morning, Jeannie walked out to Mum's garage with him. She couldn't believe what she saw—the handlebars and the entire front of the bike were turned about thirty-five degrees to the left from where Neil had laid it down on its right side…and he'd ridden it over fifty miles like that! They returned home by train—with the bike—sending it on to Coventry, where it was collected for repair at the Triumph factory.

Neil told Jeannie, "Now you know why I always tell you to step off the bike if ever I have to lie it down!"

Then there was the time when Jeannie was staying with her mother. He called her from a public call box:

"Can you come and fetch me with Mum's car—and bring a tow rope? I'm just your side of Taunton but I was riding downhill between some steep banks when a dog ran down and across the road right in front of me. The bike won't start and I can't see what's wrong in the dark. The rear light still works, though, so you can give me a tow."

She took the car, and found him. He had to steer the bike with one hand and hold the rope with the other. She couldn't see him in the rear view mirror, other than from the lights of approaching vehicles—and there was not much traffic in those days. Suddenly she realized he wasn't there! She stopped and turned around at the next junction.

When she reached him a few miles back, he said, "We're not competing in a cross-country race, you know; we're just trying to arrive alive tonight at your Mum's house—with the bike." One guess—what happened next? They sold the two 500cc. bikes and bought a Triumph Thunderbird 650cc.

Thereafter Jeannie rode pillion and Tammy occupied one pannier—complete with a sweater and goggles!

CHAPTER 22A

DECISIONS

Jeannie didn't mind giving up the Triumph Speed Twin and the Tiger 100 for the Triumph 650cc Thunderbird; she much preferred riding pillion anyway, and it was such a great bike. They transferred the panniers to it and Tammy occupied his place of honor in one of them, going everywhere they went on the bike—that is, until the fateful day when he ran over their bank into the lane and bit the neighbor's Alsation on the neck. He had no fear—but you can't have dogs biting people or other dogs, and the property was too large to fence adequately. He was Neil's dog and he had been a part of the family since Neil bought him as company for his mother until she died. So it fell to Jeannie to take him to the vet that last time. Neil was devastated; he loved the little dog, feisty though he was.

But a month or so later, it was "pay-back time." For some reason, Jeannie had to go around to the neighbors' house. She saw the Alsation in front of her as she walked up the driveway, but the dog knew her and she wasn't afraid of dogs anyway. She had nearly reached the house when it rushed through some bushes and out behind her, jumped up and bit her hard through her thin summer clothes on the upper part of one leg. She could feel it bleeding. The neighbors came rushing out upon hearing her scream.

She said, "Don't worry, I'll be all right, but I'll go to the hospital and get a tetanus shot—just in case." Neil took her in as soon as he came home.

They apologized for the dog's actions—and that was that, until the dog did the same thing to another lady, who threatened to sue the neighbors. Result—the end of any dangerous dogs living along the lane.

At the end of July, Neil said, "Let's take the bike and ride to Scotland for the two-week holiday when all the factories are closed in the Midlands and your work will be, too. The last time I went was when I took my pre-war Triumph all the way from Dorset to Edinburgh at the end of my last year at school. I sent my school trunk to Chesterfield by train and picked it up there, by bus, when I got back. We'll go up the West Coast and come back through Edinburgh, where we can stop and see my school friend who, with his wife, now owns about half of East Lothian—two old Scots families intermarried, all with farms."

Jeannie was always game for anything he suggested, but particularly when it involved the bike. Now, having both of the panniers for packing space, since she didn't have to cater to poor little Tammy any more, she was able to include clothes suitable for hotel overnight stops. Besides, the bike was powerful enough for any of the more obscure routes she knew Neil would favor…but she was hardly prepared for the Devil's Elbow up and over the mountains leading to Applecross in Ross and Cromarty.

The far north of Scotland from Fort William in the west to Inverness on the east coast is almost cut off by a series of lochs, Loch Linnhe, Loch Lochy in the west and Loch Ness at the east end, joined by land at Invergarry.

Maps of the British Isles are available on the Internet. The only difference is that at the time of Neil and Jeannie's adventures there were no motorways—freeways.

Neil told Jeannie, "This time we'll take the road from Carlisle, just below the Solway Firth which divides Scotland from England on the west coast, to Dumfries and onward to Kilmarnock, so that we skirt the City of Glasgow; then we'll cross the Firth of Clyde on the most convenient ferry and aim for Inverary in Argyllshire."

"That seems like an awfully long ride from Carlisle," said Jeannie. "Let's see how we get on because we could stay one night at Kilmarnock, south of the Clyde, or Ardrossan on the coast and then go on to Inverary the next day; there's no real rush, we've got a couple of weeks, and we could explore the area a bit more instead of just rushing through it."

"Okay. That makes sense," said Neil. "It's not going to be the only time we'll come and enjoy Scotland. I can feel the blood rushing through my veins—I just love it; every time, it's "home" to me. Pops' family was from Perth on the Firth of Tay but his mother was a Fraser from Aberdeen. That's why they sent me to school in Edinburgh. I loved it there."

Jeannie laughed. "You sound just like Daddy," she said.

The ferry system up the west coast serviced the area efficiently—if at times, in those days, somewhat precariously—avoiding the effort and many miles of circuitous narrow roads.

The entire adventure was breathtaking, the views fabulous, every bend in the road providing new excitement, very little traffic, the local people friendly and curious about the young adventurers and their modern mode of transport; their overnight sojourns a fairy tale in themselves—rarely in hotels, more often in private crofts offering bed, breakfast and an evening meal—generally "high tea," where the owners were only too happy to answer questions and offer suggestions; in fact they could have extended many of their stays. Instead, they promised to return—one day.

They stayed at Kilmarnock that night, crossed the Clyde, and rode on to Inverary for the following night. It didn't look far on the map but the "main" roads were nearly all single-lane with passing places and if you were on a downhill stretch you always gave way to anyone climbing, regardless of the location of the passing place. Leaving Inverary, they had intended taking the coast road to Oban but decided to take the shorter route via Dalmally and save any spare time they had for "wandering" further north. So far, the weather had been tempting for such delays, but they knew they could not rely on that to continue.

At that time, in the 'fifties, Oban was the fishing capital of the Highlands—not the most attractive town in itself but, in addition to fabulous views of the Firth of Lorne, it was the access port for steamers to the Isle of Mull, largest of the islands off the west coast, and the outer islands of North and South Uist, including Lewis to the north and a scattering tail of islands to the south—not all inhabited but providing excellent fishing grounds, all comprising the Hebrides—next stop Iceland.

They spent one night at Oban, then followed the coast road beside Loch Linnhe to Fort William, making use of a ferry at Connel and Ballachulish, most ferries consisting of a floating platform holding only two vehicles, towed by a motorboat.

Neil said, "We'll spend the night at Fort William and then we'll ride out to Mallaig. That road is a cul-de-sac but it is steeped in history and the sands at Mallaig are some of the finest in all of Scotland; the view will be different on the return journey because we'll be looking at Ben Nevis in the background ...don't worry, I'm not going to take you up there, it's in the Grampians, over 4,400 feet high, the highest in Britain and it doesn't have any sort of a road."

They explored Fort William briefly the next morning and Jeannie bought a shaped shawl for her mother and a Hunting Fraser scarf for Neil—the name describing the pattern of the weave—and they kept their reservation at Fort William for a second night. The ride to Mallaig was glorious, initially along the northern shore of Loch Eil, then through open country to Glenfinnan, where they stopped to climb the historical monument at the head of Loch Shiel. It was built in 1815 to commemorate the Jacobites who fought and were killed during the 1745 uprising. Prince Charles Edward Stuart—Bonnie Prince Charlie—raised his standard on August 19, 1745, marking the start of his campaign to restore the exiled Stuarts to the throne of Britain.

There was not a soul in sight as they climbed the spiral staircase to the low-railed balcony at the top of the monument. Jeannie leaned back against Neil, who put his arms around her, as they stood and gazed down the length of Loch Shiel.

"I will never forget this moment," she said, "it is so awe-inspiring. You can hear the horses pawing the ground, and the pipes and drums of Prince Charlie's men as he raises the flag at the head of their column; it's all resonating in the surrounding hills, sad but beautiful."

Neil kissed her neck. "There's a great deal about war which is sad," he said, "we're lucky to have one another. Be careful going down those stairs, they are very small and narrow. I'd better go first in case you trip."

They rode on to Arisaig, where there were beech trees with their bright green leaves shining in the sunlight, and yellow gorse reflecting a golden glow, but they left it all behind as they turned sharp right along the coast at the end of Loch Morar to their destination at Mallaig. Neil was correct—the sands were amazing—soft, fine and almost white.

"Let's find somewhere to get some lunch and then we'll make our way back," he said, "we have a long ride tomorrow."

To them both, it was heaven on earth; they loved the peace and quiet and ethereal beauty with no unwanted crowds to disrupt their thoughts.

"I'm so glad we made this trip," she told Neil, "I'm sure that one day it will not be like this any more, but we'll have our memories—nothing can change that."

They were lying in bed in Fort William for the second night. He turned and, putting his arms around her, made love to her.

"This is just to add to our memories," he said.

They studied the map again over breakfast.

"Let's go to the Isle of Skye before we leave the west coast," Neil suggested, "it's just over a hundred mile run but you know what that's like in this countryside, and we have to cross over to it by ferry at Kyle of Lochalsh, so it will be late afternoon by the time we get there."

CHAPTER 22B

DECISIONS

Neil and Jeannie left Fort William immediately after breakfast and set off along the road running north-east which would have taken them to Inverness on the east coast had they not turned off it at Invergarry and continued along the north shore of Loch Garry, taking the steep, hilly road across The Saddle, then descending to Loch Duich, and ultimately the Kyle of Lochalsh—scenery which had to be seen to be believed.

At that time the only way to access the Isle of Skye was by way of a ferry across the Kyle of Lochalsh. They took the ferry and, since it was then late in the day, stayed at a little house at Kyleakin, a few miles up the road.

"I want to take you to see Dunvegan Castle tomorrow," said Neil, "it has been occupied by the MacLeods since the 1200s, and the MacLeod of MacLeod—the Head of the Clan—lives there to this day. We can't spend too long on Skye because we've been away seven nights already and we have to get across to Inverness and down the east coast, but I've promised myself that I'll show you Applecross in Ross and Cromarty first; it is hemmed in by mountains, apart from one narrow road of hairpin bends, which is the only access apart from the sea, known as the Inner Sound, between Raasay Island and the Highlands."

"Why do you specifically want to go there?" said Jeannie. "There are plenty of incredible places to see without going to that remote area."

"Because it's a challenge, and it's really only viable to attempt on a bike."

So, after he had taken her to see Dunvegan, known as the oldest inhabited castle in Scotland, they went back across the Kyle of Lochalsh by ferry and headed north to Strome Ferry, which only carried one vehicle at a time across Loch Carron, after which the principal road led to Dingwall, on the east coast, but Neil only stayed on that for a short distance before turning left for Applecross.

Jeannie could see the outline of the road ahead—a zig-zag of hairpin bends, each supported by a rock wall, which appeared to be going up a perpendicular cliff. I'll shut my eyes, she thought, and open them when we get to the top—he's crazy! But it was not to be as easy as that; in spite of leaning forward, she could feel herself sliding off the back of the bike. I can't get off and walk, it's too steep, I'll roll down the hill! He's in the lowest gear all the way. Supposing that isn't low enough?

Neil negotiated the next bend, and stopped next to the wall. "We're riding into the clouds, but if this isn't the top, we're very near it," he said. "What do you think about it?"

Jeannie grabbed her courage with both hands, trying to apply logic rather than what would appear to be her personal opinion—she wanted to leave him with some pride, after all.

"We don't know how much further it is and even if we have made it to the top, which I think we have, we can't see anything in the cloud. We don't know what conditions will be like across the top or going down the other side, and even if we make it to Applecross we don't know if there will be anywhere to stay, and if it rains we may be stuck there…" and, to tell the truth, she said to herself, I don't want to spend the rest of my life in Applecross; at that precise moment life in the caravan seemed like heaven.

"That makes sense," said Neil, "so we'll turn around and go back?"

It could have been a question but she pretended it was a statement.

"All right, darling," she said, "anything you say."

That night they spent in Dingwall—but they didn't leave the Devil's Elbow road to Applecross until he had taken a photo of her with the bike—in the fog!

It was such a temptation to spend more time in the Highlands, many of the names were familiar to Jeannie, either from her own travels as a child with her parents, or hearing her father talk about them—Glen Affric, Invermorriston, Aviemore—but Neil interrupted her thoughts by saying,

"We'll drop down from Inverness through Grantown and Tomintoul to Ballater and we'll be able to see Balmoral Castle which was built for Queen Victoria and her husband, Prince Albert, towards the end of the nineteenth century, and it's been an Autumn home for the Royal Family ever since."

This area is full of history. Today, anyone with a computer can be occupied for hours. Neil and Jeannie's trip was long before the existence of computers and the hundreds of folks who are encouraged to explore Scotland as a result.

Neil continued to explain to Jeannie, "The road will take us past Braemar and across the moors to Pitlochry, and we can go down through Dunkeld to Perth and Stirling, and then along the coast of the Firth of Forth to Edinburgh—not all in one day, of course, but that's the general route. We've got five or six days to get home. Don't forget, this won't be the only time we'll come to Scotland!"

That was the general route they took, promising themselves that they would traverse the Lowlands on another trip, but this time they would spend two or three nights in Haddington, East Lothian, so that they could explore Edinburgh and visit with Neil's erstwhile school friend in East Lothian.

Inevitably, they went to Edinburgh Castle.

Neil said, "I want to go to the Scottish National War Memorial. It was originally the medieval St. Mary's Church but it was adapted in 1923 by Sir Robert Lorimer to commemorate Scots and those serving with the Scottish regiments who died in the First World War—the "Great War,"—and subsequent conflicts. I know I'll find the names of some of my school friends there, and I'd like to pay them my respects—since I'm one of those who survived World War II to do so."

They spent over an hour at the Memorial and Neil found the names of about ten of his friends, all whom he knew at school in Edinburgh, some who later were with him in Dorset; it was so emotional for him.

"I feel almost guilty still to be alive," he told Jeannie. "They were such fine people. My name might have been in that book, had it not been for the fact that I volunteered that year I was in Birmingham and walked into a recruitment office there."

Jeannie squeezed his hand, "It's no fault of yours, darling," she said, "you gave up seven years of your life to the war. It's just important that we live a decent life and do what we can to make sure our children and other people's children have some opportunity in life, so that your friends did not die in vain."

He hugged her and kissed her there, in front of the open register with the names of his friends, "You're such a comfort to me," he said.

They walked out, hand-in-hand, and explored those parts of the Castle open to the public.

The Castle stands up on the basalt plug of an extinct volcano estimated to have risen about 450 million years ago, protected on the south, west and north by sheer cliffs about 260 feet above the surrounding countryside, making the Castle almost impregnable since its only accessible route lies east. There is much detailed information easily available today by inputting Scotland-Edinburgh Castle-History into a browser.

"Let's ride down The Royal Mile, which connects Edinburgh Castle with the Palace of Holyrood House. 'The largest, longest and finest street for Buildings and Number of Inhabitants, not only in Britain, but in the World . . . Daniel Defoe, 1723,'" said Jeannie, quoting something she'd read—somewhere.

They traversed The Royal Mile, all the time very conscious of the history surrounding them, which they could spend weeks exploring if they had the time.

Neil said, "I'll find a phone and call my school friend. Maybe we can ride out to East Lothian to see his family. There was a wonderful old mansion on the estate when I rode up to Edinburgh from Dorset in 1937; I don't know whether they are still living in it, though."

In the end they stayed in Haddington and found an intriguing pub for an evening meal, thinking they'd explore the coast from Dirleton, through Dunbar and perhaps down to Berwick the next day and then go to see Gordon and Anna in the afternoon; but anyway Neil decided to call them in the morning before they set out to go anywhere.

They were given a great welcome as soon as Neil said they were in the neighborhood. A family party was planned for that evening because the eldest of the sons and his girl friend had just announced their engagement to be married—there were five sons and one daughter; she lived at home. The eldest had his own farm. Ultimately, two others farmed in the neighborhood, the youngest worked on his father's, and one son in East Anglia, England, each specializing in his choice of farming, but Neil and Jeannie learned all that in the future. That evening was just a joyful celebration.

Neil and Jeannie arrived early enough to be shown around the place. There was a gated entrance to the estate, with a gatekeeper's lodge. As they followed the driveway, Neil pointed out where the original house stood. It had evidently been demolished since 1937, when he was there. Now it was many years later and much changed. The grounds were still magnificent, with a small forest of lovely old trees on the left as they entered. It transpired that much of an old existing building—the groundskeeper's cottage—which Neil scarcely recognized, was modernized and rebuilt. He recalled its location, opening up to a huge private walled garden in one direction, with rolling farmlands in the other.

Gordon had farming in his blood, so it was little wonder that his sons followed in his footsteps and benefited from his capable and knowledgeable mind. Neil explained to Jeannie that Gordon had to leave school at sixteen because his father was ill. He died shortly afterwards, leaving his young son responsible for the family property—land upon which many of the new extensions of Edinburgh were subsequently built. The additional farms in East Lothian were acquired since then.

Neil and Jeannie rode the bike back to the hotel where they were staying in Haddington, knowing that they would be bidding a reluctant farewell to Scotland the next day. They were about a hundred miles from the Border with Northumberland if they decided to cross it at Carter Bar, in the Cheviot Hills. Neil wanted to go that way because it avoided principal towns and was such lovely countryside. Jeannie remembered it subsequently for the Highland Cattle with their huge horns and shaggy coats.

They crossed the old Roman Wall just before Corbridge, which had been built by the Romans between what is now Carlisle, nearly on the west coast and Newcastle-upon-Tyne on the east coast, to stop the Picts from invading England. Amazingly, a large part of the Wall still stands. They stopped to take a closer look at it.

Jeannie said, "We admire so many of today's achievements, but you know, Hadrian ruled from AD117 to AD138 and he arrived in Britain in AD122 and caused 73 miles of wall to be built along what was then the north-west frontier of the "Province of Britain" to separate the Romans from "the Barbarians"—actually the Picts to the north. Imagine that!"

"If my memory serves me correctly from all those years ago at school in Edinburgh, when we were taken to explore the Wall," Neil said, "it runs from Wallsend-on-Tyne on the east coast to Bowness on Solway Firth on the west coast, and then an extra 26 miles down the Cumbrian coast from Bowness; the Romans certainly intended to keep the Picts out. I believe it was in use until the end of Roman rule in Britain in AD410."

Jeannie laughed. "I didn't know you were a historian," she said.

"I'm not. "It's just that in those days we were expected to learn what we were taught," he said, "so there are certain things you just never forget; they're tucked away in your brain until something stirs the memory."

"Do you remember the first time you kissed me?"

"Yes. It was after your Mum invited me back for dinner the second time and you walked down the lane with me because you said I might get lost! That was just an excuse. I saw through that maneuver—"Pussy-cat, pussy-cat . . ." He danced away to avoid her playful slap.

"I still love you," she said.

"I'm glad to hear that. It would be an awfully long way for you to have to walk home. Jump on the bike. It's about 30 miles to Durham. We'll stay there for the night and you can prove it to me after we've had some supper."

They were back in England again and ready to head south for home after breakfast the next morning. The weather still remained fine and Jeannie settled down to enjoy the ride; she never had reason to doubt Neil's skill on a bike.

She thought of all the many trips to Scotland in the late '40s or early'50s, before they had family responsibilities and were still celebrating their freedom, when the only straight roads were the old Roman ones; the remainder wound around the banks, hedges or stone walls of properties—depending upon the raw materials available in the different Counties.

They rode the "500," "Tiger Twin," or "Thunderbird"—always a Triumph—up the glorious West Coast, first through the Lake District of Cumberland—now Cumbria—to Carlisle, and then loch to loch by way of ever more devious single track roads, with "Passing Places," where you gave way to other traffic, or vice versa.

The scenery left them breathless with its beauty, and the sight of the old stone castles made their imagination run wild with stories of the Battles of the Clans. Often they returned via Inverness and Balmoral to Edinburgh, then through East Lothian and across the Border at Carter Bar into Northumberland and Yorkshire, joining the Great North Road which ran as a huge switchback for miles—the Romans built roads straight, up hill and down dale. Neil accelerated down through the dip for the thrill of it, climbing fast up the other side—leaving Jeannie's stomach behind somewhere on the way! She thought, I knew there was a reason I didn't like to go on the Big Dipper!

Today, she thought, Here we go again! And braced herself for the thrill.

CHAPTER 23

CHANGES

As Jeannie grew more confident of her skills, they even entertained friends in the caravan—mostly Neil's friends—who thought it really "neat" to be able to eat a proper meal and—sometimes—stay for the night in a "bed." On those occasions Neil and Jeannie gave up their own precious bed, opened the wardrobe doors across the van for privacy, and slept on the other bed, which they only made up for such occasions—or if Jeannie's Mum came to stay for a few days.

On one such occasion, Jeannie told her mother, "You know, I really fancy smoked haddock—the kind they're famous for in the Isle of Man—we ate it on our honeymoon."

Mum laughed, and said, "You're pregnant. If you fancy something weird and specific like that, you've got to be pregnant. About time, that was nearly four years ago."

She was very kind, but Jeannie had to listen to too many "old wives" tales. Mum had lost her first baby, Jeannie's brother, and she went to Southend just after the Great War, when Jeannie's cousins were born because "Aunt Audrey" her younger sister, "was always the weak one." Subsequently Aunt Audrey lived to be nearly one hundred and just missed the Queen's Telegram—she had always been nurtured by the family, and outlived all but her sons.

They were still living in the caravan when Jeannie told her Mum she fancied smoked haddock for dinner. Mum drove home the next day and Jeannie waited until she had the doctor's confirmation before she told Neil she was pregnant.

She was more concerned about the restrictions a baby would put on their lives than anything else—or rather, on ***her*** life; she and Neil had gone everywhere together but what would happen now? Her movements would be restricted to pushing a pram along to the village store, or possibly down the hill to the bus stop to shop in Redditch once a week and then pushing it wearily up the hill again. She would no longer have a job and all the interests that entailed. And what about Neil? He'd soon be pretty bored coming home and sitting in the caravan every night.

At least, that is what she thought.

"We're going to have a baby," she said.

"Really? When? Are you sure?"

She told him about the visit to the doctor and his projection that the baby would be due roughly mid-April next year and that he had made arrangements for her to go into hospital.

He was quiet for a few minutes, then he said, "Now we might be able to apply for a permit to build our house; I think I read somewhere that the County Council disapproves of people living in a caravan with a baby."

Paralyzing fear suddenly struck Jeannie.

"Do you mean we'd have to move out? Where would we go?"

Rentals in the United Kingdom were not a foregone conclusion; there were only homes leased by the County as residences, not temporary shelter.

"I don't think so—as long as we've shown the intent to build. We're already living on our land, with approval to do that. I'll have to go and make some inquiries. What about you? Are you feeling okay? You haven't mentioned anything?"

She thought—practical, as always; he never panics.

She said, "I love you, darling."

He said, "I love you, too—that's why it isn't really a surprise. I guess we weren't quite as careful as we thought we were. Now we'll have to concentrate on getting the house. At least you're not having the baby alone, while I was abroad!" He hugged her, and laughed.

They already had the plans from the architect, well known to the County Council, so Neil simply submitted them with an accompanying letter explaining their need, due to the anticipated baby.

The response came within about three weeks. They had a choice: either make the home smaller or build half a house now and the remainder later, when the materials situation may have improved. They opted for the latter. It would be more expensive but it suited their purposes better than building it all at one time, which would also sabotage the design. Their architect recommended a reliable builder whom he had used previously so they made daily inspections as the building progressed. It was opportune to be "on site."

For one thing, they had the windows lowered, saying they wanted to see out of them when sitting down. It seemed obvious, but fashions change over time; the architect had designed them higher. The kitchen had a solid-fuel range. They were on the end of the line for electricity and power fluctuated when demand was high—apart from the fact that unions always seemed to choose to go on strike in the winter, when it was cold. The range warmed the kitchen and also water in radiators. It was not the most convenient range on which to cook, but they had to weigh the downside with the upside and there would be times in the future when they would be envied.

A few years later Jeannie recalled a dinner party to which they had invited eight guests, the first of whom arrived at the door just as all the lights went out. By then, they had the rest of the house built, which included a large living room/lounge leading into an enclosed patio/loggia for additional space. The lounge had a large open fireplace with a controllable under-floor draft. That particular evening the light from the fire lit up the entire room. Neil found the propane gaslights they used with the camping equipment to provide a warm glow in the dining room, and put the propane stove in the kitchen in case Jeannie needed it. Their guests voted it to be one of the most successful and fun dinner parties anyone had attended!

Currently, the construction helped to take Jeannie's mind off her physical problems—but the baby would arrive before the building was completed. She knew roughly as much about having a baby as she had known about cooking, and she'd solved that problem so she figured

Half a house

it would all work out in the end. It was the process she had to cope with—she didn't even anticipate the pain.

Neil was in the caravan with her on the evening of April 15 1952, and Jeannie was getting more and more nervous; she'd had those heaving pains all day and they were getting more frequent and closer together.

"I think you'd better drive me to the hospital," she said when she felt she couldn't stand it any more. "It's not that I want to go in there, but I'm afraid of what's going to happen if I don't get there in time."

"It's okay, just take a deep breath and relax. You've got your personal stuff ready to take with you, haven't you? Give it to me, and hold my hand going out to the sidecar. I don't want you tripping over something."

He drove her to the hospital with care and waited while they wheeled her into a ward by herself, undressed her and put on a hospital gown; then he came in and kissed her goodbye, squeezing her hand to reassure her.

Then it started—wave after wave of pain—not a hope of going to sleep. The night nurse told her to stop making so much fuss. You're just an old misery, she thought, and in the end she said,

"It's all right for you, you don't have a clue what it feels like; you've never had a baby, have you?"

"No, but I've seen plenty of ladies who have, and they haven't made all this fuss."

"Well, this is my first baby, and I don't know what's going on, and you're not telling me," said Jeannie, crying in frustration and anxiety.

It went on until 3:30 PM the next afternoon, by which time the doctor, the daytime ward nurse, and one of the maternity nurses were at her side, trying to give her encouragement but having little discussions amongst themselves which did nothing to allay Jeannie's fears. I'm going to die in the attempt, she thought, but then there was a huge, overwhelming pain and they said, ***PUSH—AGAIN—PUSH,*** and suddenly it was all over, and she heard her little baby's cry. She was worn out, glad to be cleaned up and able to lie back and relax. She ran her hands down her body—nearly flat again, she thought, with relief.

"Don't you want to see your baby?" It was the maternity nurse. "It's a girl, and she's in the crib on your left."

Jeannie rolled over to look. "Six pounds, thirteen ounces—and perfect," said the nurse. The baby had dark hair, like Neil—well, like them both, really—curled around the top of her head like a rose, the skin looked more like Neil's than hers, and those eyes—a baby version of his; Jeannie's were hazel. The baby closed them, and went to sleep again, rolled up expertly in a little soft blanket to keep her safe and warm.

Neil came straight to the hospital after finishing work. "She's lovely," he said, "you did a good job—though Helen was a blond Grecian goddess, and somehow I don't think this little mite is going to be either blond or a goddess; we can always keep 'Helen' as her middle name." They were both recalling his mother's dying wish—her own name for the first girl.

Three years later they still had not been able to finish the house, but half a house was much better and more spacious than living in the caravan. Neil had arranged the sale of that and he had demolished the adjacent structure, so Jeannie worked on the front garden since she was at home with her little girl, who walked when she was eleven months old.

Now, she was pregnant again and due to have their second child, three years later. This time they arranged for her to have the baby at home, with the District Nurse in attendance. Mum drove from Devonshire to take care of the house and everything else. This time was much better because she knew what was going to happen and was not frightened. It was the baby who was a worry for the first week—and the District Nurse, who disappeared with a nervous breakdown the very next day. But they overcame both problems and were now delighted to have a girl and a boy—Helen and Douglas!

"I think we should have three children," said Jeannie, "so if anything happens to one of them the other two will have each other. We've got three years between these two, so we don't need to wait quite as long to have the third one."

The house was built well back from the lane, so the driveway was about sixty yards long, with a wide sweep at the front of the house, giving plenty of room to park and turn around. It was covered with black cinders as a foundation for tarmac or gravel. The cinders rolled into the soil over time. They'd finish the drive after the house was done.

Mum stayed with them for a couple of weeks but planned to drive back to Devonshire the next day. Neil arranged to have nine tons of cinder delivered—and Jeannie was about three months pregnant. These days she knew within a couple of weeks when she was pregnant because her nipples began to feel sore, and this time the baby would be born about eighteen months after Douglas.

That morning she saw the truck back into the driveway, but before she could do anything with her two kids in order to run down and tell the driver where to dump the cinder, he tipped the back up and it was all in a pile in the middle of the driveway. She thought—what a stupid place to dump it—Neil will not be able to drive in, let alone the milkman or the postman, and Mum won't be able to drive out tomorrow.

"Mum, please can you keep an eye on the kids and I'll go and shovel the cinders; I need to spread them out because no-one can move in the driveway with them as they are."

By the time Neil came home she had almost finished spreading the nine tons of cinders and Mum was in the middle of preparing their evening meal.

Jeannie was very tired and Neil scolded her for shoveling and barrowing the cinders.

"Never mind, it's done now. I'll be okay after I've slept," she said.

The next morning Jeannie dressed and fed the children, as usual, and Mum left for her home in Devonshire after Neil had gone to work. She still didn't feel too good so she relaxed in an armchair while the children played. Then she went to the bathroom—and noticed blood in the toilet as she stood up. I must call the doctor, she thought.

She put Douglas in the pushchair and told her daughter to hold onto it as they walked along the lane to the phone box at the other end of the village, by the last house. She spoke to the doctor's Nurse, who said she would give the doctor her message, but that in the meantime she must go to bed and lie down.

"I can't do that—I've got two other little children," she said, "I'll have to lie on the floor until my husband comes home."

Neil arrived, distraught when he saw her, but she said, "Drive down to the phone box and call Mum. Ask her if she can possibly drive back again—because I don't know what's going to happen and I can't look after the kids."

He did that, and told Jeannie, "She said she'll turn around and come straight back as quickly as she can."

"Poor thing. That's awful—she's 75 and she will have had a four and a half hour trip each way."

Mum arrived at 11:00 PM, and a half-hour later Jeannie, lying in bed, began to have a miscarriage which lasted until about four in the morning—and was "worse than having any baby," she said afterwards.

Mum stayed for another ten days, until Jeannie could cope with the kids and food and the house, but Jeannie told Neil she felt so depressed.

"Never mind," he said, just concentrate on getting yourself better. There's plenty of time to have another baby. We'll see if we can get the rest of the house built, and that will give you something different to think about."

He was right on that score. She lost Douglas one day and found him at the top of an exterior ladder to the upper floor. She didn't shout at him in case he looked down and lost his balance. She couldn't go up after him; heights petrified her. She talked him down so he reached the ground safely—full of excitement over his adventure. That was just the beginning. He was adventurous all his life.

Living in the house while the rest of it was being built was not fun. The noise was awful. Doorways had to be knocked through the current outside double wall from the hallway into the lounge, and to replace the window with a door from the hallway into the loggia, so there was brick-dust everywhere.

The bricklayers and carpenters worked to the sound of music—their choice of music—ceaselessly, all day long. Jeannie, Helen and Douglas were confined to the kitchen, with dining room furniture stored in it, when they were unable to be outside—that being the most distant point from all the activity. She was deprived of almost all emotion by the time Neil arrived home after work. How do you manage to have a meal ready with a welcoming smile at the end of an exhausting day when all you want to do is curl up in a corner and howl? He understood, but it was a nerve-wracking experience for both of them.

She said: "It might have been better if we'd kept the caravan and squeezed into that until all this was over?"

"It's easy to have hindsight; also the County would have frowned on that solution."

Like most good and bad experiences, eventually there is an end. When the house was finished it was gorgeous.

"We'll get a beautiful new fireplace for the lounge and to replace the one in the dining room. Since the house is designed with air space under the floors, the fires have under-floor draft, to act like bellows to get the flames going within minutes of being lit; the ash-pans can be lifted out and emptied, the floors are all tongued and grooved Australian oak—which is not "rationed." It gives us a large master bedroom over the lounge, and the enclosed balcony over the loggia will do double duty as an extra fourth bedroom." Neil was excited, and relieved.

Finally, they had the home of their dreams—for that day and age anyway.

Eighteen months later, on March 22 1958, Duncan arrived fairly effortlessly, to complete their family, as planned.

So now they had three children, with three years between each of them.

It was 1960 when it happened. Neil waited until the children were in bed and asleep before he broke the news to Jeannie.

"I've been asked to go to Australia," he said, "to assist in opening up a new Assembly Plant."

"That should be exciting," said Jeannie, ready to go to the ends of the earth with him.

"The money's good, of course, but they want me to go out there alone; they won't pay for my family to join me until I've been out there two years."

Jeannie's heart sank. She didn't want to stand in the way of opportunity for him, but the thought of losing him for another two whole years and bringing up three little children alone—in this big house, living on a large piece of land...? Right out in the country...?

"How do you feel about it? Do you ***want*** to go?

The home of their dreams

" I don't mind going; it could be interesting, and the pay's good, but I don't want to leave you here to cope on your own.

" If the money is the main consideration, I'll go back to work when Duncan is six and has been at school for a whole year. In the meantime I'll go back to College on a daily basis. We've been forced apart so long, I can't bear the thought of losing you again."

Neil said, "It's partly a change of scene, but things may get better here too, and we've got a lovely house which we own—it's not as though we owe a fortune on it—and plenty of friends. Do you want to go back to work?"

"Well, I've kept myself pretty well occupied with the Women's Institute and raising money for a new village hall ***without*** getting paid anything for it, so I guess it would be nice to do something whereby I'll get compensated for my efforts," she said, half joking, "and it would be nice to feel we could take the kids abroad without having to stretch things too much; the wider their experience of the world, the better it is for them."

"So you want me to turn it down, then? Personally, I think it's a job for a single guy, rather than someone like me, with a family. I'll make that point."

Ultimately, it did go to a single guy, and the following year Neil had a promotion, which included a Staff car and traveling to Coventry every day, adding about two hours to his working day and dangerous in the winter months with ice or snow on the ground. But they were together as a family, and that was what mattered most.

Jeannie decided she would get a Teaching Diploma, amongst other things; she knew she had the ability to teach, considering all her army experience, but she wanted to be able to give seniors the benefit of her life experiences when they were stepping out into the world looking for their first job; she knew she would probably end up teaching Shorthand, Typewriting, Commerce, First Year Economics and Commercial English at a Technical College.

It was better than that. She taught part-time at two different Technical Colleges. Then an opportunity arose for her to apply for a full-time position at a Senior Girls' school, where the unique and educationally creative Principal had persuaded the City Board of Education that an additional two years at school, after the 16-year-old requirement for leaving, could benefit her students by giving them an entry to a working life. She proposed a choice between two separate two-year Courses: Commercial Studies and Nursing.

After two years' teaching at that school, Jeannie was promoted to Head of Department, because the existing Head of Department became Deputy Principal. It would be the only school in the City offering such an opportunity, but after its subsequent success, other schools followed suit and some sent their teachers to study Jeannie's curriculum and ***modus operandi***.

She enjoyed it and also extended the educational side into extracurricular activities, such as visits to the Manchester Ship Canal and to the caverns in Derbyshire, the London Stock Exchange, the Tower of London, the Silver Vaults, the Crown Jewels, Westminster Abbey, St. Paul's Cathedral—not all at the same time, but a selection of visits for different school years, the crowning glory being a trip on the Thames, or the Changing of the Guard at Buckingham Palace, and always an evening visit to a theater production, finally catching the midnight train back to Birmingham. To students who had never traveled anywhere, it was a day to be remembered.

Jeannie herself endeavored to stay current with various events in order to impart her experiences to the students. One never-to-be-forgotten adventure was going down a coalmine at Durham, in northeast England.

Coal is the result of thousands of years of compressed decayed vegetable matter, and wherever it is found had at one time been the site of an ancient forest.

The coalmine was just outside Durham, a famous English university town in the industrial northeast surrounded by shipyards and steel mills. It was the Easter break, and in the best interest of obtaining practical experience to impart to her Senior Commerce students, Jeannie joined a group of 18 men and just one other woman on an Educational Course concerning a coalmine; the Course including visits on-board commercial shipping, and a steel mill.

The wind was straight off the North Sea, bringing with it snow and rain blowing parallel to the ground. Jeannie asked herself what on earth she was doing there? It was hard enough to comprehend how men work consistently under such bleak conditions to produce the raw materials to ensure that store shelves are filled, and cars, trucks and ship parts continue to be manufactured on their assembly lines.

Jeannie and her group dressed in miners' coveralls, boots, gloves and caps with a lamp on the forehead as they descended into the mine in the same cage the miners used. When the cage reached its destination their miner guide told them that they had to walk the rest of the way to the coalface where the miners worked. The walls of coal dripped with moisture and their small lamps provided the only light as they trudged down a gradual slope for about a half-mile. Jeannie dreaded a tiring, slippery walk back up!

At the coalface the miners sweated, stripped to the waist, the coal dust forming black rivulets down their bodies and arms. They hacked away with steel picks at the coal, which was then shoveled onto a continually moving belt about two feet wide, with a small gap between each shovel of coal. The belt moved uphill into the gloom where the group could hear the coal tipping off it, while the continuous belt relentlessly completed its non-stop circle.

The miners waved to them and jokingly invited the group to join them, saying they hoped they enjoyed their trip! Their miner guide explained some of the technicalities of the mine, including the daily amount produced, problems encountered, numbers of workers employed and length of the shifts.

Finally he said, "Time we were getting back."

There was a concerted groan as they anticipated the long, uphill, slippery trudge to the cage—it had been bad enough going downhill, never mind climbing back up!

"You don't have to walk all the way up there," he said, "you're going back on the belt. That's the way the miners end their day. We want to give you the genuine experience!"

There was a small wooden platform adjacent to but slightly above the coal belt, from which they were instructed to jump onto the moving belt, and warned to be prepared to jump upwards off the belt onto another small wooden platform at the point where the belt discharged its loads of coal. This will be one of the most frightening experiences of my life, thought Jeannie—right up with dodging shrapnel during World War II! But what was the alternative? None was offered.

At her turn, Jeannie jumped fearfully onto the moving belt in a gap between the shovels of coal, knowing that a miscalculation could send her over the edge into the trough below. Then—how would she get out? She knelt on one knee on the wobbly belt, keeping the other foot at the ready to push mightily upon reaching the small wooden platform they were warned to expect at the discharge point.

It was not easy to balance on that narrow moving belt. The moment came to jump up and off. The thought of being discharged into oblivion with the coal gave her strength and determination she didn't know she possessed.

Helping hands reached down to ensure that she didn't slip backwards and, with a breath of relief, she joined the rest of the party for the upward journey in the miners' cage to fresh air and daylight.

The cold wind and driven snow were unbelievably welcome after the musty smell of damp coal and the unspoken fear of impending disaster. The group managed a somewhat hysterical laugh as they regarded each other—faces streaked with coal-dust!

As the years went by, Unions ensured that laws were passed to facilitate the safety of both the miners and the curious public.

Jeannie did not regret her unique experience, knowing she could impart to her students the humility and gratitude they should all feel towards those who choose, or are obliged, to spend their days and risk their lives extracting carbonized vegetable matter—coal—from the bowels of the earth so that others may benefit from its usefulness and the joy of a cheerful warm fire on a wintry night.

Those post-war years were filled with adventures.

CHAPTER 24

TURNING LIMITATIONS INTO OPPORTUNITIES

The cottage, ensuring environmental safety, and exciting sandy beaches of the Lleyn Peninsular in North Wales—together with the kindness of their friends in permitting them use of it—provided Neil and Jeannie and their young family with summer vacations to be the envy of many less fortunate.

They piled into Neil's car, equipped with buckets and spades, holiday clothes, some indoor games, cans of food, and high spirits for the long and somewhat tedious drive each year, but they looked forward to it with optimistic anticipation for the familiar surroundings upon arrival. Young children are generally more content with the daily possibilities of known sights and sounds. It was a thrill to them to visit the friendly owner of the village store, who called them by name, and to discover books and games not on the shelves the previous year. They could name other beaches and places they enjoyed previously, and ask to go there again.

For all those reasons, it was relaxing for Neil and Jeannie, who often invited close friends for a weekend, or went to visit friends or relatives visiting other small towns in the neighborhood. It was a traditional haven for them all until Duncan, the youngest, was about six. That year, it rained, and it rained—which is why they all remembered it.

Summer beach vacations with three young children in a friend's rented cottage on the Lleyn Peninsular in North Wales are hard to beat when the sun shines; however, the operative word is "when." Having exhausted the village store's supply and their own creative energy on "wet day" games the past year, Neil and Jeannie decided to seek pastures new in the campsites of Europe, intending to follow the sun.

To add to the experience of the venture they decided to introduce their young family—13, 10 and 7—a girl and two boys—to erecting a shelter rather than towing one with built-in luxuries, offering little in the way of achievement. But they did decide to buy a small trailer, in which to carry a rented tent, a kerosene lamp, a variety of food in cans, tarpaulins to put on the ground, a 2-burner propane gas cooker—to sit on the ground—in fact they would all be sitting on the ground, and lying on the ground in sleeping bags on tarpaulins that year. They soon learned the ground became hard very quickly.

To add to a foreign vacation experience, there was, in the "Sixties," a low limit to the funds to be taken out of Britain to go anywhere by any means; another primary reason for the decision to camp.

They decided to take the shortest ferry crossing—Dover to Calais—but to their dismay, discovered there was no time for a meal on the ferry. It was dark when they arrived in France, too hungry and tired to deal with the tent but, confident the kids would fall asleep in the comfy car, they decided to get as far South in search of the sun as possible and to make up for the disaster with a good breakfast.

They bypassed Paris on secondary roads and wound down the windows to enjoy the fresh country air. By 5:00 AM, passing through the villages, they could smell French bread baking. By 5:30 AM, the kids were all awake.

"What is that smell?"

"I'm hungry?"

"Everyone's riding bicycles!"

"Look at that old man on his bike…he's got a long loaf of bread sticking up at the back."

"That lady's carried her bread in the basket on the front. Look, it's all different shapes." "Don't they have sliced bread in France?"

"I'm hungry."

"Can't we stop, . . . ***please?*** I'm hungry."

"Look, there's an outdoor market," said Jeannie, "we'll get some tomatoes and peaches and apples and cheeses and we'll find some hot coffee for Daddy and myself, and some hot chocolate for all of you at that small coffee shop, and you can choose your own croissants from the patisserie."

The kids bounced up and down with excitement and the thought of choosing their own food.

Out in the country again, Neil pulled over at the side of the road and they sat on some soft grass under a tree to enjoy the impromptu feast.

Neil drove the right-hand drive car—built for driving on the left in the UK—but this was the mainland of Europe where everyone drives on the right, so Jeannie tried to be a good navigator. Inevitably, they took a wrong turn occasionally.

"I've got to turn around," said Neil. Then—"The trailer's jack-knifed. Jump out and unhook it, Jeannie. Hook it up again when I've straightened out. It's too small to control and I can't see it when reversing. We're ***not*** going to be using it again."

They had five weeks' vacation time so decided the Mediterranean coast of Spain would be their ultimate destination, via Andorra in the Pyrenees, returning via the coastal route to France.

In the "Sixties" a set of Michelin Road Maps, specifically those identifying and classifying campsites in all countries you intend to explore, provided another learning curve. Sites varied from those having showers with hot and cold water, separate toilets for men or women, paved roads with night lighting, identified plots for erecting a tent, to sites with only sinks and a cold water faucet, toilets—simply a hole in the ground with a concrete "footprint" on either side. They called them "Peter and Paul's footsteps." There was a chain with a ring at the end connected to an invisible water tank up in the roof somewhere. After rescuing one of the kids clinging to the wooden wall at one camp—reminiscent of a gecko with poor suction pads—they discovered that often the water "flushed" the entire floor, requiring beating a hasty retreat or leaping up the wall until the "flood" subsided.

But that was all later. In any event bath tissue was not provided, and neither was soap. Their first stop was at a camp in France in early afternoon. Duncan, the younger boy, took on the responsibility of investigating the ablutions and returned, declaring loudly and triumphantly for all to hear,

"It's Peter an' Paul's footsteps, Mum!"

That turned out to be the very least of their problems.

"Open the trailer please, Douglas," said Neil.

"Oh! It stinks! That lamp has leaked kerosene all over the folded tent and the tarpaulins and the cans of food."

"Quick, look for a hosepipe and water."

With a certain amount of inward embarrassment but outward aplomb, they dragged the trailer and its contents to the nearest faucet. They washed and liquid-soaped what they could and found a couple of towels in the trunk of the car to dry everything off—but it didn't kill the smell.

"We're getting rid of that lamp," said Jeannie, with the kids chorusing: "Yeah!"—They preferred to survive with flashlights until an alternative means of lighting was found—any practical alternative with no smell.

Then the tent had to be erected for the very first time. They decided—wisely as it turned out—to rent rather than buy a tent initially. There were poles and ropes and metal pegs and a somewhat well worn instruction sheet. They laid everything out on the ground and tried to figure out a logical way of dealing with it—all too aware of a very critical and somewhat amused audience.

In an hour it would be dark, and they were beginning to panic, but they had not counted on the natural camaraderie of the camping community, who let them struggle for a while. But when it became obvious that the tent was going to win, three young men—two French and one Dutch—without even a glance at the instruction sheet, had the poles firmly in place and the tent ready for occupancy.

Neil commented, "We should have made time before renting, to research the shape and size of a tent to suit our needs, asked for the erection of it to be demonstrated, and then given it plenty of practice on the lawn."

Jeannie, not wanting his vacation to be ruined, said, "Never mind, we left in a rush but even small tents can present problems. We'll be okay. We've just got to remember the tricks of the trade. Does anyone remember how those guys tackled it? They were so quick."

"Yes. They laid the poles in the approximate locations—one at each corner and one in the middle of each side..."

"And then two of them stood up two corner poles while the third guy stretched out the guy lines..."

"Then they did the same thing on the opposite side of the tent ..."

"But they only had the bottom half of each pole standing up when they laid the folded tent across them—the poles sort of folded in half attached with a spring..."

"Yes," said Douglas, who had been listening intently to the conversation, "because we wouldn't be able to reach if the poles were at full height."

"Well done," Neil patted him on the back, "so then what happened?"

"They opened the tent across all the poles..."

"Then they went inside and lifted up two poles at a time to their full height," added his sister.

"Then they came out and pulled on all the strings and pushed the pegs in the ground to hold the strings ...'guy lines' corrected his brother ...tight." Duncan was not to be outdone and he looked at his Dad for approval.

"Do you think you could help me erect the tent, now?" asked Neil.

"Yes," chorused the kids.

Neil assigned each member of his family a pole and told them all to remember which one was his or her responsibility. The reverse process packed up the tent—loosening the guy lines, reducing the height of the poles to half their extendable height, then folding the tent on the frame to keep it clean—adopting the same technique as a matter of routine so that when the tent was going to be used it could be laid on the frame before the poles were extended to final height. That efficient process contributed to a feeling of absolute joy, triumph and satisfaction—especially in front of a critical audience. What an achievement!

"Let's time ourselves to see how fast we can deal with the tent," said Douglas.

On future vacations, within five minutes they were blowing up their air mattresses with a pump hooked up to the car's electrical system.

They enjoyed the drive over the Pyrenees the following day, and camped upon reaching Andorra at the top—7,000 feet elevation—explored the small town before darkness fell, treating themselves to a real meal in a convenient little restaurant.

In the "Sixties" most travelers used the easier coastal route, and today that route boasts a freeway all the way down the Mediterranean coast to Barcelona, and beyond, but the more adventurous drive through Andorra, though their numbers have increased a thousand-fold and it is fortuitous to arrive early for a camping spot.

They researched a camp ground right on the Mediterranean at Tamarit, where a rocky headland sporting a genuine Spanish castle provided a long, sandy bay on one side of it. Here, the amenities were quite good. They could drive right to the designated camping spot, even though the "road" just consisted of compressed sand, and by now they felt reasonably confident of the tent erection process—being watched by the critical eyes of their next-door German neighbor and his wife.

They cooked their own meal—on the ground, and sat around—on the ground, eating it, while their neighbors luxuriated in comfortable folding chairs on either side of a little table holding a bright gas lamp, above which a small model airplane circled, providing a cooling breeze with its propeller as a fan, whilst effectively keeping flying insects at bay. Typically, the German neighbors were very organized.

A day or so later they spent in Barcelona, exploring the castle, two churches, a street market, advertisements for a bullfight and experiencing a major traffic jam. They discovered that the Spanish are not patient people like the British, who tend to have a stoic attitude when faced with an annoying crisis. In spite of being ignorant of the cause of the jam, every driver hit his horn—and held his hand there. The resulting cacophony was deafening.

Finally, on the way back to the camp, they spied lowering black clouds and feared the worst. Sure enough, they entered to a downpour. The dry ground didn't absorb the rain and it ran right through their tent—on a slight slope—washing sand over the tarpaulins on the floor and threatening to soak the sleeping bags. Frantically, they tried to dig a ditch to divert the water with bare hands and spoons—having no other means.

Suddenly, their silent savior, the German neighbor, came to the rescue with trenching tool in hand, and a shovel he handed to Neil. They watched the German's practiced actions with feelings ranging from mortification to envy—as one might absorb the technique of a skilled tennis player. Beneath it was undying gratitude—finally they would be dry.

Like lightning, he scooped away a trench all around the tent and let the tent sheet drop into it. Then quickly, he showed them how to build up a wall of sand on the interior to keep the water out so it would run down the trench.

Next day they bought their new friends a huge basket of fruit, nuts, cookies and German lager. The previously dour guy held up the trenching tool and the shovel and said, in German:

"Don't leave home without them!" He gave a triumphant laugh, in which they all joined.

Don't leave home without them! They always looked at the land when pitching the tent.

"If there's a slope," said Neil "the door must face downhill. We'll dig the trench immediately—not wait until it rains. It would help to have a flysheet—a separate sheet to go over the tent with space for air between it and the tent sheeting. That would keep the interior cooler in a hot climate."

That was the first of many camping trips with the children. They bought a large tent with separate interior "room dividers" all across the back, leaving plenty of living space in the front half; a folding cooker stand, folding chairs and table, inflatable mattresses and other practical comforts; a trenching tool and shovel but—literally the "crowning glory"—a large roof rack with a wood base, high sides, and its own cover, to carry all the camping equipment, so they had no worries about towing anything—the principal reason for not investing in a caravan in the first place. They had been frustrated many times by a long line of traffic on British roads, inevitably with a car and trailer at the head of it—plodding along at minimal speed.

Clothes and cans of food fit in the trunk of the car. They made many friends, British, German and Dutch, including a doctor and his wife and family, who towed their boat, with whom the kids learned to water-ski.

Usually, they made the four-hour crossing from Newhaven to Dieppe, giving time to have a proper meal on board, and the kids chorused: "Now our vacation has really begun!"

Neil and Jeannie took them all over Western Europe, and also they each went with a separate school party—their daughter, Helen, to Norway, Sweden, Denmark and Russia, before the ending of the "Cold War"; the elder boy, Douglas, to Italy; the younger one, Duncan, to Austria. When they were old enough to drive and had finished school, Neil and Jeannie took his company car with all the camping equipment and had a long vacation on their own, meeting the boys at Dieppe, where they took over and their trusting parents sailed back as passengers to Newhaven, where the boys parked another car for the drive home.

Trusting? Or crazy? It taught them independence. In the meantime, their older sister had flown to friends in the United States to create a new life for herself.

Today, many travelers make the crossing by way of the "Chunnel"—the Channel Tunnel between England and France—but they miss half the fun. Jeannie was teaching in the "Sixties" and was packed up and ready to go the very day the term ended, returning a week before the Autumn term commenced. She was too exhausted to waste a week at home, knowing she would achieve nothing prior to the vacation. The adrenalin of all the family was always high—driving from "Shakespeare Country" to the South Coast—as more than once they were the last to board the ferry!

Worried about a challenging vacation? Life is too short for the faint-hearted. All the memories are worth the effort, and children never forget a happy childhood with a learning curve.

However, consider the following, it's known as the ***Channel Express***. Britain's high-speed ***Eurostar*** rail service, which used to run from Waterloo Station, now commences from St. Pancras International Station. The Victorian, striped-brick structure, was given a major face-lift at the cost of about $1.6 million a few years ago, the inspiration of Sir

Norman Foster, a well-known architect, making the train station almost a destination in itself, with its Arcade of representative British shops, including ***Boots, Marks & Spencer, and Thomas Pink***. Additionally featured—a Champagne bar, reputedly the longest in Europe, at nearly 300 feet, and an elegant first-class departure lounge. The silent ***Eurostar*** trains are purported to be the first in the world to go 100 per cent carbon neutral.

For more information, go to ***raileurope.com***.

They had been home a couple of weeks, when Jeannie was in the hallway as the 'phone rang. A familiar voice said, "I'm just calling to let you know that Daddy died this morning at Llangwnnadl."

Jeannie, visualizing a virile man in his early sixties, said, "Oh my god! How did that happen?"

"He was out in his boat alone, baiting his lobster pots, when the cord to one of the floats got tangled around the outboard motor. He leaned over the end of the boat to deal with it—and fell in. As you know, he couldn't swim, but in any case he was wearing thigh-length rubber wading boots. They filled with water, making them like lead weights, dragging him down. A helicopter was dispatched from Anglesey, but there wasn't a hope of saving him. Mum witnessed it all from the cliff-top."

Jeannie cried, every time she thought about it, for a month.

But, he was doing the thing he loved in the place he loved best. We should all be so fortunate when our time comes.

None of them ever visited Llangwnnadl again.

CHAPTER 25

INTERLUDE

At eighty-four years of age, Jeannie's Mum moved from Exeter to Neil and Jeannie's large home in Warwickshire, not far from Stratford-upon-Avon. The final straw to her living alone had been a fall down the stairs resulting in cracked ribs, and Jeannie's sojourn, with the children, for six weeks while she recovered—leaving Neil to fend alone.

Mum was an active parishioner—to be sorely missed at all church functions, so Jeannie endeavored to duplicate her interests within her new environment. She held a "Coffee Morning" at the house, to which she invited active members of the community and introduced her mother to them. They were happy to learn of someone with the potential to participate in the activities of the village.

All Jeannie's efforts were in vain. Although Mum took an energetic interest in the garden, she did not wander beyond the gate. This became a draining responsibility because Mum's social activities then rested with Neil and Jeannie, who both had full-time jobs and three children to look after.

At Easter 1966, when the children were at home for Easter Break from school, and Neil had several days off work, Jeannie decided to take her mother to Ireland—Eire—the Irish Republic, in southern Ireland, not Northern Ireland which became a part of Great Britain since British troops were sent over there at the time of the potato famine to stop so many Irish invading Liverpool.

She also thought it would be an opportunity to give Neil's beloved Auntie Flo an Easter vacation, so she took one of the cars and made arrangements for the crossing from Liverpool to Dublin.

Unfortunately, after a few days' driving and sightseeing, Auntie became seriously ill, and Jeannie asked the owner of the little hotel where they were staying to send for the doctor. After examining Auntie, he said, "You'd best get the old lady on the plane; she's going to die and you be in a foreign country."

Jeannie arranged that in a hurry, and had her airlifted back on a stretcher, calling Neil to get his doctor cousin to meet her at the airport in England, while she and mother continued their vacation.

A few weeks after they returned by boat, with the car, the latest Irish uprising began, with bombs and guns and other fearsome things, which went on for years. A good thing I heeded the doctor's advice, she thought.

Now, on Easter Sunday, the bells were pealing. Everyone was going to church, many walking miles and miles along rutted roads, the women in their long, black gowns and the men in their Sunday best, also black. When they reached the nearest of many Catholic churches, they found it surrounded by a rock wall, with bicycles stacked all around it, at least six deep. Horses, freed from their harness and carts, grazed among the tombstones.

Jeannie and Mom ate sandwiches and coffee they'd purchased earlier, then after lunch, with service ended, they went inside such a church. It was magnificent. Gorgeous stained glass windows, polished pews, immaculate altar cloths, paintings, prayer books and kneelers, shining brass and copper collection plates and candlesticks. The sun, shining through the windows, lit the church with rainbows.

In contrast, the solitary Protestant church in the nearest little town, had one bell to toll, plain glass windows, and a simple interior.

However, Eire had recently joined the "Common Market" as one of the first five countries to do so. Today it is known as EU, or European Union, consisting of most of Western Europe. From being pathetically poor, Eire also began to reap the benefit of welcoming the Japanese, who were thus able to produce many electrical goods, then to be sold in Europe without paying import duty, since they were "Made in Eire".

Today, Eire has changed in the same way that the Hawaiian Islands have changed—fortunately or unfortunately—depending upon how it is perceived. Jeannie was glad she had been able to see it in all its natural beauty. However, the populace is more affluent from the tourist trade. It was commonplace to see a tiny white-washed stone croft with thatched roof, a man walking a donkey with panniers filled with peat or stacked high with hay-bales, followed by a solitary cow and, of course, a dog. Jeannie took photos to remember it.

Eire reminded Jeannie of a shallow basin—higher land and low mountains towards the coast, peat moors and some bogs inland, where undoubtedly there had been forests in years past. No wonder it was called the "Emerald Isle"—she had never seen anywhere so green.

They explored the mountains, where men awaited them eagerly with ponies and traps to transport them along the rough roads and to tell them tales of local lore, but after one such ride, Jeannie decided she could tackle other routes by car; she had driven up more challenging roads in Scotland. Owners of the local transport did their best to dissuade her, but Jeannie knew that was because they would be missing out on remuneration—undoubtedly needed—rather than the fact that the roads were unsuitable for a car—let alone a woman driver!

Once, when they stopped to admire a view, they were suddenly surrounded by numerous gypsy children, and realized they had stopped near a gypsy encampment. Mum wound down her window to give them some wrapped toffees, after which they formed a group—obviously having done that on more than one occasion—for Jeannie to take a photo of them. She didn't leave the car, but she wound down her window to take the photo. Later, Jeannie reached into the pocket of that door—and found that two large sticks of pink and white peppermint rock were missing! She knew the culprit—a small child who had clambered up to the window while she was taking the photo, reaching down into the door!

The southern coast road took them through Cork—always to be remembered at that time for newspapers and rubbish blowing in the wind, probably because the township could not afford to employ workers to keep the streets clean. The situation improved as they followed the road north through Waterford, famous for its beautiful cut glass bowls, vases and wineglasses, called Waterford Crystal. Jeannie's Mum had a set of antique wine glasses and more than one cut glass bowl.

The return crossing from Dublin to Liverpool was better than the experience Neil and Jeannie had returning from the Isle of Man, but the Irish Sea was a force to be reckoned with most of the time.

On another occasion—actually prior to Mum's move from Devonshire permanently—Jeannie suggested a trip by car to Scotland, which Mum had not visited since Daddy died in 1940. Mum drove herself to their home; Jeannie taking over from there.

In the process of packing Mum's car, Jeannie noticed a familiar small suitcase on the back seat. It had accompanied her everywhere throughout her years in the army.

"Thank you for bringing my suitcase finally, Mum. I'm sorry I left it at your house for so long."

"I brought it because it's such a convenient size for me to use," said her mother.

Jeannie's heart missed a beat with fear and doubt.

"What did you do with all my letters from everybody during the war, and my old address books and other mementoes?"

" Oh, I just burned them all. You married him," she said, "so what was the point in keeping all that stuff? "

" They weren't just Neil's letters," Jeannie said. " They were from lots of other people I knew. How could you do that? They weren't yours to burn, and in any case, you didn't even have the courtesy to call and ask me first."

"him" she said; she didn't even call Neil by his name.

And—two precious, sentimental pieces of paper: One, torn from an old writing block, had been folded and folded into a small square because she wanted it to fit into a pocket of her dress at the time she was eight, staying with Grandma at her old Norfolk inn. Annie, the Gypsy Fortune Teller, had given it to her. The other, the top sheet of a large yellow lined writing pad, where Neil had written his name and home address diagonally across it, right in the middle.

To Jeannie they represented two vivid memories.

I'm sure she read them all, Jeannie thought. She felt sick to her stomach. There was an irreplaceable letter from Len Richardson, who worked for her father; it was a first-hand description of his struggle back through the beaches at Dunkirk—more vivid than anything Neil told her—he preferred to forget it. And, a letter from Bobbie Martin, whom she'd met on a train journey, when he returned from North Africa after fighting Field Marshall Rommel's army and was subsequently shipped to Italy—letters containing first-hand reminiscences—so valuable in trying to recall life at that time.

She saw Bobbie two or three times since the war ended. He returned to his job as a long-distance truck driver and he looked her up when his travels took him through Exeter. There were all the letters from her cousin, stationed in Gibraltar, at the entrance from the Atlantic to the Mediterranean Sea. Letters from her Irish girlfriend who married a British Army Captain in the King's Chapel of the Savoy and subsequently moved abroad with him. Now Jeannie no longer had her contact address. Lives—at one time so close; now—forever lost. Forget Scotland, she thought, furious and very upset. All she had left were memories.

But she did take her mother to Scotland, to retrace her father's footsteps as far as her mother's fading memory would permit, and she didn't mention the suitcase and its contents again, although she thought about it a lot. Instead, she chose to remember the 22 Karat wedding ring she wore on her left hand, and her father's camera, and the "comfort packages" Mum sent to Neil when he was still in Britain. In fact, they went to the Braemar Gathering—famous Highland Games—with Princess Margaret—Elizabeth's younger sister—in attendance, and occupied privileged places in the adjacent canopied seating. It was pure luck they happened to be in the right place at the right time, and Mum was thrilled. Jeannie wished Neil could have been there. He was an expert at tossing the caber and putting the shot and other such Scottish skills.

Another summer, Jeannie decided to take her mother to the mainland of Europe, since she had never crossed the Channel, although her ancestors on her father's side were French. Now, she was sailing from Immingham, in Yorkshire, to Amsterdam, in Holland. The ship was from a Belgian line, and very comfortable. They had the experience of sailing through locks in the Kiel Canal to reach Amsterdam.

Jeannie drove down through the Netherlands to the beautiful old town of Maastricht, where they broke their journey for the night. The next morning she continued south through the small but delightful country of Luxembourg, afterwards following the Mosel River to Koblentz, where it joins the Rhine. They did not go to Koblentz then, but spent that night at a "gasthaus"—inn—overlooking the Mosel.

The gasthaus was a lovely old wood building with huge open beams in its dining room. Jeannie read the German menu and ordered the same meal for each of them. It was served on large, colorful oval plates. Jeannie noticed that her mother ate the vegetables in the center of the plate but did not touch the long sausages arranged at the top and bottom, following the shape of the plate.

"Mum, why aren't you eating the sausages?"

"Where are they?"

"At the upper and lower edges of the plate."

"Oh!" She pushed her fork into a sausage. "I thought they were the pattern on the plate."

At that moment Jeannie realized how bad Mum's close sight had become, and determined to take her to an ophthalmologist when they got home.

After breakfast the next morning, Jeannie drove into Koblentz, parked the car and, holding Mum's arm, told her they were going to take a trip on the Rhine. They got on the boat and found seats in the bow so that Mum could see as much as possible, her long sight being an improvement on her short sight.

It was a wonderful trip, past impressive old stone castles high up on the east side of the river and colorful villages where passengers embarked and disembarked. They rounded a corner where the "lorelei"—maidens, in German fables—were reputed to distract the boatswain so that he ran into rocks where supposedly they would capture him to make love to him and prevent his return to his own village!

They returned the way they had come, but sailing on the other side of the river, collected the car at Koblentz, and stayed at the same gasthaus for a second night.

Jeannie followed the Rhine south the next day through Heidelberg, where they explored part of the old city and bought some genuine china Hummel figures—named for their creator—a postman and a seated girl—for which the place is famous. Then on to Baden Baden, where she took a scenic secondary road down through the Black Forest to Konstanz, on the lake of the same name, otherwise known as Bodensee.

Villages all through the Black Forest are architectural gems with steep roofs so that the snow in winter will not weigh heavily on them, and hundreds of logs are stacked under overhangs ready for winter fires. Bright geraniums grow in wire baskets hanging over balconies on each house, adding color everywhere. They spent that night in Konstanz. Jeannie decided to take the ferry across the lake into Switzerland the following morning, and she drove as far as Lucerne, a lovely town on a lake of the same name. They walked across a roofed pedestrian bridge containing overhead paintings for which it is famous. They stayed that night in Lucerne.

But it is impossible to leave Switzerland without mentioning the cows, since one encountered a whole herd frequently on the road, being moved from one location to another.

"Listen to the bells, Mum, and look at the cows as they pass."

They heard them before seeing them, since each wore a bell, hanging low from its neck, intensifying in size and sound to suit the herdsman's whim; he knew every animal by the sound of its bell—a useful appendage in countryside where they roamed free for miles, often out of sight, and a tuneful accompaniment to a slow traverse in a peaceful, green world.

It was time for Jeannie to make her way to Le Havre to catch the ferry back to England, so she took the road to Basle, deciding to aim for Dijon and then for the Route Peripherique—the circular elevated road around Paris. She'd been on it before, driving south with Neil. The experience got the adrenalin pumping. Drivers picked up speed immediately to join the circumnavigators doing at least 70 MPH, whilst being prepared to get off at the correct "pont"—"bridge"—failing that—being subjected to the entire circular route, hoping to get off the second time of asking! She knew it was useless to ask Mum to look out for the "pont" so she trusted she would notice the sign for Rouen before it was too late.

She managed it, and continued on the two-lane road to Le Havre, on the coast—to be faced with a sign indicating there were no ferries. There was a major dock strike in Britain. Jeannie asked whether there was anywhere they could catch a freight plane, because of the car. They were lucky to find one with just two seats for passengers.

So, Mum had two "once in a lifetime" experiences—visiting the mainland of Europe, and flying in an airplane!

Maybe it was a good thing she couldn't see too well.

CHAPTER 26

LIFE-CHANGING TIMES

Many things changed throughout the Western World during the 1960's and 1970's affecting Neil and Jeannie's life and that of their young family. On the lighter side of things it was having a great many friends in their age group, though not all with children, and the fact that Jeannie, whilst at home with the children, had the time and the energy to get involved with fund-raising for a new Peace Hall. The Hall in use had been built at the end of the Great War—WWI—so being a wooden building, it had seen better days.

It was the center of all events in the little village, which had an active Women's Institute, a very well supported Amateur Dramatic Society, a Bridge Club, Chess Club and, due to the fact that the population was small, many were members of more than one gathering, and success was such that people from surrounding villages supported many events. Jeannie supported the first two.

By this time, Dana, the source of some concern to Jeannie in reference to her relationship with Neil both at work and when he moved to Alcester after his landlady absconded with the milkman, had married the Head of Department for whom she worked. In fact, Neil and Jeannie were invited to the wedding and Jeannie made the three-tier wedding cake as a wedding present, having it professionally decorated. Subsequently, Dana, now retired, having no children of her own, was happy enough to help out Jeannie in looking after them to enable Jeannie to participate in village affairs. Circumstances change events!

Jeannie complained mildly to Neil that although she put a lot of effort into events, such as local dances, with the object of a new Peace Hall in sight, she was unable to enjoy the fruits of her labor because he didn't dance! Never one to shirk a challenge, and always one to complete it to perfection, Neil suggested they should take professional dancing lessons. When Jeannie had, figuratively speaking, picked herself up from the floor with shock at his ready submission, she got to work making the appropriate appointments, resulting in a lesson one evening a week and serious practice in a Birmingham ballroom one other night a week—Neil's idea. She had also to organize a reliable baby-sitter for the children—the latter with varying success, as might be expected. For instance, they returned unexpectedly early one night—to find that baby-sitter's—uninvited—boyfriend lying on the sofa in a compromising position!

They were getting dressed to go to a local dance competition one night, when Helen, who had been watching television while her brothers were in bed, came running into the hallway,

"President Kennedy's been shot! President Kennedy's been shot!"

They all ran to look at the "Special Announcement," interrupting regular programming, a sinking feeling in the pit of their stomachs. The United States of America was a long way away, but even Helen, eleven years old, realized it was an earth-shaking catastrophe. Neil and Jeannie spread the unwelcome news to others at the dance; it had a dampening effect on the whole evening. People always remember where they were when events such as this take place.

At this point, in this chapter CNN's program on August 25, 2009 was interrupted to announce the death of the fourth, and youngest, brother, Senator Edward—"Teddy"—Kennedy. Jeannie said she was glad he died in his own bed in Hyannis Port, with his family around him, rather than being shot—or shot at, in an airplane like the oldest brother, Joseph, during WWII—particularly since his very public life for nearly fifty years had put him at risk.

A basic group of Neil and Jeannie's friends, each with their own additional acquaintances, held dinner parties at home on a regular basis.

By this time Jeannie had become quite an expert cook who enjoyed experimenting with new recipes. The latest holiday phase was taking slide photos in color. During winter evenings they all shared these with their friends, introducing them to new holiday venues.

In 1969, when Helen was 17, she became restless. School trips, and the young people she met on them, opened her eyes to the world, and made her realize the possibilities offered by places other than Great Britain or Europe.

The first person she met, through a group of her own friends, was a young Belgian called Franz who had returned to England recently from America, and spoke fluent English with an American accent. He ingratiated himself with Douglas and Duncan when Helen brought him home because he knew so many card games, which he made a point of teaching them. He said he was twenty-six, and also seemed to have made a hit with Helen's circle of acquaintances.

About three months passed, when suddenly Franz and Helen announced that they wanted to get married. Helen needed her parents' permission since she was still not eighteen. Franz made a good case for himself and appeared confident of being able to support them both. Helen was a restless teenager looking for adventure, with no specific career in her future, though she was bright and ambitious.

With considerable misgivings and a certain reluctance, Neil and Jeannie agreed to the wedding, thinking it might be better to give in than to object, since the chances were that their daughter would follow her own desires the minute she was eighteen in any case. It was to be a civil ceremony, not a church wedding, which avoided the calling of banns, followed by a reception for close friends in the hall of a local inn catering to such occasions. Congratulations and gifts began to arrive from distant friends and relatives.

The evening Helen and Franz went into the city to see a film, Jeannie suddenly looked at Neil and said she didn't feel comfortable about the situation—something just didn't seem to "click." She knew it was only intuition, but Neil suggested calling the people in Florida to find out whether the story told by Franz was true—that he had been a traveling companion to an older lady but he left for Europe when she returned home.

They had no 'phone number but they had her rather unusual name and the town where she lived—this was in the days before the Internet and its search possibilities—but within an hour they were talking to members of the lady's family. What they heard did not reassure them. Jeannie went upstairs and opened a large suitcase Franz had brought with him. She looked through it, and right at the bottom found documents and photographs. The documents were in German and the photos were of Franz with a young lady. Neil and Jeannie managed to decipher the documents sufficiently to realize that Franz was married, and presumed that the young lady was his wife.

Jeannie remembered vividly what happened when they entered the house. Neil waited until they were inside, and locked the door behind them. Ignoring Helen, he ordered Franz upstairs to collect all his things and bring them down immediately.

Jeannie told Helen, "He's married."

Neil took the case from him and put it in the trunk of the car.

Then, brusquely, he said, "Get in."

He had plenty of experience dealing with worse characters!

Neil drove all the four hundred mile round trip to Dover and back that night, to put Franz on a channel ferry. He warned him not to attempt to return to Britain because he would be arrested at any port or airport through which he tried to enter.

The next day Jeannie canceled everything planned and returned the gifts.

They breathed a sigh of relief at having avoided a near tragedy. Any expenses were cheap compared to what might have happened.

Shortly thereafter, it appeared to Helen that opportunity knocked in the form of a person her father had known at school.

Gerry—not his real name—was the son of Russian immigrants who escaped from Russia during the 1917 revolution and ended up in Canada, where he was born, and then sent to a private school. At about 14 years of age, he absconded from school and wandered around the United States by himself. When his parents eventually caught up with him, they decided to send him to an English Public School, where he stood less chance of doing another "disappearing act."

Neil was Head Prefect of MacDougall House, and Gerry was put in his charge—not an enviable job for Neil, but evidently Gerry respected him during that time because he stayed in touch with sporadic letters. He served in the Aleutian Islands during the war.

Years later, after WWII, Jeannie met Gerry when he showed up in London with his wife. She and Neil drove from their home in Warwickshire to meet them at the Savoy Hotel, where they stayed for a long weekend. They drove the visitors to Windsor Great Park to see the October colors of the trees, and historic Windsor Castle. One evening they saw a show at one of London's famous theaters, enjoying a very successful run—"A Funny Thing Happened on the Way to the Forum." After that association, and a Dinner Dance at the hotel another evening, Jeannie decided she didn't like Gerry—he was too much of a "controlling, over-bearing" type, even to the point of trying to influence Neil's life. His wife was delightful—much too nice for him. Jeannie made Neil aware of her feelings. He didn't disagree.

A few months passed, and Gerry called them at home, saying he was "in the neighborhood." Being the sociable types that they were, they invited him to stay for two or three nights. He was by himself, and he latched onto Helen—seventeen and impressionable—like a limpet. Subsequently, he wrote to her. The minute she was eighteen—like Cinderella when the clock struck midnight—she flew to the United States to stay at Gerry's place on the ocean in Mobile—they didn't know Gerry's wife had divorced him. He took Helen all over the US and Canada, but they did not hear a word from her—other than the odd card—and they only heard what really happened to her much later. She disappeared from their lives at eighteen! Over time, Gerry used his influence to obtain a Resident Alien card for her, and after five years she obtained her Citizenship on her own account.

Finally, she called and said she was getting married—no, not to him—to escape from him. The young man was from Mobile—a baseball player for a well-known team—and his parents and many relatives were thrilled that he wanted to marry a British girl.

They then had a little son, so Helen and little Neil traveled where the team moved. However, it was to be short-lived. Her husband was injured and could no longer play, and Helen found herself working to keep all three of them. She didn't foresee that as much of a life so, determined to divorce him, she decided she had to move them all to California.

In California, Los Angeles by all accounts, promised an easier chance to get divorced, and more opportunities for work for Helen, plus pre-school eventually for her son.

Neil shipped a brand new MG-BGT sports car out to her in Los Angeles. Unfortunately, she was at their rented apartment the day the divorce papers were served. Her husband was furious. She picked up her purse and the baby, jumped into her car and drove off.

She didn't have a problem finding work in Los Angeles, but she had to find a baby-sitter for the little boy, drop him off every day, and collect him every evening. At one point, she had three different jobs, to make ends meet. The baby-sitter loved the little boy and stayed in touch for many years.

In the end she met an English guy who was setting up a chain of restaurants. Actually, he had been in the British papers—as the first person to go door-to-door selling vacuum cleaners to "stay-at-home Mums"—with which he did very well until either the husbands ran him out of town or the vacuum cleaners needed spare parts or repairs; he had no follow-up for that.

You can't keep someone down with initiative like that—though when he left England he couldn't go back because he owed taxes there. He opened up a restaurant in Los Angeles. It became really popular and diners lined up to get in.

Helen was only about twenty-one but very personable, so she obtained a job as a cashier and was also in charge of the female employees—for hiring and firing and paying. It entailed long hours and hard graft, though, but there was always a room in the evenings for the little boy—and a volunteer member of staff to take care of him.

She and her employer opened up several other such restaurants, but the first one had the reputation and greatest success.

One winter night, in 1974, the 'phone rang at home and Jeannie woke up. She had to dash downstairs to answer it because her Mum had the upstairs line in her room—and cell-phones didn't exist then.

"Hello?" She said.

"I called to let you know I'm moving to Hawaii."

"Okay," said Helen's mother, "we'll come and see you in the summer, so let us know where you are."

"Do you mean that?"

"Yes, of course."

"I'll let you know," she said.

Neil rolled over as Jeannie got back into bed. "Who was that?"

"Helen. She said she's moving to Hawaii. I told her we'd fly over to see her in the summer."

"Oh, okay," he said, and turned over and went back to sleep.

Summer 1975 was the first time they visited Maui. Meanwhile, the boys took Neil's car, a close boyfriend, and their respective girlfriends, and went back to Tamarit, camping, for the umpteenth time.

Jeannie arranged for her mother to enter a private nursing home while they were away.

Neil and Jeannie went to Cook's Travel Agency in Solihull, as being the most convenient branch of the reputable firm to deal with, saying that they needed to make reservations to fly to Maui. The request caused a minor upheaval that day in 1975, nobody at Cook's ever having heard of Maui. Fortunately, Helen assisted matters by saying they had first to land in Honolulu, then take a flight on a local airline—Hawaiian Air or Aloha Airlines—to Maui.

The information opened up other alternatives. Neil decided they would fly into San Francisco, rent a car there to drive south to Los Angeles via the scenic Route 101, and fly from Los Angeles to Honolulu.

Their summer vacation was all falling into place, and they were looking forward to something different but, like many things in Jeannie's life, it all seemed too good to be true—too easy on the surface. Then they received a frantic call from Helen just before school's one week holiday at Whitsun—Jeannie was teaching all through this time.

Although Helen had custody of her son under the divorce decree and her "ex" had visiting rights, she had agreed that little Neil could stay with his father in Los Angeles for a couple of weeks. She had a friend nearby who would keep an eye on things and make sure the child was all right.

In the meantime, Helen was going to Alaska with Wade, a builder whom she met on Maui. He was considering a job with the Alaska Pipeline because the money was so good. However, the extreme cold and the risks involved did not combine in a positive way for Helen, and she persuaded Wade to give up the idea and to be content with his good job in the warmth of Hawaii. Then Helen received a phone call from her friend in Los Angeles telling her that her "ex" had absconded with the little boy—she did not know where. Helen knew immediately where—to the large family in Mobile. She had no doubt about that.

She got in touch with an attorney in Mobile explaining what had happened, only then to be informed that her "ex" was taking her to Court in order to try and obtain total custody himself. It meant that she would have to appear in Court—alone.

"Mum, could you possibly manage to fly over to go to Court with me?"

Jeannie had a Visitor Visa because of the intended summer trip, so she flew in to Atlanta, and changed planes there for Mobile. It was her first visit to America. The young man who sat next to her on that short flight started talking to her almost immediately. Jeannie thought how friendly Americans were. You could sit on a train in England and nobody would say a word—except in wartime, of course. British people tended to be reserved.

Helen met her at Mobile, frantic with worry. They went to Helen's attorney's office, which appeared to be a cluttered dingy disaster—books and papers everywhere, seemingly accumulated over years—but he was a caring old guy.

"I'm arranging for a change of venue, and a different Judge, for the Hearing. Someone who is not prejudiced against women," he said.

They duly showed up at the courthouse, only to find about twenty members of the family there. Little Neil tried to run to his mother as soon as he saw her, but was held back. A few minutes later they all filed in—Helen and Jeannie sitting to the left of the aisle and all the others to the right; the child remained outside in the hallway with a relative. It was a cavernous building, the seating like pews in an old church.

All were required to rise as the Judge entered. He was a short man, barely able to see over the top of his rostrum. He listened to the points of view of the family—cutting some off short if they were too loquacious. Helen kept her plea short and to the point, as instructed by her attorney—including wearing a suitably sober dress purchased for the occasion.

The Judge came to his formal decision and dismissed the family, whilst requiring Helen and Jeannie to remain in their seats. Then the double doors opened at the far end of the courtroom and the little boy, just three years old, ran all the way down the aisle alone and jumped onto his mother's lap.

"Let's get out of here," said Helen, "I don't feel safe anywhere around these people. We'll fly to Los Angeles, and you can fly home from there. It's a long way round for you but safer, and an easier flight to Maui for me."

They stayed one night with a friend in Los Angeles and then Jeannie flew directly back to London and Helen to Maui, vowing not to let the child out of her sight again. She made him learn her telephone number and to trust a member of the police if anyone at any time tried to take him away, no matter who tried to do so, or what they said to him. He learned that over and over again.

The next time Jeannie visited America was with Neil, in the summer, as planned.

Helen, of course, was very familiar with Los Angeles, so she arranged for her parents to stay with a friend not far from the airport, who offered to make sure they would go to Disneyland before leaving. The friend also had a "California King" bed—the largest bed Neil and Jeannie had ever seen in their world travels so far!

"Fine, if you're getting divorced," was Neil's comment, as he waved goodnight to Jeannie from the far side of the bed!

It had its influence though—they ordered a Queen-size bed without a footboard as soon as they returned home, and wondered how they had managed to live with traditional British beds with head and footboards all those years, considering Neil's height. He no longer suffered from periodic leg cramps.

The local flight from Honolulu was interesting, accompanied by Hawaiian music and Flight Attendants dressed in colorful, long mu'u mu'us, the pilot flying the turboprop low so they were able to see the coast of Oahu and the islands of Molokai and Lanai before turning into the wind across the central plain to land at Maui's airport, where they followed "native footprints" painted on the tarmac to guide them to the "Arrivals" entrance—astonished to see a large Banyan tree growing out of the roof of the building.

Instantly, they felt the ambience of the place; tension and the cares of the world fell away. They had arrived safely on a little island, having flown halfway around the world, now in the center of the Pacific, further away from any major landmass than anywhere else.

Jeannie thought, this is where Daddy wanted to be. All these years later, his grandchild brought us here. Jeannie's entire life seemed to be predestined. Maybe the steering wheel had something to do with it?

Helen met them with an old blue open-top car—"a typical Maui cruiser," she said, and a big white fluffy dog, "Kona," with whom Jeannie shared the back seat. They crossed the center of the island, the narrow two-lane road bisecting acres and acres of green sugarcane waving in the wind, with mountains to the north and south, until finally they reached a magnificent coastline and the infinity of the blue Pacific, interrupted only by the little islands of Kahoolawe and Lanai and the tiny crater top, Molokini.

They drove south along the coast road with nothing destroying the view, other than a few buildings at each end, and Azeka's Store, with the Post Office adjacent, just beyond the halfway mark. It was an old single story wood building, with a couple of gas pumps in front of it, the inevitable coconut palm trees in the background, and Yee's Orchard opposite. A few houses were built along by the ocean and on the volcano side of the one road; other than those, the pastureland belonged to kiawe trees and cactus, dried up by the heat of the sun and little rain at that time of the year.

They turned left up the lower slopes of the dormant volcano, Haleakala, climbing to about 550 feet elevation.

"This is a new subdivision, called "Maui Meadows," said Helen. "Prior to this, the land belonged to Ulupalakua Ranch, above us. I'm sharing a rental house here with a friend I met on the beach. I was just sitting there with little Neil when this big fluffy dog came up to me—and you know what a sucker I am for dogs—and its owner said,

"My name's 'Wade,' what's yours?"

"He's a builder, and they're going to develop condominiums along the coast; he works for the developer. Actually, he's Irish from Boston originally, with an elder brother and four sisters; he's the youngest. His father was a Colonel in the army, so he had a strict military upbringing. He was two or three years in Vietnam, and then he worked in the West Indies, but decided he wanted a change, so he moved to Maui, in Hawaii. He's a bit taller than you, Daddy, and nice-looking. I hope you'll like him."

She turned left into the driveway. It was a single story Pole house, raised up, so there was plenty of room to park underneath. She carried one of the cases and Neil carried the other one, following Helen up the wood steps to a railed balcony running around the house. Glass slider doors opened to a kitchen and living room with high, peaked ceilings and a beautiful polished wood floor, and sliders to a deck on the opposite wall—with a view to die for.

The land dropped away to the coast road and the ocean they had just left. It was peaceful, with scarcely a sound. She led the way into a bedroom at one end of the house, and showed them the separate bathroom. Little Neil's bedroom was adjacent, the main bedroom being at the opposite end of the house, with its own bathroom—a fairly standard layout, Jeannie discovered much later.

They dumped the suitcases in the bedroom, and then sat in the living room with Helen, who brought them all tall cold drinks.

"This wasn't the first place I found," she said, "in fact it was sort by accident I arrived on the island of Maui. I was at the airport in Honolulu, trying to decide which island to go to, when a young guy came and sat down beside me. He asked me where I was going and I told him I was trying to make up my mind. He said,

"Catch a flight to Maui. I was there for a year; it's the nicest of the islands."

"So, that's what I did."

"I had the child, my typewriter, a suitcase, and a small pop-up tent, so at Maui airport I rented a car and asked where I could camp. They directed me to Baldwin Beach, where there's a small campground."

" Next morning I thought I'd try to find a rental of some sort and I drove upcountry—up Haleakala. I came to a very small village and went into a Chinese store to find something to eat and to ask the owner if he knew of any rentals. A lady, shopping in there, said to me,

"Where are you staying?" When I told her I was camping at Baldwin Beach she was horrified.

"You can't camp there with the child," she said, "you must come and stay with my husband and myself while you look for a rental. My name is Inez Ashdown."

"So I stayed with them for three weeks. They were very kind. It turned out she was a historian, who had written books about Hawaii. Before World War II, her husband leased land from the Territory—Hawaii wasn't a State until 1959—and tried to get a ranch going on the island of Kahoolawe—built a ranch house there, in fact, and took some cattle over, and planted Norfolk Pine and Eucalyptus trees and seeded grass; water was the problem and trees attract clouds. But then, during the war, Kahoolawe was used for bombing practice, so he had to leave the island and there are so many spent shells and undiscovered ordnance that it is not safe to go there. Inez wrote a book about Kahoolawe as she remembered it. I found a rental in Kihei at first, but then I met Wade and we decided to move to Maui Meadows."

Helen then said, "I must cook supper. Wade will be back soon and he'll be hungry. Unpack and make yourselves at home, and then come and sit in the living room or out on the deck, and watch the sunset. It sets around 6:45 PM at this time of the year."

"I'm running the bar of a restaurant down on the coast five evenings a week, so you can come down there with me and get something to eat and drink one evening; it's nice because it's right on the ocean. I've been making wall hangings for the place because it's only just been opened and the owners wanted to make it look a bit 'different.'"

Neil and Jeannie looked at each other across the bed, both thinking the same thing—is this really our daughter who has suddenly become so versatile and self-sufficient?

They had to remind themselves that it had been five years since she left home to live in America.

CHAPTER 27

REMINISCENCES OF A MAUI VACATION

At this point in their lives, Neil and Jeannie did not know when, if ever, they would return to Maui so, bearing in mind the current trend to record vacations on slide film, the better to explain a vacation to friends, they took photos of anything and everything which might help to provide a clear history of their somewhat unusual adventure into—almost—uncharted territory.

Helen had acquired an American WWII Army Jeep, which traversed dirt roads without hesitancy, so they used it to venture along the dirt track, the continuation of the coast road below Maui Meadows where they were staying in Helen's rented Pole house.

Pole houses are of a somewhat unique design incredibly suited to building on rocky or uneven terrain, particularly in a hot climate, where the need to keep the sun off glass is paramount and the ability to take advantage of any breeze beneficial. In Jeannie's mind nothing could compete with it, yet there were those new to the tropics who still persisted in building Malibu mansions in which air conditioning was required to survive in spite of being surrounded by ocean where the air should be pure.

As far as construction, the poles are raised first, usually standing on a concrete block and held in place by right-angled steel brackets. Pole height can counter any deviation in ground level. Next, weight-bearing beams are carried by a notch in the poles plus a bolt for additional stability, for both floors and roof, walls being installed last, allowing for almost any permutation of room size. Roofs have a minimum three feet overhang—often extended to four or even six feet to provide a shady place to sit—and since a deck frequently surrounds the entire house—one can move if seeking shade or breeze. The peak, all of its length, is ventilated with screened space between it and a little "roof" of its own.

Jeannie thought a prime advantage was that it kept the bugs, rats and mice out because, if necessary, a sticky substance could be placed around the poles. Fine wire mesh screens deterred flying insects when windows or sliders were opened. Ceiling fans in every room ensured air circulation. Living in the humidity of the tropics was a whole new learning experience.

In 1975, Maui had barely been discovered by the traveling public, most of whom preferred to enjoy the beaches and nightlife of Waikiki, on Oahu, where the city of Honolulu far exceeded the size and notoriety of the old whaling town of Lahaina in West Maui, the original capital of the islands. That suited Neil and Jeannie just fine; neither of them sought cities or crowds. Peace, quiet, natural beauty and a little interesting history mixed in with some sunshine constituted their idea of a summer vacation—anywhere. That had always been one of the most satisfying things about their relationship, and the children fell in with it for the most part.

Wailuku, about eight miles directly across the flat center of Maui, was still the County Town, with its Law Courts, attorneys, County buildings and anything else connected with running the place, but commercial shipping and—latterly—an airport had necessitated the development of Kahului, lying in the Central Valley, with a harbor, stores and supply houses, a hospital, police department, homes and schools. So that is where Neil and Jeannie ventured in the Jeep one day with Helen, to shop.

They were halfway back across the cane fields when there was an ominous knocking sound, and Helen pulled over onto a stretch of rough grass at the side of the road—in the middle of "nowhere."

"Sounds as though one of the big-end bearings on the crankshaft has gone," said Neil. "You can't go on driving it like that."

The wind blowing the tall sugar cane, added to the feeling of isolation, but Helen said, with the utmost confidence,

"Don't worry. The first person to come along the road will stop."

They waited for about ten minutes; a truck appeared in the distance. Its driver, dressed in a grubby T-shirt and wearing dark glasses in the glaring sunlight, stopped.

"Where be goin'? Need a tow?"

Helen said, "Great! Thanks for stopping. Kihei will do—road's flat to there. Then I can get help."

He reached for a coil of rope in the bed of the truck and Neil jumped down to help attach it to the truck and the Jeep: "Looks as though you travel prepared?"

"'s'okay. 's way us live—helpin' each other."

Neil climbed in beside him. Helen steered the Jeep, Jeannie next to her, with little Neil on her lap.

"I told you so," Helen said. "No-one has to wait long for help, here."

Wade was certainly a tall man—about 6 feet 7 inches, thought Jeannie—a mine of inconsequential information, no matter the subject—demanding if he chose to be, but he had a certain charm; no doubt the Irish in him!

He and Helen decided to take their visitors to Hana on Sunday, driving south-west along the coast, with its view of the outer islands, and returning by way of the winding, hilly, east coast, cut into the cliff-side for much of its route. They decided that the "Maui cruiser" might not make it all the way and that it would be better to take a rental car—in spite of the fact that a rental was only supposed to take the paved easterly road. They found the most roomy car available, Wade pushed the passenger seat back as far as it would go, to cater to his tall frame, and Jeannie suggested Neil sit behind Helen, who was driving and liked to have the seatback upright; Jeannie could sit with her legs diagonally across onto his side, if necessary.

They had to drive across the island and halfway up Haleakala in order then to drop down onto the southwest coast; there was no more direct route. The views, of course, were amazing, and the visitors wanted to stop every few minutes to record them until Wade reminded them they were trying to get to Hana for lunch, not an evening meal!

They must be content to take photos from the moving car. The road up Haleakala was narrow but had two lanes. Going down through ranches, it was a narrow dirt road, and there were times when they had difficulty getting around corners due to the width and length of the car. Climbing, the corner was completely blind, so it was a trip reminiscent of some of those made in Scotland—apart from the brilliant Pacific views.

Lunch was welcome—and earned—by the time they entered the Hana Hotel, where Wade was apparently a presence to be reckoned with, judging by the prompt and detailed service they received. The building had a feeling of the Old West, and Jeannie couldn't help wondering if he'd beaten someone at a card game!

It was at least a two-hour drive back to Kahului on the coast road on a good day, but a scenic wonder. There were 56 bridges—each of them with a single lane for traffic, and more blind curves than you could ever imagine; a road it is almost easier to drive at night, where headlights forewarn the presence of an approaching vehicle. In 1975 there was greater danger of a deer or a rock-fall than of a vehicle.

Another day, in the "Maui Cruiser" with Helen, they explored the west end of the island, starting at Wailuku and taking the one precarious route all the way to Lahaina. It was then a dirt road all the way, mainly cut into the cliffs—fine for dogs and horses! Parts reminded Jeannie of Cornwall, in England's west country. The steep track descended into the little fishing village of Kahakuloa—with its own tiny wooden church—and climbed abruptly out of it. The beach on that northeast shore consisted of pebbles rubbed flat and smooth from friction caused by the tides. A few wooden houses lined one side of the road and a valley, where a fast flowing stream ran into the ocean.

The track undulated along the cliff-top, offering occasional opportunities to explore intriguing rocky outcrops and springs of fresh water, all the time with phenomenal coastal and ocean views made ethereal by the constant brilliant blue of sea and sky.

As they neared Lahaina, they could see that development was beginning to take place.

"This is called Kaanapali," Helen explained. "One hotel has just been finished. We'll drive up here for a luau before you leave. You'll be able to hear Hawaiian music and see hula dancing and how a whole pig is cooked in the ground. It's traditional but now they do it once a week to entertain guests."

In Lahaina, Helen explained how it had been a port for whaling ships. The visitors stopped to get some lunch at the Pioneer Inn, which was built at that time. They walked along Front Street, where some of the stores still overhang the water as the waves lap the seawall. On the other side of the street was the Missionary House, now open for visitors to see the austere interior. Missionaries were sent from the East Coast because Hawaiians were considered heathens for worshipping their own gods and dancing nearly naked and barefoot. Imagine what it must have been like for them to be made to wear voluminous Victorian dresses with lace up to their throats, and long sleeves, in ninety-degree temperatures!

The Prison still stands just outside town, surrounded by a rock wall—at one time occupied, no doubt, by more than one drunken sailor upon his return from a whaling expedition.

The town was pretty because of the old buildings and many flowering trees with sweet-smelling blossoms, but it was very hot, due to being sheltered from the northeast trade winds by the West Maui Mountains. Jeannie was quite happy to drive back to Maui Meadows, where it seemed there was nearly always a breeze, even on the hottest day.

The beaches there were wonderful, too, with sand, safe bathing, and gently lapping waves. The very first hotel—the Intercontinental—was being built in Wailea, the next tiny village south of Kihei—and Wade was busy working on it.

At the entry to the Wailea area was a new eight-story concrete condominium, with a restaurant and a few shops on the first floor, and a nice swimming pool. A condominium consists of self-contained apartments, which can be sold and owned separately by individuals. They can then either live there or rent them for weeks at a time to vacationers, whilst paying a maintenance fee for the upkeep of the building and grounds. It was a new concept for Maui at that time, but soon almost the entire coastline would be occupied by a variety of condominiums.

Jeannie thought she would have plenty of material and photographs for her Commerce classes at school as a result of this vacation, quite apart from being able to entertain friends at dinner parties.

CHAPTER 28

NORMANDY, THE CAR—AND THE END OF THE ROAD?

In 1974, Neil and Jeannie were traveling on their own again, so they took Jeannie's new Austin Mini, having run up about 150,000 miles on the original one, which sat like an outgrown baby carriage on one side of the turn-around at the top of the driveway, until one day Douglas asked his father,

"Daddy, can I strip it down and rebuild it, please? I'm sure I can find some parts in a scrap-yard."

Neil never did anything by halves. He thought privately it would be a golden opportunity for his older son to learn how to build a car—but he wanted the boy to own something rewarding for his pains.

Minis did not have a chassis—a frame on which everything else was built—which was how all cars had been constructed up until the advent of the Mini, so by the time Douglas had stripped it all down, he was left with four wheels, a sub-frame, a transverse engine and its adjacent gearbox—the two latter having seen better days—so Neil based his son's next needs on the sub-frame; they would rebuild the car from that point.

He obtained the parts of the car—legally, of course—in the order in which they needed to be assembled, and if Douglas was unable to figure that out, Neil told him. The exciting part was when it came to the engine. There was a "hotted-up" sports car version, bench-tested in the workshop so, to his son's total delight, Neil obtained that and brought it home for him.

Douglas rebuilt the car right down to the interior trim; even as a youngster he had patience for detail. Finally, the only thing left structurally, was painting. Neil arranged for it to go into the paint-shop, from which it emerged lime-yellow with black trim. The Tax Department re-registered it as a three-year old vehicle.

"Mum, do you want to come for a run with me?" said her proud son, after Jeannie had admired his handiwork.

"I'd love to." Jeannie sat in the passenger seat, fastening the seatbelt tightly.

The engine sounded as though it was about to start up on a racetrack which, of course, was exactly how it was meant to sound, since, on the bench, it had been built for a sports car. Douglas lifted his foot off the clutch, dropping the car into gear, as he accelerated—and Jeannie felt as though she was flying out of the rear window, the torque was so great.

"Slow down!" she said. "You'll kill yourself with this thing!

He just laughed. "It's great, isn't it? Daddy knew what he was doing when he got this engine for me. There won't be another car on the road like this."

"You'll need a new set of tires in a month if you drive it like that," said Jeannie, "and I'm not buying them for you!"

After the initial "showing-off" period with his envious friends, Douglas treated his new creation like the justifiably proud owner he was.

His brother, not to be outdone, even if just a step behind all the time, sold his motorbike and acquired a van he proceeded to inject with new life, mainly in the form of attention to body dents, plugs and paint! When you also acquire a girlfriend, four wheels are often preferable to two unless, like his parents, gas was rationed and they lived miles apart.

The boys didn't just each have a girlfriend, they had an entourage of both sexes. Case in point: their parents' friends, Hetty and Phil, were driving home to Derbyshire from Cornwall. Hetty was pregnant, and tired, so they decided to stop by to see Neil and Jeannie, knowing they would be welcome and could break their journey for the night.

They turned into the driveway, to find it packed with cars, trucks and motorbikes! They decided Neil and Jeannie were having a party, so they continued on their way. In actual fact, they were sitting in the lounge—alone! The "traffic" all belonged to the boys' friends! It seemed as though their home was a regular ***rendez-vous***, but Neil and Jeannie didn't mind—at least they knew where the boys were! Or they went out as a foursome with their two girlfriends.

So, in 1974 their parents decided they would explore Normandy and the wine country, having driven through both regions many times but never having spent much time there. It was fun with the huge tent for just the two of them, and Jeannie's new Mini. Keeping the traveling time down, they had more time for exploration—and each other. They visited many of the towns and the countryside familiar during World War II, much of which had been a safe haven for escapees, with the devoted assistance of the French Resistance, through whom many would-be prisoners were safely smuggled across the English Channel to the United Kingdom. Before returning home, they drove to Averanches, which was the site of Mulberry Harbour 'B', evidence of which was still visible when the Channel waves were calm.

They arranged to meet the boys at Le Havre this time and to ride the ferry back as passengers to Newhaven, where they found the large "spare car" which they kept for emergency in case one of the other four broke down and one of the family was unable to get to work. Living out in the country, though wonderful, had its own problems as far as transport was concerned.

The boys and their girlfriends set off joyfully on vacation in Neil's company car, complete with the all-too-familiar camping equipment, while Neil and Jeannie drove home; Jeannie with a week to prepare for the new school year. Neil didn't have that luxury; he had a business meeting in Coventry the next day.

The 'phone rang at about 4:30 PM.

"Please come and pick me up from Coventry," he said, "my car's been stolen out of the parking lot."

The police found it about a week later in the back streets of Birmingham. It was not damaged but there was no petrol in it—and Duncan's fishing rod was missing. Things could have been worse. At least Neil had it back so that Jeannie could use her own car to get to school.

They collected Mum from the retirement home—being told firmly there would be no mutual concession regarding her return in the future. Apparently she had made a nuisance of herself. Jeannie thought, this is the end of the road—next time it will have to be the hospital, this is the third place where she has worn out her welcome.

It had all happened since Mum suffered a nervous breakdown after her cataract operation, but since they were abroad each year, the people who ran each facility kept Mum there until Neil and Jeannie returned. Mum tried to explain her operation experience to Jeannie, which seemed to be too gruesome to even think about, with no improvement to her sight since she refused contact lenses or thick glasses, and was worse off than with gradual deterioration of her sight.

She had other physical problems of very old age, which made caring for her very difficult. She was ninety-five, able to walk and dress herself. She lived on the ground floor only, and a nurse came in to give her a "bed bath." She was able to eat everything Jeannie prepared, and she lived with Neil and Jeannie for eleven years. It was sad to see her incapacitated when they remembered how she had been when she lived in Exeter, and all the years before that.

But Jeannie had to consider Neil, too. He needed their annual vacation. Life was not easy for him at work and it seemed to her he was under too much stress. Long hours and union problems—and he dropped asleep in a chair almost every evening, not having the energy to join in discussions with his sons. Jeannie managed to find a care home for Mum when they went to Maui in 1975, but that was to be the last time.

In 1976 Jeannie asked Mum's doctor to arrange for her to stay in a hospital while they were away. The boys were at home this time, each of them with a job to go to daily. As soon as their parents arrived home from another holiday in Europe, they said that the hospital called to request Jeannie, as next of kin, to go there immediately.

When Jeannie entered the ward she was told that Mum was in a coma. She had collapsed when walking back from the bathroom the previous week, but she recovered from that and they kept her in bed. Then she lost consciousness and had been in a coma ever since.

She was propped up in bed and her eyes were closed. The Ward Nurse said,

"She will be able to hear you; hearing is always the last sense to go."

Jeannie kissed her Mum on the forehead and, holding her hand, she said,

"Mum, this is Jeannie. We're home again; we just got back and I came straight over to the hospital to see you. Have a good night's sleep and I'll see you in the morning."

She kissed her again and asked the Ward Nurse to call if there was any change.

A half hour later, Jeannie had just arrived home when the 'phone rang. The Ward Nurse said,

"Your mother has just passed away; she waited for you to come home, you see."

Jeannie accepted how superstitious the nurses became in a ward constantly dealing with death.

Jeannie said, "Thank you for letting me know. I'll leave a message for my undertaker; he's standing by, waiting to hear from me. As you know, I arranged for that when I left, just in case mother died before we got home."

"You should never have gone, knowing she might die." The Ward Nurse was irate.

"I do not have to justify my actions to you," said Jeannie. "She was in the best place, in a hospital. My husband and I have looked after her for twelve years and there was no more we could do. I have a living family, all of whom need my care. I will make sure she goes to join the one she loved—my father—who lies waiting for her in Devonshire."

Jeannie didn't explain what she meant; it was of no concern to the nurse. She arranged with the undertaker for the hearse to transport the coffin to the local village church in Devonshire, where it would remain for the service on Saturday, and in the meantime she arranged for the grave to be opened to receive the coffin. The village undertaker remembered her family, even though none of them had lived there since her mother left for the house in Exeter after World War II. She ordered wreaths, to travel on the coffin in the hearse, which would remain on the coffin for the church service.

Jeannie was astounded at the number of people who attended the service, and the beautiful wreaths placed around the coffin. Her family had been very well-known and there were already graves in the cemetery for Aunt Martha, Mum's older sister, and her husband; Grandma, who had lived with Aunt Martha in "The Bungalow" after Mum and Dad built "High Hills" and moved into it; her Aunt Alice, Daddy's sister, who had a heart attack and died when she was staying with them in 1939; and her uncle, who took over Daddy's business; and Daddy himself, who was interred in a double grave in January 1940—it lay just to the right of the lych gate, the entry to the cemetery. The grave had now been opened to receive Mum's coffin. Jeannie arranged for Mum's name to join Daddy's on the gravestone, and the date of her demise.

Neil and Jeannie stood at the church door to thank everyone who attended the service; she said her Mum would be so honored that they came. She thought that the local undertaker must have spread the news; the present Rector would not have known Mum and the Vicar in Exeter had already moved on to another Parish.

They followed the hearse to the cemetery for the interment and left the wreaths to be arranged on the grave when the soil had been replaced.

Neil and Jeannie drove into Exeter and stayed at the Rougemont Hotel for the night. On Sunday morning they returned to the cemetery and Neil took a photo of his wife saying a final goodbye to her mother, who played a large part in their lives before she ever came to live with them for twelve years.

Although they were glad that her suffering for the past five years had ended for all of them, it was very sad. She had spent 36 years without Jeannie's father. Before he died in January 1940, she had a happily married life of just 30 years—minus four years when the Great War had stolen him from her for Service abroad to his country.

We tend to take so much for granted and seldom realize how fragile life can be.

CHAPTER 29

HOUSE SWAP

In May 1977 Jeannie received a letter from Helen in Maui. The neighbors, John and Juliet, living across the street in Maui Meadows were planning a vacation in England and Scotland in August and they wondered if they could arrange a "house swap" with Neil and Jeannie since Helen had mentioned they might be visiting Maui again in August?

Correspondence ensued. Jeannie ended up planning their entire trip for them, including making reservations at suitable hotels en route for a trip by car—Neil's car—encompassing the Lake District in Cumbria, two-thirds of Scotland, bringing them back through Edinburgh, and south through Yorkshire and Lincolnshire, full circle to Neil and Jeannie's lovely country home on a hilltop about twenty miles from Stratford-upon-Avon.

Neil and Jeannie arranged to meet them upon arrival at Brown's Hotel, where they were to stay in London. Their anticipated arrival brought back memories of the first visit to Maui in 1975.

Only a few moments passed before Juliet opened the door wide in response to the Canterbury chimes of the bell. The carefully painted red lips expressed her welcoming smile, but the mischievous blue eyes confirmed its sincerity.

"Do come in," she said, "how wonderful to meet you at last. We've heard so much about you. Now, I want to learn all about your trip—and your first impressions of Maui!"

This was Jeannie's initial introduction to Juliet. In the weeks and years to follow she was to experience many facets of her life but throughout it all she radiated kindness and joy and expressed a genuine interest in others, no matter their station in life. Always vivacious and sweet, Juliet saw goodness in everyone and appeared blind to the machinations of those who would take advantage of her seemingly innocent nature.

Although in her late sixties, Juliet maintained the elegance and grace of her days as a model, and when, in the privacy of her home, she allowed her lovely wavy hair to cascade over her bare shoulders, one could well understand how her outwardly staid husband found her irresistible. She had an exquisite taste in clothes and wore her hair high on her head with several blossoms pinned jauntily into it, emphasizing her long neck and chiseled features.

Neil and Jeannie left home quite early for London because it was Neil's intention to drive out along the Thames for lunch. They picked up John and Juliet at Brown's Hotel and Neil explained how they were going to spend the day; they were thrilled at the thought. As always, Jeannie was intrigued by the ease with which Neil found his way; it didn't matter where they went in Britain or Europe, he seemed to have an intuitive sense of direction. They arrived at a restaurant straddling a portion of the river, offering an interesting view of the river traffic—in fact so much so that the visitors were reluctant to leave.

That evening they all shared a taxi to the "Cave" restaurant in the Strand, so called because it was located below ground. It offered a dance floor and an excellent pianist.

Halfway through the meal, Juliet approached the pianist and asked whether he could play Hawaiian music. He responded that he used to be a musician on a cruise ship and would be happy to play for her. She stepped alone and barefoot onto the intimate dance floor and gently swayed into a graceful hula. Waiters, in their black pants, white shirts and bow ties stood back against the walls, watching, some still balancing a silver tray on one upraised hand. The clatter of knives and forks on china ceased as diners stopped eating, and the only sound was the gentle melody of the piano. There was a moment's silence when the tune came to an end, and then the entire room erupted into applause, followed by the clinking of glasses and appreciative laughter. It felt as though Juliet, in her inimitable way, had made friends of a roomful of strangers.

Later, the four of them went upstairs to their two respective bedrooms at Brown's. Juliet's husband preceded her and held back the door for her to enter. With a little sensuous sway of her hips she stepped into the room, turning her head for a brief moment to blow Neil and Jeannie a 'goodnight' kiss with a broad smile and a twinkle in those devastating blue eyes.

The next day they all left London after breakfast and Neil and Jeannie took their guests home, and introduced them to their sons, who would be there to take care of things when John and Juliet returned from their exciting trip to Scotland. At the same time, Neil and Jeannie prepared to leave for Maui.

Jeannie was careful to select direct routes, avoiding cities, to make the trip as easy as possible to navigate, since their guests had never driven anywhere in Europe, let alone in Great Britain on the left side of the road; they had never dealt with roundabouts—circles—and they were accustomed to a car with automatic transmission, not a stick shift. There were very few cars with automatic transmission in Great Britain at that time. Due to the hilly nature of the roads, it was not considered desirable.

None of this had ever presented problems to Neil and Jeannie, who accepted driving on the right in almost every other country in Western Europe—even with a right-hand drive car—as "normal"—and going around roundabouts in the opposite direction because you were driving on the other side of the street. It didn't faze them in the least. And as far as Douglas and Duncan were concerned, they'd never given it a thought either.

But of course America is a large country and comparatively few of its citizens, in spite of having traveled abroad, ever drive anywhere else on the opposite side of the road. Neil promised that he would give their visitors a little practice before letting them loose on British roads, including getting into and out of roundabouts; apart from their safety—he was concerned for his poor car!

Then Helen called on the 'phone and spoke with her father. She and Wade married on Maui in 1976 and he obtained his General Contractor's license, with the thought of running his own business instead of working for someone else. They qualified for a mortgage to buy the land on the rising ground above the pole house they were renting, and were building a pole house style cottage on it "for your retirement, Daddy." They had run out of money.

Neil discussed all this with Jeannie and said he preferred to take out a small loan against their house to using cash or investments, since they owned their property free and clear. It was not a normal thing to do in England, and the bank required that Neil should have a thorough medical examination. This was how they discovered that he had an enlarged heart and dangerously high blood pressure—in fact so dangerously high that his doctor didn't want Neil to fly.

They had their airline tickets and they'd made all the arrangements for the visitors to stay in the house with the boys, who were both working, so in the end the doctor gave Neil medication to take and made him promise not to exert himself at all and to go back and consult with him when he returned.

The extreme danger did not even sink in with Neil and Jeannie. He had always been so incredibly strong and healthy, and in those days in Great Britain, regular check-ups just didn't happen. They blamed the fact that Neil was frequently tired, and could barely manage to finish an evening meal before falling asleep, on work related stress. It never occurred to Neil that he should mention these symptoms to his doctor. They didn't link anything to the high blood pressure because they didn't know that was what high blood pressure did to a person. In subsequent, more enlightened times, this all seems crazy—but that's the way it was in 1977.

Everything worked out well in regard to the house-swap. The boys and their girlfriends had great fun with the visitors when they returned safely from their Scottish trip, introducing them to various colorful "pubs" and trying to make them understand that in Britain you didn't have to tip the barman! Not in 1977, anyway. It was also the beginning of the era whereby the best of the pubs provided an evening meal, leading to the eventual demise of many restaurants unlicensed for the sale of liquor.

The visitors were intrigued by activity in the orchard behind the house, taking their nightly cocktails, to watch quietly, while seated in a couple of garden chairs, the wild rabbits and hares in the moonlight.

The hares stood on their haunches to eat the bark on the fruit trees, probably because it contained sap, ignorant and uncaring that such activity might kill the tree if they gnawed all the way around it! Jeannie had to surround the base of the trees with wire netting when she returned.

Neil and Jeannie enjoyed a relaxing vacation during their second visit to Maui. Wade had commenced working independently and was in the process of building several private luxury homes with his own construction crew. Few people occupied the nearest beaches and they both went home with a tropical tan and even more stories relating to life in the tropics.

CHAPTER 30

REPLANTING ROOTS

On April 1 1978, Douglas and his long time girl friend, Sandi, were married by way of a lovely formal church wedding and a beautiful reception at a country inn catering to such occasions. There were many guests of both families and the young couple spent a brief honeymoon in the Cotswolds, since the groom planned to leave for Maui to join Helen and Wade in his construction enterprise, with the bride following as soon as he got settled with work and somewhere to live. They both had Resident Alien cards, and since she was a trained Dental Hygienist she did not anticipate it would be difficult for her to find work. Douglas stayed with his sister when she was in California, before she decided to move to Hawaii, and, of course, he met Wade when he and Helen flew back for a vacation in 1976 after grandma died.

In 1978, work for both Neil and Jeannie turned from bad to worse. Union troubles were invading not only industry, but education as well. Jeannie was Secretary of the second largest Teachers' Union, City of Birmingham Branch, for the past two or three years and oversaw the amalgamation of the male and female teachers of that Branch of the union in the process, making several trips by train to headquarters in London.

The other catastrophe was the retirement of the school's Principal, who was always so supportive of creative ideas benefiting the students in any way, and obtained the necessary funds from the City to implement them.

A school building never provides the inspiration in any context; everything depends upon the knowledge, creativity and dedication of the people within it.

The Principal's replacement had no desire to follow through with her predecessor's creative ideas, preferring to concentrate on the required basic education for students to the school-leaving age of sixteen. She didn't interrupt the existing extended Courses, but accepted that the entire school system throughout Britain was gradually being changed, so that Grammar schools and Secondary Modern Schools were replaced by Comprehensive Schools catering to all abilities, rather than, as existed, the necessity for students to take exams at the young age of eleven in order to determine the type of education available to them subsequently. Jeannie didn't expect to be short of a job, but she knew, ultimately, it would entail a change of venue—most likely to a Technical College, catering to any extended courses, which would no longer prevail at any High School.

That summer Neil and Jeannie were on their own once again exploring Western Europe spending time in Switzerland, staying at Interlaken, taking the rack railway up the Jungfrau and enjoying the beauty and solitude of the mountains, then slowly wending their way back through France. With over a week to spare before they crossed the English Channel to drive home, Neil said,

"Maybe we should call home to make sure the house is still standing."

It was a joke, because Duncan and his girlfriend, Carrie, were at home.

Jeannie made the call, and Duncan answered the 'phone.

"Everything's fine," he said in answer to her question, "but Helen is due here in four or five days—before you're due back anyway."

After she put the 'phone down and explained what was going on, Neil said,

"We'd better go back. It's a shame for her to fly all that way and then to have to wait for us to arrive. We've had a pretty good vacation and the weather doesn't seem very promising now anyway."

So that is what they did. As they were driving back through France, Jeannie said,

"I've got a gut feeling this is the last time we're going to be doing this; she's come back to move us. If we go, we'll have to take Duncan with us; he won't want to stay here alone because, for one thing, we'll sell the property."

Neil didn't make any comment but she noticed his lips move into a tiny smile.

Jeannie watched the familiar peaceful countryside as they kept a steady pace along the road, and she thought about the reason they anticipated Helen had come home so unexpectedly. She recalled Annie, the Gypsy Fortune Teller at her grandma's old Norfolk inn . . .

" . . . and you will be married to a tall, handsome man and you will have three children but one of them will leave you. Then you will travel a very long way from here, and you will live in the sunshine with lots of dark-skinned people. You will be very happy, and then—and then—I can't tell you any more . . ."

Neil reached for her hand and squeezed it tightly. "You're very quiet," he said, "what's the matter?"

"I was thinking about something that happened years ago, when I was a little kid, just eight years old, it sort of gave me the creeps. What are you going to say if Helen wants us to move?"

"What do you want me to say?"

"You'll think of something. Whatever you want to do, I'll just come along for the ride. You haven't disappointed me so far. I love you, darling."

"I love you, too. There's the ferry—and we're not going to be last on this time! Are you hungry? If we get something to eat it will save stopping on the way home, and perhaps there'll be time for a roll in the hay before we get a good night's sleep!"

"You have a one-track mind," she said.

They arrived home safely and unpacked their personal things from the car the next day. Jeannie always hated that job, partly because of the finality of it "until the next time" and partly because there was so much to sort out and so much laundry to do! Duncan took the car and the camping equipment for a brief vacation with his girlfriend, Carrie.

Then the 'phone rang.

"I'm at the train station in Birmingham," said Helen. "I'm going to catch the City bus out to Northfield. I've only got a carry-on bag so it's not a problem. I didn't think you'd be home yet, that's why I caught the train from London. Can someone come and pick me up?"

"I'll go and fetch her," Neil said, and Jeannie repeated that into the 'phone.

Helen preceded Neil into the house.

"This is a surprise," said Jeannie. "What brings you all this way so suddenly?"

Helen said, "I've only got a couple of weeks so I can't waste any time; a friend came to take care of little Neil. I've come to help you make arrangements to move. Daddy, you're not well and you can't go on working until you drop.

Wade's going to be busy and we could do with some help estimating jobs. I obtained my citizenship all those years ago so it would help you with immigration; Douglas has come over to help with the work and I'm sure Duncan can soon learn to use a backhoe, with his training and experience with heavy equipment."

"We need to get the yard cleaned up and fresh gravel spread on the driveway, ready for you to put the house on the market. Let's look in the paper to find guys who'll come and do that. Who will you get to sell the place, and what are you going to do with all the furniture?"

It hit them like a bombshell, but they suddenly realized this was "the way out." It was unlike Neil not to have some questions or suggestions. Jeannie couldn't recall his ever having denied her anything—totally—she tended to "jump in where angels fear to tread" so he would modify things a bit—always for the better—but he had never said, "No."

Later, she commented to Helen—"Did you notice that Daddy didn't say 'Yes,—but' as he always does, and then adds his special provision? He just said that he'd arrange for a new Triumph Spitfire sports car to be exported to you before we move to Hawaii. This will be the last opportunity he'll have to do so before he retires. It shows he realizes he needs to stop working."

"It's not quite so easy for me or for Duncan because all my students are dependent upon me for their Finals this year, and it's important for Duncan to have this year's practical experience to add to his resume. His job offers good potential so he may be reluctant to leave."

Helen followed her instincts, and the next day a small army of workers descended on the yard, trimming hedges, weeding and cleaning it up, and they spread loads of medium-sized cream-colored gravel on the driveway.

It looked so clean and elegant that Jeannie said, "I don't know why we didn't have that done ages ago so that we could have enjoyed it. I guess we were both too busy working to think about it and to realize how nice it would look."

She was nearly in tears at the thought of having to leave, because that little bit of additional attention made her realize what a lovely property Neil had provided for them all with his decision to buy the land and build, all those years ago. It set off the lovely Tudor-style home to perfection. Now that leaving was so imminent she was looking at their home with new eyes—no wonder everyone had admired it, especially since it was furnished with antiques inherited from their two families.

A salesman from a real estate company, with branches in Birmingham and towns in Worcestershire and Warwickshire, responded to their call. They arrived at an acceptable asking price and arranged with him to install a sign down by the entrance, and to put all their antiques, including china, into an antique sale after the property sold.

Then they began to turn out the house, starting at the top, room by room, sorting out the things they would keep and those they would dispose of, either to friends or to places which would benefit—such as the local library, which gladly took an entire collection of books which had belonged to Neil's father.

They packed boxes to be shipped to Hawaii in a crate. They held a Garage Sale—unique in England—the alternative being a Jumble Sale at the Village Hall. But their sale included a unique collection of 78rpm and 33rpm records—many of them precious memories of brief wartime leaves together in the little bungalow in the yard at Jeannie's Mum's house in Devonshire—eagerly snatched up in their entirety by an avid collector. And they almost filled a huge dumpster three times with trash.

At the end of the second week Helen had to fly back—and Jeannie faced the first day of the Autumn Term—knowing only too well that she had made no preparation for it. It was the second day that it hit her—***I cannot deal with this; it is too much work and I've lost all my inspiration. I've been working too hard for too many years, and I just can't face it any more.***

She collapsed into tears when she knocked at the door of the Principal's office.

"Go home. You cannot be in school like that. I will get your Department Deputy to take over until you are fit to return."

She didn't know how she managed to drive home. At one point she found she had steered the car up onto the sidewalk. The next conscious moment was after the tires hit a raised pedestrian crossing. She thought, I've got to get off the main road; I'll drive up the lanes to our home. Thankfully, she reached the driveway, and left the car in the turnaround at the top by the house.

Neil came home from work and found her lying on the bed in hysterics. It was so out of character for her to be like that, he didn't know what to do.

Duncan came home and, seeing the "For Sale" sign at the entrance and the new gravel, thought he'd turned into the wrong driveway! Carrie told them afterwards that Duncan's first words were: "I'm not going; I'm staying here."

Jeannie did not return to school that term. She received sedatives from the doctor, and Duncan's girlfriend, Carrie, saved everyone's life and sanity by living at the house, cooking the evening meals and generally looking after everything, while Jeannie descended helplessly into "zombieland." It had all been too much, too fast—and too great a shock to the system. She had a nervous breakdown.

Sandi flew out of Heath Row to join Douglas, who was working with Wade and Helen on Maui—only to be asked, two days after her arrival, for a divorce from Douglas, who had met a photographer Helen knew in California, who was now recording the visit to Maui of an established mainland musical group. With no compunction about his situation, or her 12-year seniority, she told Helen she would not leave Maui without Douglas—having promised him an exciting future in the Hollywood "scene" where—she said—he would have the opportunity to study lighting for stage and film.

Helen was left to pick up the pieces for her ex-sister-in-law whom she got established working as a dental hygienist with the foremost dental surgeon in Maui.

The house sold in October. Neighbors across the lane whom they scarcely knew were visiting Tasmania prior to moving there, and were happy to let Neil, Jeannie and Duncan stay in their centrally heated home during the winter months, complete with their two precious cats, "Tiddles" and "Toots."

Weeks passed. The fact that she would be unlikely to be granted entry into the United States with a doubtful mental record forced Jeannie to pull out of the breakdown. In November, she and Neil had to go for interviews in London at the American Embassy, complete with medical reports.

Jeannie had the most wonderful American doctor. She told him, as briefly as possible, what had happened.

He patted her on the knee, and said, kindly, "My dear, you're ***just like*** my wife—you try to ***do*** too much. You'll be fine."

Late that year, Neil and Jeannie covered the country from north to south and east to west, saying "goodbye" to friends and relatives.

Jeannie's cousin, Martha—named for their aunt—said, "How can you leave your 'roots'?"

Jeannie told her, "You can take a plant and nurture it, give it soil it loves and water it each day, and it will put out new roots. Don't worry."

She was a long way from feeling "right" but destiny had stepped in and pointed the way; there was no turning back.

Neil was given a suitable, somewhat envious send-off at work, and Duncan, Carrie and Jeannie saw him off when he flew from Heath Row in January 1979, leaving Jeannie to "wind up" everything.

Next, she received a color photo of him seated happily in the Triumph Spitfire, with the brilliant blue Pacific in the background.

Jeannie kept telling herself—I'm not a superstitious person, but ever since that phone call when we were in Europe and learned that Helen was coming home, I kept thinking about the gypsy woman, Annie, and what she said when I was eight years old. It's the same sort of feeling you get here in Hawaii if you move a rock from a Heiau—Hawaiian place of worship to the gods.

Jeannie managed to drag herself back to school in January to see her students successfully through their Finals that June.

She and Duncan, having discovered there was no simple way of flying "Tiddles" and "Toots" into Hawaii without months of quarantine—a total experience too traumatic for them to endure—took them to the local vet, leaving them purring on the veterinary table—oblivious to their destiny—while Jeannie and Duncan walked back to the car, sobbing.

At Easter break, when they could all get away from work, Jeannie, Duncan and Carrie decided to make a last nostalgic trip to North Wales—including crossing to the Isle of Anglesey, where they climbed around the ancient walls of the castle. After that, they all agreed to take a trip up the rack railway to the top of Snowdon. It was still very cold at that time of the year and the tops of the mountains were covered with snow, the sunshine contributing to beauty but not warmth.

For Jeannie, everything she did held a wrenching sadness. Having made some wonderful trips to Maui, she and Neil were half prepared for the move, though it was a major, major decision and upheaval.

They were both adventurers, so the fact that they could actually live in Hawaii had its attraction—but, they had a magnificent home, full of treasures, in a gorgeous location, and many friends. They needed a "push" to make the decision. That came, unfortunately, in the form of Neil's health, which was more important to Jeannie than all the possessions in the world. She wanted the strain to leave his face and happiness to take its place.

For Jeannie, Duncan and Carrie, the final few weeks in June were spent in Kirstie's home up on the Lickey Hills, since she had gone to her beloved Llangwnnadl for the summer.

Carrie said she would fly over to Maui for a vacation sometime next year, 1980, when Duncan was settled. His twenty-first birthday was in March and Carrie provided him with a beautiful birthday cake in the shape of the figures '21'. They had been together since 1975, when they were both seventeen. Jeannie took Neil and the two boys to a Christmas dance at the school where she taught, and Carrie was a student in the extended Commerce Course.

Subsequently, she told the story of the first time Duncan brought her home. He turned the car into the driveway and she said, "Where are you going?"

"Home."

Faced with the long driveway and the lovely house belonging to her "Commerce teacher," she said, "I can't go in there!" And she slid down in the seat, hiding from sight.

"Come on, don't be silly."

Reluctantly, she gave in, and he took her through the house into the Lounge—the main sitting room.

"Sit down," he said.

"Where?"

She looked around at all the antique furniture—all of it comfortable—but not the sort of stuff she was used to sitting on! She was unsure what was expected of her.

"Anywhere."

And he plopped down on the sofa, finally giving up and leading the way.

Jeannie and Duncan entered the United States via New York's Kennedy Airport, laden with additional luggage in the form of army surplus kitbags, stuffed to the brim, as being stronger and more practical than suitcases. They just hoped they would not have to unpack anything going through Customs.

The contents were meager possessions, mere remnants of a prior lifetime.

They received welcome assistance from a luggage handler, sending their bags through to Kahului, on Maui, via Los Angeles and Honolulu.

Neil and Helen met them at the airport with hugs all round, a truck, and the Triumph Spitfire, so Jeannie arrived at her new home in style, chauffeured by the most precious man in her life. As long as he was there to spend it with her, nothing else mattered.

He carried her suitcase into the cottage saying, "Get out of those clothes; you won't be needing them any more."

Jeannie packed a colorful, long mu'u-mu'u near the top of the suitcase, bought when they vacationed on Maui in 1975. She slipped that on and he took her by the hand, leading her to the new pool, to be entered from the first floor level of the main house, when completed.

She sat at the edge, splashing her feet in the water, looking out at the extensive view of the blue Pacific and the outer islands of Kahoolawe and Lanai, enjoying the comforting warmth of the late afternoon sun, when her husband pulled her into the water by her ankles and, putting his arms around her, said "Welcome home!"

Jeannie still has that dress, and Daddy's steering wheel hangs on the redwood cottage wall in Maui, Hawaii, which is where he always intended it to be—awaiting the next fork in the road...

APPENDIX

Chapter 1
Rupert Brooke, a British soldier in Europe during the Great War, wrote much of his creative work at that time. Heading for Chapter I is taken from a line in his poem: The Soldier
Chapter 2 – "itinerant gypsies" constantly on the move from place to place. The Education Acts in England after the war made it compulsory for the gypsy children to attend school, so they did not roam any more in England, though they were still roaming in the Irish Republic in 1966 when Jeannie visited there.
"Lorna Doone" – heroine of a famous West Country book of the same name.
"Prime Minister" – Head of the Party in power in Britain.

"Preparatory School" – like Middle School, but a Private School.

"battledress jacket" – informal, or working uniform, comfortable and loose-fitting.

Chapter 3 – "Boer War. Boers were South Africans of Dutch extraction. It was a war between Great Britain and the Transvaal, 1880-1881, a province in the north-east of South Africa.
"horseless-carriage" – early name for a car in Britain.
"High Hills" became a small private hotel in peacetime. The Austin Motor Company launched the Austin 7 – a small car with a hard top or

a soft top, 7 hp and very reasonably priced; many families toured with it in the summer months.

In Private Boarding Schools ("Public Schools" in the UK) the senior students normally occupied accommodation, two to a room, for sleeping, in daytime as a study.

Chapter 6
"biscuits" – together, a mattress.
N.A.A.F.I, - Navy, Army and Air Force Institutes providing services to the armed forces, including a canteen providing light meals and snacks.

"the tube" – commonly used name for the underground railway.

"teatime" – a light meal, generally served at 4.00 pm, such as cucumber sandwiches, and cookies or small cakes, together with a pot of Indian or China tea.

Chapter 11
"two large taps" – faucettes
"flannels" – face cloths.

"King Kong" – the first black and white version; the later, second version, was in color.

"C.S.D." – Command Supply Depot.

"Limited Access Zone" – once you're in, you're in and once you're out, you're out – without special permission to move.

Chapter 14
Google search: Mulberry Harbours (note spelling)
Combinedops Mulberry Harbour
Image: Allied Invasion Force:jpg
Sketch: Mulberry B

Detailed information can be found under Combined Operations through Google Search, as shown above, principally from Wikipedia, the free Encyclopedia, plus books as referenced below.

"A Harbour called Mulberry"—Sir Bruce White
"Some Aspects of the Design of Flexible Bridging, including 'Whale' Floating Roadways"—Allan Beckett
"Untold Stories of D-Day"—National Geographic June 2002
"D-Day: US Army's 1st Infantry Division's Desperate Hours on Omaha Beach"
The film "Saving Private Ryan" shows the difficulties faced by the US 1st Infantry Division's desperate hours on Omaha beach largely caused by the storm destruction of Mulberry A

.

Chapter 21
"transverse engine"—lying across the car, rather than "inline" front to rear.
"sans sidecar"—"sans"—without (French)

Chapter 30
"first floor"—in America, this is the floor above the "ground floor"; in England the ground floor is the "first floor" and the next floor is the "second floor."

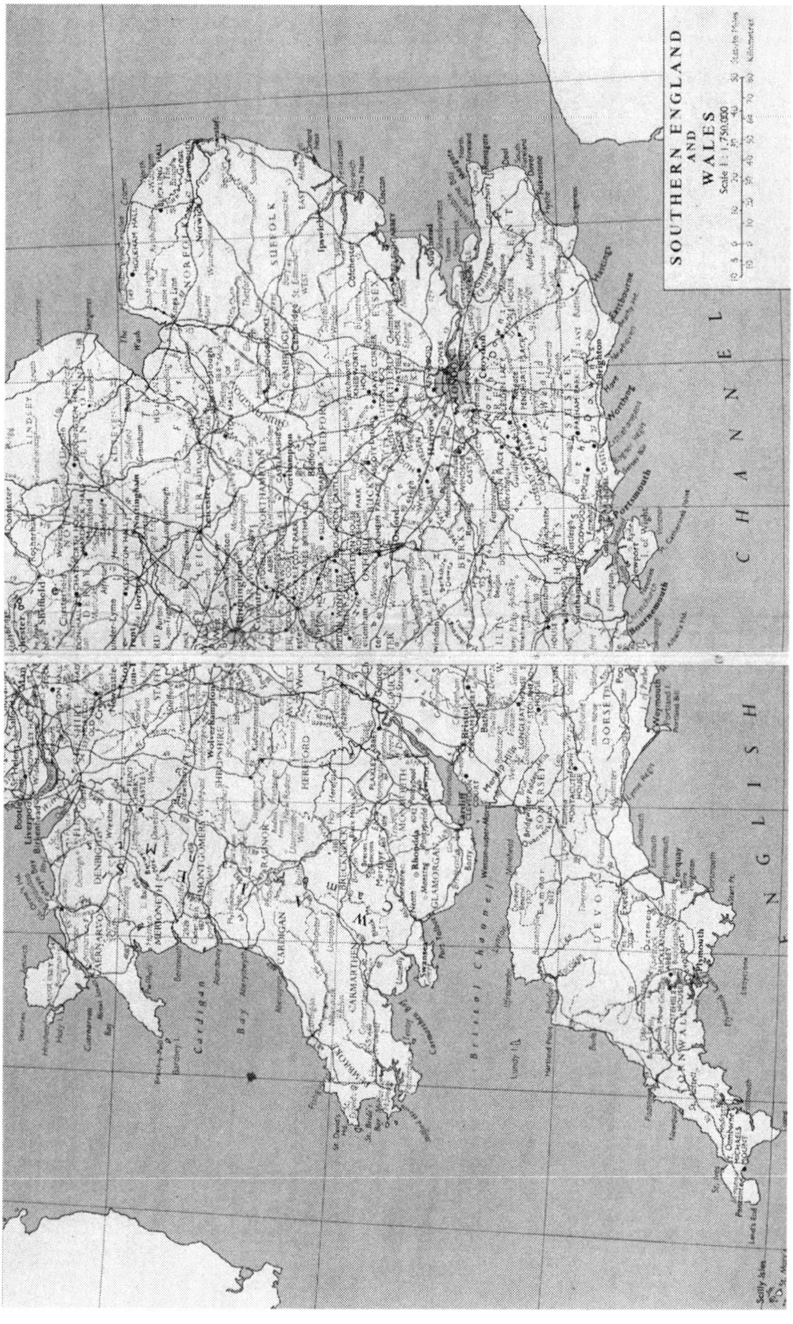

Southern England, including Wales

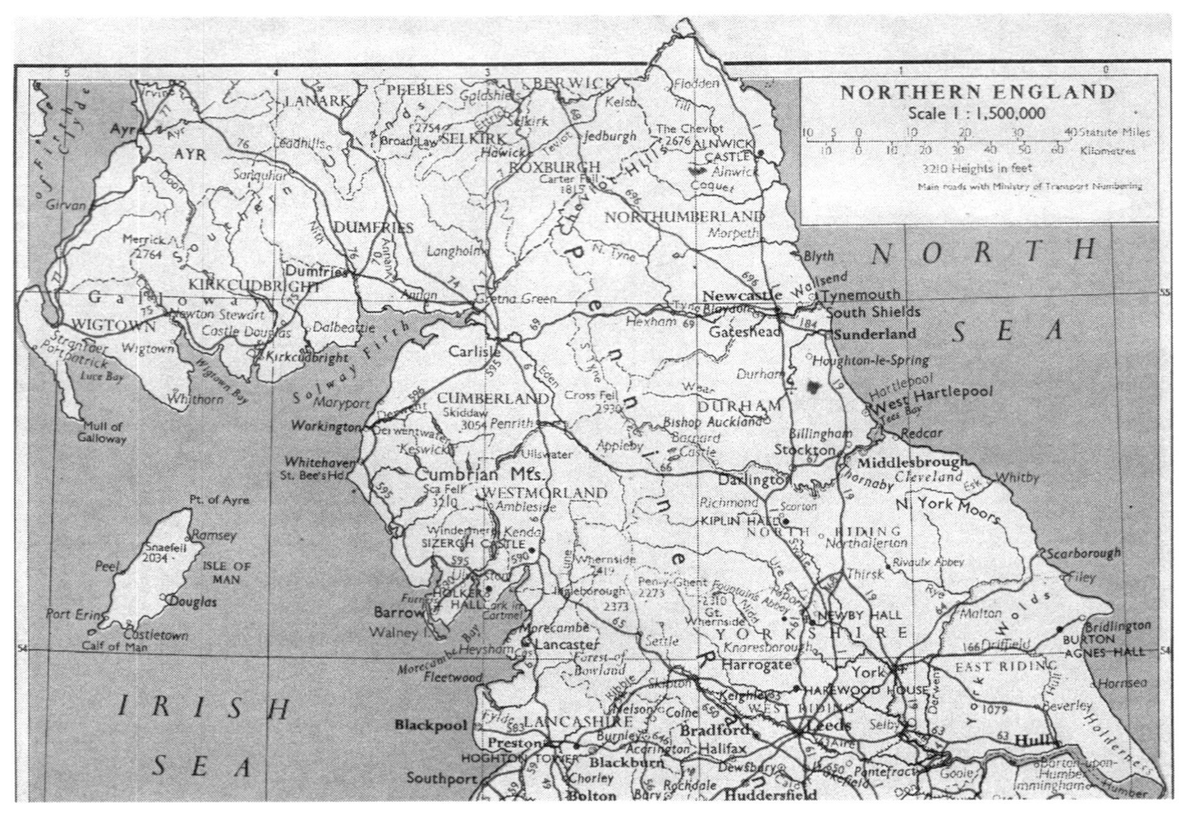

Northern England

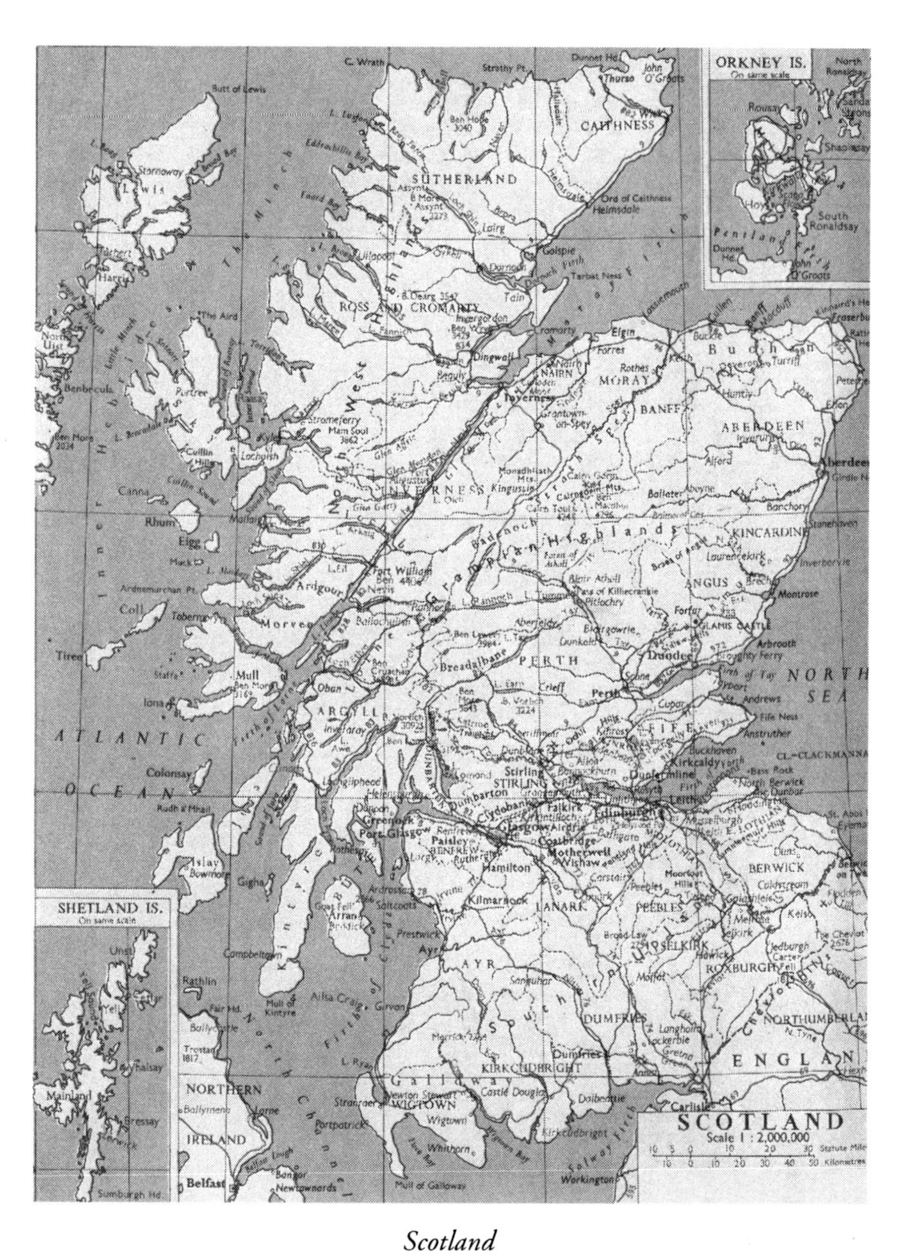
ORKNEY IS.
On same scale
SHETLAND IS.
On same scale
SCOTLAND
Scale 1 : 2,000,000
Statute Miles
Kilometres
C. Wrath
Strathy Pt.
Dunnet Hd.
John O'Groats
Thurso
Butt of Lewis
CAITHNESS
SUTHERLAND
Stornoway
Lewis
Harris
Ord of Caithness
Helmsdale
Golspie
Dornoch
Tarbat Ness
Tain
Lairg
Ullapool
ROSS AND CROMARTY
Invergordon
Cromarty
Dingwall
Elgin
Forres
Nairn
NAIRN
Rothes
MORAY
BANFF
Buckie
Banff
Macduff
Turriff
Fraserburgh
Huntly
ABERDEEN
Inverurie
Alford
Aberdeen
Inverness
Grantown-on-Spey
Stromeferry
Mam Soul
3862
Benbecula
Portree
Kyle
Lochalsh
Cuillin Hills
Canna
Rhum
Eigg
Muck
Mallaig
INVERNESS
Kingussie
Cairngorm Mts.
Cairn Toul
Ballater
Aboyne
Banchory
Stonehaven
KINCARDINE
Laurencekirk
Inverbervie
Brechin
Montrose
ANGUS
Forfar
GLAMIS CASTLE
Arbroath
Dundee
Broughty Ferry
Grampian Highlands
Badenoch
Fort William
Ben Nevis
Ardgour
Ardnamurchan Pt.
Coll
Tobermory
Morven
Tiree
Staffa
Mull
Iona
Ballachulish
L. Rannoch
Pitlochry
Blair Athell
Pass of Killiecrankie
Aberfeldy
Dunkeld
Blairgowrie
Ben Lawers
Breadalbane
PERTH
Perth
Scone
Crieff
Oban
ARGYLL
Inveraray
L. Awe
ATLANTIC
OCEAN
Colonsay
Lochgilphead
Helensburgh
Dumbarton
Stirling
STIRLING
Falkirk
Dunfermline
Kirkcaldy
FIFE
Cupar
St Andrews
Fife Ness
Anstruther
Buckhaven
North Berwick
Dunbar
Leith
Edinburgh
Clydebank
Glasgow
Greenock
Port Glasgow
Paisley
Coatbridge
Airdrie
Motherwell
Wishaw
Hamilton
Rutherglen
RENFREW
Islay
Bowmore
Gigha
Rothesay
Ardrossan
Saltcoats
Arran
Kilmarnock
LANARK
PEEBLES
Peebles
SELKIRK
Selkirk
Galashiels
Melrose
Kelso
BERWICK
Coldstream
Hawick
ROXBURGH
Jedburgh
The Cheviot
Campbeltown
Kintyre
Mull of Kintyre
Prestwick
Ayr
AYR
Sanquhar
Moffat
Girvan
Ailsa Craig
Rathlin
Fair Hd.
Ballycastle
NORTHERN
IRELAND
Larne
Belfast
Bangor
Newtownards
Stranraer
Portpatrick
Newton Stewart
WIGTOWN
Wigtown
Whithorn
Mull of Galloway
Castle Douglas
KIRKCUDBRIGHT
Kirkcudbright
Dumfries
DUMFRIES
Dalbeattie
Langholm
Lockerbie
Gretna
Annan
Carlisle
Workington
NORTHUMBERLAND
ENGLAND
NORTH SEA
Unst
Yell
Mainland
Bressay
Sumburgh Hd.
Rousay
Hoy
South Ronaldsay
Pentland Firth

Scotland

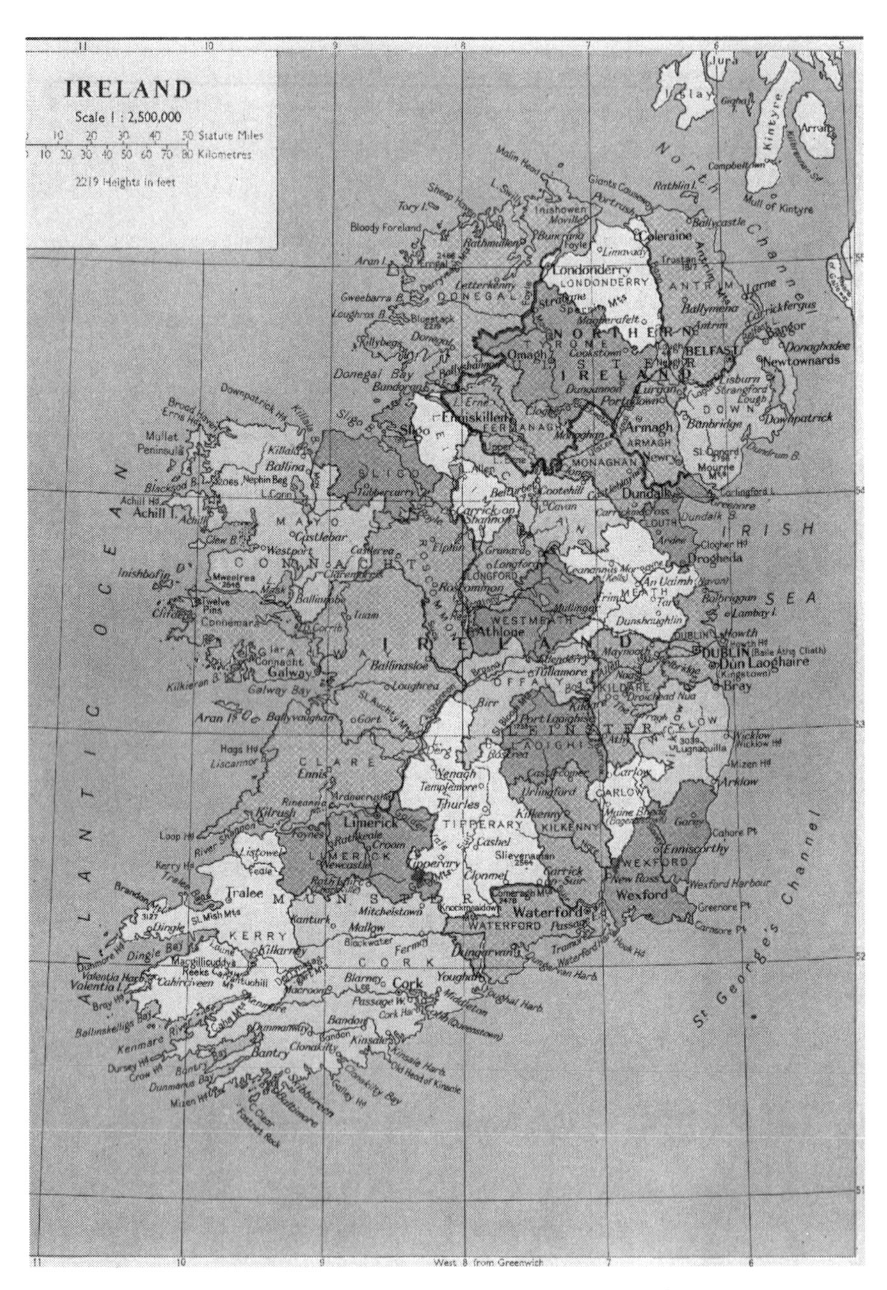

Northern Ireland and Republic of Ireland

AUTHOR BIOGRAPHY

I lived in England throughout the time of the book—a factual novel. Some names of persons, though most deceased, are changed to preserve privacy.

Following a demanding business life, in England and Hawaii, I studied through Long Ridge Writers Group, Redding CT, living permanently in Maui, Hawaii since 1979.

Lightning Source UK Ltd.
Milton Keynes UK
15 August 2010

158463UK00001B/64/P

9 781450 238434